DARK ENTRY

First in the thrilling new
Kit Marlowe historical mystery series

Cambridge, 1583. About to graduate from
Corpus Christi, the young Christopher
Marlowe spends his days studying and his
nights carousing with old friends. But when
one of them is discovered lying dead in his
King's College room, mouth open in a silent
scream, Marlowe refuses to accept the
official verdict of suicide. Calling on the help
of his mentor, Sir Roger Manwood, Justice of
the Peace, and the queen's magus, Dr John
Dee, a poison expert, Marlowe sets out to
prove that his friend was murdered...

DARK ENTRY

M. J. Trow

Severn House Large Print
London & New York

This first large print edition published 2012
in Great Britain and the USA by
SEVERN HOUSE PUBLISHERS LTD of
9-15 High Street, Sutton, Surrey, SM1 1DF.
First world regular print edition published 2011 by
Severn House Publishers Ltd., London and New York.

British Library Cataloguing in Publication Data

Trow, M. J.
   Dark entry. -- (A Kit Marlowe historical mystery)
   1. Marlowe, Christopher, 1564-1593--Fiction. 2. Dee, John,
   1527-1608--Fiction. 3. Manwood, Roger, 1524 or 5-1592--
   Fiction. 4. University of Cambridge--Fiction. 5. Murder--
   Investigation--England--Cambridge--Fiction. 6. Cambridge
   (England)--History--16th century--Fiction. 7. Detective
   and mystery stories. 8. Large type books.
   I. Title II. Series
   823.9'2-dc23

   ISBN-13: 978-0-7278-9923-1

Severn House Publishers support The Forest Stewardship Council
[FSC], the leading international forest certification organisation. All
our titles that are printed on Greenpeace-approved FSC-certified paper
carry the FSC logo.

MIX
Paper from
responsible sources
FSC® C018575

Printed and bound in Great Britain by the
MPG Books Group, Bodmin, Cornwall.

ONE

It was pitch black in that alleyway. What moon there was blinked between the clouds of that summer, leaving its ghost behind with a slight stain of silver on the sky. And all cats were equally grey.

He checked the street one last time. He heard their feet clattering on the cobbles of Bene't Street behind him; one set of footsteps slithering and sliding, the hobnails on the soles scoring the stones, the other set firm, even and determined, eating up the yards until they reached the wall. He heard the stifled laughter of old, that stupid bray that Henry had when he was in his cups. He didn't have to see them to know what was going on. Henry would have to be quiet and that was Tom's job; dear old, dependable Tom. Matt? Well, Matt would probably be balancing on the college wall by now, tiptoeing through the daisies. And why not? It isn't everyday a man becomes a Bachelor of Arts in the greatest university in the world.

'Kit!'

Shit! Tom hadn't been quick enough. That was Henry's voice, booming and giggling at the same time, bouncing off the walls of The Court,

5

echoing in the traceries of King's and Catherine's across the road. No time to lose now. The Proctors had ears like bats. He felt rather than saw the gnarled old branch, worn smooth by the scrabbling hands of generations of roisterers. He hauled himself up, feeling his hair tangle in the twigs and he'd just hooked one booted leg over the parapet when he saw them. He tucked the trailing foot beneath him and immediately regretted it, as he felt the blood-flow slow and cease. Within minutes he would be in the grip of pins and needles. One minute more and his leg would be in that strange limbo of complete anaesthesia and pain.

Beams of light danced from their lanterns, flashing on the thick window panes of The Court. He froze, willing the leaves to stop moving. In his three years at this place, out on the town at the Eagle, the Boar, the Cap, he'd never been caught. And now, on the eve of his greatness, was not the time to try his luck.

He recognized their footfalls – Lomas of the heavy tread; Darryl, the scamperer. And he knew their voices too.

'Where are they?' he heard Darryl hiss in the darkness near the Master's Lodge.

The footsteps stopped. 'They'll be cutting across the churchyard.' This was Lomas, crafty, everywhere, never wrong.

He knew the Proctor had got it right again. Tom would have realized they were making too much noise, rolling home under the fleeting moon and he would have pushed Matt and

Henry through the gateway and across the graves of St Bene't's churchyard, so that their drunken feet padded on grass and saved them all from a beating.

The lantern beams switched direction, away from his corner, moving eerily north as the Proctors laid their ambush. He couldn't move, couldn't change position despite the sudden agony of cramp in his calf. His teeth flashed gritted in a single sweep of the moon over the faintly gleaming grey stone of The Court. Looking up through the tangle of branches, he saw the clouds had gone.

'Shhh!'

That was Henry again, the only man in Cambridge whose sibilance was louder than thunder. He'd have no chance to save them now. And if he wanted to save himself, he'd have to shift fast. He knew what they'd do, the Proctors. Darryl would nip behind a buttress, crouch there like the malevolent toad he was. Lomas would be inside, waiting on the stairs like the mouth of Hell itself, ready to swallow scholars whole.

That ploy gave him a minute, perhaps two, to get across the lawn and on to the staircase. And that lawn was suddenly bright under the moon, all cover blown, all hope extinguished. In a desperate moment, he snatched the dagger from the sheath at his back and threw it at the far wall. It clattered on the stonework and landed on the flagstones below.

The lantern beams merged, having crossed and crossed again and he saw the black shapes converge. Their robed shadows danced, huge and macabre, over the lawn. He hauled himself free of the clawing branches, willing his sleeping leg to work, and he ran.

Behind him, even as he hit the ground, he heard the ruckus. Running feet that were not his own scraped and thumped among the shouts and curses. He was under the archway and bounding up the twisted stairs three at a time, wincing at each thud when his numb foot came down. He crashed in through the door, hauling off the flash doublet as he went, tearing at the laces that fastened his shirt. He floundered in the cluttered darkness of the room, looking in vain for his nightshirt, finding only Matt's. He dragged it over his head, scattering leaves and twigs and he pulled on his nightcap. Now ... the performance.

'Lomas? Darryl?' an enraged but still sleepy head poked out from an upstairs casement. 'What's going on?'

The scuffling stopped and five faces looked up at him, eerily lit by the still dancing lantern beams.

'You tell us, Master Marlowe,' Lomas sneered. Henry Bromerick had just kicked him in the shins and anyway, the Proctor was never at his best in the early hours.

'Have you no idea of the time, man?' Marlowe said with an outrage in his voice born of long years of playing the innocent whilst being thoroughly guilty. 'I have lectures with Professor Johns after breakfast. He won't take kindly to me yawning all through the morning; he's a

8

sensitive soul.' Marlowe leaned further over the sill, shielding his eyes in the lantern-light. 'Matthew Parker, is that you?'

'Yes, Kit,' Parker replied obediently, still struggling half-heartedly in the grip of Proctor Darryl and staring a bleak future in the face.

'Tut tut.' Marlowe shook his head and withdrew a little into the shadow of his dark room, to hide his smile. 'Roistering again, eh? And your grandfather Archbishop of Canterbury! Whatever next? Please go about your business more quietly, gentlemen. This is Corpus Christi, don't forget. We have a reputation to uphold.' And he leaned forward again, to pull the window closed.

'Master Marlowe.' Lomas stopped him. 'Is this yours?' He was holding something up in the half-moonlight.

'What is it?' Marlowe peered down, squinting his eyes so as to see whatever it was more clearly.

'It's a dagger, Master Marlowe.' Lomas was patience itself.

'A dagger?' Marlowe frowned and shook his head, causing a small twig to dislodge and skitter off the sill towards the upturned faces below. 'Now, what would I want with a dagger?'

They stood in a sheepish line in the Master's Lodge, caught out, embarrassed, humiliated, expecting the worst. A lazy golden dawn had crept over Corpus Christi College an hour earlier as the Constable of the Watch had called it a night

9

and gone home. And here they were, the three who were to have graduated today, standing silent and motionless in their grey fustian college robes, with the badge of the pelican and lilies.

Dr Norgate might have been a hundred as far as these three were concerned. They were eighteen; he was ... a hundred. He peered at them over the rim of his spectacles and leaned back in his chair, looking for all the world as if he'd been frozen in time and festooned with cobwebs. Behind him on oak shelves stood the serried ranks of the works of the scholars of antiquity – Herodotus, Aristotle, Euclid, Plinys elder and younger, Plato and a hundred others. There were no cobwebs on those volumes, no dust on the leather. Rumour had it that Dr Norgate read them all every day, could recite them for hours – and knew where the printers' errors were.

The great man cleared his throat. 'Henry Bromerick,' he said softly.

'Sir.'

Bromerick was having difficulty focusing. How many had he sunk at the George? How many more at the Eagle? It was a great night ... probably. He couldn't quite remember. There'd been a party at the Blue Boar, of that he was certain. Quite certain. He mentally shook himself and tried to concentrate on the Master, tried to make the two dim images of the man merge into one and stay there.

Norgate looked him up and down. The boy

was very large, like his appetites, his brown hair cropped under his scholar's cap, his eyes tinged red.

'A scholar of King's School, Canterbury.' Norgate was reading from the parchment on the table in front of him. 'Secundus Convictus, pensioner ... nay, Matthew Parker scholar, no less.'

'Sir.' Bromerick was happier with just monosyllables this morning. To have your curriculum vitae read to you was akin to a death sentence. Would the Master of Corpus be showing him the instruments of torture next?

'Dr Lyler speaks highly of your Hebrew.'

Bromerick blinked. 'Does he, sir?' This came as a surprise to Bromerick. Had the great man got him mixed up with somebody else?

Norgate waved him back into line. 'Thomas Colwell,' he said.

Tom Colwell was smaller than Bromerick, blond and wiry. His grey eyes were clear when he was sober and his mind was like a razor. But today was not a good day. He'd just thrown up spectacularly in the shrubbery outside the door and for all it was June, he shivered.

'The King's School, Canterbury,' Norgate said with a certain sense of having been here before. 'Matthew Parker scholar. Professor Johns is impressed by your rhetoric in the Discourses.'

'That's very kind of him, sir,' Colwell managed through his chattering teeth.

'Isn't it?' a voice rasped from the corner of the room. All eyes, even Norgate's, swivelled to Dr Gabriel Harvey, sprawled in his academic

11

finery. He stared back, defiant, his eyes cold and his mouth hard. Harvey had been waiting for this moment for three years. Three years to bring these rule-breakers, these delinquents, to book. Somehow, they'd got away with it before, creeping out on the tiles of Cambridge when the sheer exhaustion of academic rigour should have had them stretched out, dead to the world, in their truckle beds. And he was far from happy that there was one name missing from the roster of roisterers on the Master's desk. That prize still waited to be claimed.

'Matthew Parker,' Norgate said.

The scholar stood forward. He wore the permanently pained expression of all the male members of his family under his curling hair, as though he was about to meet his maker and regretted all the sins he'd committed in his young life. And now, he was.

'Pensioner,' Norgate said, shifting the parchment in front of him. 'Scholar of the King's School, Canterbury. Recipient of the Matthew Parker scholarship...'

'Jobs for the boys,' Harvey almost spat. He had come up the hard way, with no scholarship to pave his way, no silver christening spoon clamped between his teeth. He despised the gilded youths standing before him and didn't care who knew it.

Norgate was nodding his old, grey head. 'Your grandfather,' he told the boy, 'once sat where I am today before God and Her Majesty called him to higher office. What would he have said of his grandson's profligacy?'

Parker cleared his throat. 'He would have been appalled, sir,' he said. Matt Parker remembered his grandfather well. He was a sweet old boy who gave him toys and smelt of incense and old leather. He was too nice to be an Archbishop and certainly too nice to be Master of Corpus Christi. Parker remembered the old man's funeral when he'd stood in that huge cold vault of the cathedral and saw the tears on everyone's cheeks. He'd let the old boy down, that much was certain.

'And yet,' the Master sighed, 'Professor Johns and Dr Lyler tell me that your Dialectics are to die for.'

Harvey snorted. Parker was average at best; how could his colleagues be so easily taken in?

'What a waste.' Norgate stood up. 'Gentlemen.' The guilty three stood to attention once more, gazing steadfastly into the middle distance. 'You were found climbing over The Court wall at two of the clock this morning, worse for drink. Proctor Lomas reports that you, Bromerick, struck him on the head with your fist.'

'Flat of the hand, sir,' Bromerick blurted out, instantly regretting it. 'Flat of the...' and he stopped short, tucking the offending appendage into the front of his gown, as though to hide the evidence. Shut up, Henry, he heard the little voice inside his head saying. They cut off people's hands in this great country of ours.

'You are all good scholars,' Norgate went on, 'and today you were to have been invested by

13

our college with the degree of Bachelor of Arts.'

Gabriel Harvey smiled. He had not missed Norgate's use of the past tense and fully approved of it. There was, as he'd known all along, a God.

'You know that I could withhold your degrees?' the Master said.

There were assorted mutterings of assent from the three. They were all students of the Dialectic, well versed in the Discourses; the Master's use of the conditional gave them hope. Harvey's lopsided grin was already appearing. Perhaps he'd missed the nuance.

'I shall consider,' Norgate said and the grin vanished. There was a dull metallic clanking from across the quadrangle, from the tower of St Bene't's. 'There's the Chapel bell. Get along with you, now. You will have my decision by twelve of the clock.'

'Sir,' the scholars chorused and made for the door, doffing their caps as they went. Parker stopped at the studded woodwork. 'Sir,' he said, 'I hope it goes without saying that we're very...'

'Get out!' Harvey roared. And, with a hop and skip to catch up with the others, he did.

The Chapel bell clanged on in the golden morning and scholars crept out from the staircases, fumbling with caps and gowns, colliding with the Fellows whose rooms they shared. In some ways, Corpus Christi was a victim of its own success. The college had never been fuller, but that meant that space was at a premium. Sizars, always cold, hungry and broke, shared

14

lodgings with the Fellows for whom they skiv-
vied and scraped. Only Gabriel Harvey lodged
alone, complaining of the smell of the hoi
polloi, whose academic potential diminished
year by year.

The Master looked down from his eyrie as he
had now for more years than he cared to
remember. Then he turned back to his second in
command. 'Well, Gabriel?'

Harvey got to his feet too. 'Withhold their
degrees, Master. Throw the book at them. Damn
it, throw every book you've got. Damaging the
reputation of the college like that. We'll never
live it down.' Norgate was old school. Mentioning the reputation of Corpus was bound to
work and Harvey knew it.

But if Harvey was the Devil's advocate, then
Norgate was equally good at playing God's. 'A
few lads had too much ale,' he said quietly. 'Not
a great sin in the scheme of things, Gabriel. You
and I have seen far worse things, even here in
this university. True, it would have been better if
they'd waited until tonight to celebrate. We
don't, after all, flog our graduates...'

'...yet.' Harvey finished the sentence for him.
He looked out over The Court as the stragglers
disappeared into the Chapel doors, still just in
shadow as the morning sun crept over the grass
towards the dark interior. His eyes moved upwards and he saw a face in a far window – the
liquid eye, the sardonic, unreadable mouth, a
look that would outstare the Devil. 'Of course,'
he said, not turning away. 'I'd swap all those

15

idiots for the one who's behind it all.'

Norgate followed his gaze. The scholar in the far window bowed and doffed his cap. 'Ah, Christopher Morley.' The old man could never get his name right. 'You've never liked him, have you, Gabriel?'

'No more than I like the pestilence,' Harvey growled. He snatched up his satchel. 'It is, of course, your choice, Master,' he said, with all the cold contempt at his command. 'I must to morning service.'

'Not going to morning service today, Kit?' Professor Johns wanted to know. He wasn't all that much older than Marlowe but he had the grey skin that goes with the intellectual, a man who had long ago decided that his would be a world of books and scholarship and the scratching of quill on calfskin.

'Not today,' Marlowe said. The flash doublet had gone and he wore the grey fustian of a scholar. Across the quad, he saw that bastard Gabriel Harvey scurrying to the Chapel, hatred seeping from every pore. Every time he saw the man, he wondered what he'd done to upset him. What it was in the three years they'd known each other, teacher and pupil, that had made Harvey so detest him.

'One of these days,' Johns said, 'I shall ask you why. Why you go to Chapel so rarely.'

Marlowe turned, smiling. 'One of these days, Professor, I might tell you.'

'Professor?' Johns laughed, his blue eyes

16

twinkling. 'We're very formal today, Dominus Marlowe.'

'Ah.' The scholar held up his hand. 'Not Dominus yet, I fear.'

'This afternoon, though,' Johns said. 'I can be forgiven a little prematurity.'

'Perhaps,' Marlowe said. 'But I shan't take my degree until the lads get theirs.' He looked at the man before him, and decided to speak what was on his mind. 'Tell me, Michael, can you step in with the Master? On behalf of the lads, I mean?'

'The Parker scholars?' Johns resumed his seat by the window. 'You've always been a father figure to them, haven't you?'

'I'm older,' Marlowe said with a shrug. 'It's only natural.'

'No, there's more to it than that. They look up to you. Most of the student body does. What Marlowe does, they do.' He paused, knowing that what Marlowe did was not always a good thing. 'Were you with them last night?' he asked.

Marlowe turned to face him. 'Is the Pope the Bishop of Rome?' he asked.

Johns laughed. Then, suddenly, he was serious. 'Kit,' he said. 'Sit down, will you?'

Marlowe turned on one toe and flopped down on the window seat, leaning back against the transom and folding his arms, looking at Johns from under his half-lowered lids.

'What are you going to do with your life?' the Professor asked.

'Do?'

17

'Well, the Church, naturally,' Johns said. 'But somehow, I just don't see you...'

'In a surplice handing out the Eucharist?' Marlowe chuckled. 'No. Neither do I.'

'The law, then?' Johns suggested. 'When your new classes begin ... Or what about medicine? It's a subject that's the coming thing, believe me. All those potions and elixirs. Fascinating.'

'The theatre,' Marlowe cut in.

'What?' Johns blinked.

'Drama. Poetry. Air and fire. *That's* the coming thing.'

Johns looked as if somebody had just stabbed him in the heart. 'Not coming to Cambridge, I hope,' he said.

'Oh, no.' Marlowe chuckled. 'All that's coming to Cambridge is more of the Godly, the Puritan persuasion. If there's a tavern standing come Lady Day, I'll be astonished.'

'Don't joke, Kit,' Johns warned solemnly. 'You don't know how powerful...'

'The college authorities are? Oh, I've got a pretty good idea.'

'No,' Johns said, looking even more ashen than usual. 'I didn't mean that. Kit – promise me something.'

Marlowe shrugged. He didn't make promises, not ones he couldn't keep. It had something to do with his immortal soul.

'Conform, Kit.' Johns leaned forward to him. 'Please – *conform*.'

Marlowe pushed himself upright from where he lounged on the window seat, then stood up, stretching. 'Perhaps that word sounds better in Greek.' He smiled down at Johns. 'Or Hebrew. I'm afraid I don't understand it in English.' He crossed to the door. 'Time for breakfast,' he said. 'Michael–' he turned in the archway – 'you'll do what you can for the lads?'

And he was gone.

They stood in a hollow square as the sun sat high in the Heavens, nearly a hundred strong, the Master, Fellows and Scholars of Corpus Christi College. Only the servants were absent, busy with their duties and forbidden to watch what was to follow on pain of the same.

The scholars had all seen this before and some of them had felt it, the knotted lash with its nine tails. Gabriel Harvey stood four-square with the Master, the Fellows behind him in their tassels and gold lace, glinting in the summer sun. Funny how everybody dresses up for torture, to celebrate a Roman holiday.

The three stood in the centre, leaning forward with their wrists strapped with leather thongs to the rough wooden pyramid frame the Proctors had placed there. They were stripped to the waist, the points dangling from their woollen hose and their skin pale in the sunshine.

'Scholars of Corpus Christi.' Dr Norgate's voice was strong over the rising breeze that fluttered gowns and headgear and took some of the heat from the midday sun. 'Witness the punishment of three of your number who failed to obey the college curfew and were found the worse for drink.'

He let the words sink in, noting one or two of the older scholars who arched an eyebrow or eased a collar. This was to encourage the others; the lesson would not be lost.

'Proctors, do your duty.'

Marlowe saw the relish on Lomas' face as he began to lash. His right arm snaked back and the whip thudded across Bromerick's shoulder blades, followed almost instantly by Darryl's strike. There was a gasp from the younger boys as the knots bit home, the wicked tips of the whip cutting the pale flesh and leaving a slash of blood.

Bromerick's body convulsed and he bit down on the leather pad that Darryl had shoved unceremoniously between his teeth. As the second blow fell and the third, a single tear trickled down Bromerick's cheek. His hair was matted with sweat and his legs felt like jelly but he wasn't going to cry out. He wouldn't give them the satisfaction.

Before the last stroke, Lomas held back, shifting the haft of the cat in his hand, for more purchase for his encore. Darryl's rope sliced the air and cut diagonally across the pulp of Bromerick's back. As the scholar turned to stare defiantly at his tormentors, Lomas deliberately sent the whip high, slapping across his mouth and cheek so that the blood spurted in a sudden arc.

Marlowe moved forward, his jaw set, his body rigid. Only Michael Johns quietly standing in

20

front of him and laying a hand on his chest stopped him. *'Conform!'* he hissed.

Then, as the bleeding Bromerick slumped, exhausted and beaten on the triangle, the Proctors went to work on Colwell, then Parker. They had had to wait in an agony of helplessness and frustration, watching the pain inflicted on Bromerick and knowing it was coming to them. It seemed to go on forever, the whistling and thump of the whips, the grunts of exertion from the Proctors. In the far corner, near the Master's Lodge, there was a brief commotion as a sizar fainted. The lad turned white and pitched forward on his face. He had been unable to watch and unable to look away, all at the same time. Somebody scooped him up and propped him, with his cold, sweating forehead lolling on his updrawn knees, against a wall.

Then, all was silence, except for Lomas and Darryl, who were puffing, red-faced from their hard work. No one was sorry to see that Lomas in particular found his breath hard to catch, and the tortured whistle as he drew air into his lungs was music to many ears in the hollow square.

Kit Marlowe was not a man to make promises, but he made one to himself that morning. There would be a reckoning.

Dr Norgate stepped forward as if he were taking the service in Chapel. 'An offence like this,' he said, his voice echoing around the courtyard, 'would normally result in these scholars being sent down.'

Even the Proctors were silent now.

'However,' the Master went on, glancing in Johns' direction, 'representation has been made and these young men, fine young men as I know them to be, will be given their degrees when their wounds have healed.'

No one dared cheer or applaud. Somehow, the moment was not right. Marlowe nodded to Johns a silent thank you. Then he went to unhitch his lads from the triangle. The Master and the Fellows marched away, followed by the scholars, whispering urgently to each other about what they'd just seen.

'Next time, Master Marlowe,' Lomas sneered as he coiled his whip away.

Marlowe smiled at him, untying Bromerick's hemp first. 'Oh no, Master Proctor,' he said. 'In a few days I shall be Dominus Marlowe and if you lay a hand on me – or any of my friends – I will kill you.' And there was something in his eyes that made Lomas believe it. Marlowe closed to him, grinning widely. 'Not much moon again tonight, I'll wager. You watch your back.'

The three friends sat side by side on a bench in the Swan in Bridge Street that night and, despite the ale in front of each one, no one felt too much like celebrating. Henry Bromerick in particular had difficulty swallowing, his lips purple and swollen, his teeth scraping on each other as he tried to sip his ale. The corner of one eye was red where the cat-tip had caught it and the bruise spread down his cheek in one direction and in the other disappeared into his hair. The others' wounds were not so easy to spot, but anyone could see from the way that they sat, stiff and unmoving, that they were in great pain, hurting under the grey fustian.

'Come along now, gents.' The innkeeper was clearing away the debris of earlier revellers. 'Shouldn't you lads be on top of the world tonight?' He glanced at Bromerick and considered qualifying his remark, but thought better of it. 'Masters of Rhetoric, or whatever it is you do?'

Jack Wheeler had been keeper of the Swan since before these boys were born. He had seen generations of scholars come and go since the Queen was newly-crowned. In fact, as he never tired of telling everybody, he'd had the honour to present Her Majesty with a cup of his finest local brew on the occasion of her one and only visit to the town. He'd noted the Queen smiling at him but was too busy bowing low to be aware of her passing the cup to the Earl of Leicester who sniffed it and poured away its contents. Wheeler was still waiting for the letter with the lion and dragon seal which would allow him to write 'By Appointment' on his shingle. 'By disappointment' would have been more apt.

'We got caught last night, Jack,' Tom Colwell told him, in an admission of defeat. 'Felt a taste of the cat.'

'Not unlike your very own brew, Master Wheeler.' Kit Marlowe swept in from nowhere, back in the roisterer's doublet, remembering not to pat anybody on the back. 'I'll have a brandy. The same for my friends and...' he looked around him, frowning. 'Still no Ralph? Where is the toad's harslet?'

'Who?' Matt Parker surfaced from under the smothering golden curls of the girl who he was, very carefully, balancing on his lap.

'Whingside.' Bromerick gave it his best shot, but his lips felt like blanc mange – very painful blanc mange – and he gave up.

Marlowe smiled and ruffled his hair before hauling up a footstool to sit on. 'What Dominus Bromerick is trying to say is *Whitingside*; Ralph by Christian name. He's not here.'

'He wasn't here last night either,' Parker remembered, smiling at the girl.

The rest of the company looked at him. Had this man just received a degree from the finest university in the world, or had he not?

'That's King's men for you,' Colwell grunted. 'He'll have been carousing at the Cardinal's Cap last night. Meg–' he half-turned as best he could to the girl perched on Parker's lap – 'doesn't your sister work there?'

'She does,' Meg told him. 'Who're you looking for?'

'Ralph Whitingside,' Marlowe said.

'That tall bloke?' Meg asked, unconcerned. 'The one with the six pairs of hands?'

Marlowe smiled. 'If you say so.'

'He was in here last night. He...' She looked up and caught the eye of Jack Wheeler. He was all for extras on the bill, but he doubted Parker could afford them. She jumped up and gave the table an ineffectual wipe with her apron. 'I must go,' she said, pecking Parker on the cheek. 'His master's voice.'

'Last night?' Marlowe reached out and pulled her back by the arm. 'When?'

'I don't know for sure. One night's very much like another in this business, Master Marlowe. Latish. All I know about time is that it passes.'

'It surely does,' Marlowe agreed, letting the girl go.

'What's the matter, Kit?' Colwell asked. 'You-'ve got a faraway look on your face.'

Marlowe snapped out of it. 'Probably nothing,' he said. 'But as far as Ralph Whitingside knew we were all going to graduate today. I just thought he'd be here. It's ... ah, that's my girl!' Meg had brought their drinks. 'Gentlemen,' he said and raised his brandy. 'Here's to Doctor Gabriel Harvey.' Nobody drank. 'May he roast in Hell!'

'Gabriel Harvey!' they roared and downed their drinks in one. Except Henry Bromerick, who slopped most of his over his cheek.

Meg Hawley made her way along Jesus Lane as another dawn crept over the graves of the Grey Friars. Her step was a little unsteady and her cloak dragged through the Cambridge dust as she turned the corner. She half-expected to see her sister crossing the low fields by the river, but she wasn't there. She had probably got off early and was already snoring in her truckle bed at the

25

farm, grateful to be off her feet after a long night.

There was *someone* there, though, leaning against the red brick of Jesus Gate. He wore his doublet open and his collar was pale against the darker skin. This wasn't unusual. A client. Meg opened her cloak a little. All right, it was early morning and she was tired, but a groat was a groat at any time of the day or night and while she still had her looks and her youth she wasn't about to pass up an opportunity. She had lived on the edge of this town all her life. She knew all its alleyways and dark entries like the back of her hand. Lots of places to accommodate a gentleman ... She stopped short.

'Oh, it's you, Master Marlowe,' she said, wondering again why she always called him that. The others were Matt, Tom and Henry. The poor sizars who couldn't afford her often, or the gentlemen who'd toss her a shilling; she called them all by their first name. But Marlowe was always different. There was something danger-ous, something cold, something indefinable about Marlowe, and she'd no sooner call him Christopher than fly to the moon and back, still less Kit as his friends called him.

Her heart was pounding. The first time she had seen Marlowe, three years ago now, when he came to the town, she was drawn to him and repelled at once. He was handsome, but not in an approachable way, like the boys he was with at Corpus Christi. She and he were of an age, she thought, give or take. She always felt much older than the boys in the Swan and those in the dark alleys, who fumbled and sweated and called her pet names. But Marlowe made her feel like a child; there was something timeless about him, something old looked out of his eyes. He was always friendly, always polite and she was, if not willing, then ready to take his money. Yet ... nothing. Perhaps this was it. Perhaps this morning with the golden glow of mist was the time, and this the place.

He reached out his hand and, after only a momentary pause, she slid into the crook of his arm, ignoring the fluttering in her stomach. He held her cheek and pulled her lips close to his. She opened them, waiting, staring into those smouldering dark eyes.

'Tell me,' he whispered, 'about Ralph Whitingside.'

She blinked. Frowned. The moment had gone, as they stood there in the red-brick shadow of Jesus College and the morning climbed in the east. Meg pulled away.

'I've got to get home,' she muttered. 'My dad'll take his belt to me.'

But he reached out again and held her tight with a powerful right hand. 'You saw him the night before last,' he said, taking account of the morning which was now here.

'What of it?' She was frightened now, staring again into those hypnotic eyes. 'Let me go. You're hurting me.' She tried to wriggle free, but he held on tighter, squeezing her arm just above the elbow.

27

'Ralph,' he said softly. 'Tell me about Ralph.'
She met his gaze for a few seconds more, before squeezing her eyelids shut. A single tear showed fat and wet along her lashes before rolling down her cheek. She spoke so low he had to lean in to hear what she said. 'I love Ralph,' she sighed.

He pulled back and let her go in surprise. 'You ... love him?' he asked. Everyone knew that Ralph Whitingside would go off into the bushes with anything that flashed an ankle at him, and in some cases he hadn't even needed that encouragement. Add to that the fact that Meg was well known throughout Corpus Christi and beyond as a willing girl, if the price was right, and love seemed an odd word to be hearing.

'Yes,' she said, rubbing at her cheek to dry her tears and looking up defiantly. 'As soon as I saw him, I loved him. And he loved me the same. It's just that, well, we both know there's no future in it. He's a gentleman, I've got my intended.'

Marlowe patted her arm, almost absent-mindedly. Old Ralph, eh, and a tavern girl. Could this explain where he was, why he was hiding? He looked at her and realized she was waiting for a response, but everything that was going through his mind wasn't really for her ears. 'Hmm, yes. Lovely story. Who ever loved, that loved not at first sight? I expect you and your intended, it was like that with him, I suppose?'

'Not really.' Meg's face fell a little. 'I've known Harry all my life. He lives on the farm with us all. But Ralph...'

He took her hand, gently. 'I've known Ralph Whitingside since we were boys,' he told her. He turned her hand over, rubbing his fingertips gently over the calloused palm. 'We are kindred spirits, you and I, Meg of the golden hair, Meg of the Swan. You got these hands from the pots, didn't you? Hauling casks when you still wore hanging-sleeves. Me too. I was a pot boy at the Star back home in Canterbury. I used to pass Ralph's house on my way to work there and we'd talk. He didn't mind I was a pot boy.' He laughed and dropped her hand. 'And I didn't mind he was a gentleman's son.'

She smiled fondly. 'Ralph gets on with everyone,' she said.

Marlowe nodded. 'He saved my life once, you know. In the river, back home.' He had that faraway look in his eyes again, the one that Colwell knew and he shook himself free of the memory; the dreadful sound of the weir crashing in his ears, the pain in his filling lungs, the grip of the slimy weed round his legs. 'We should have graduated yesterday, the boys and I,' Marlowe said. He didn't have to name them. Kit Marlowe and his boys were famous in every ale house in the city. 'We'd arranged to meet Ralph on Tuesday, but he didn't turn up. He didn't turn up last night either.' He looked at her closely, narrowing his eyes. 'Do you know why?'

'No.' She felt more at ease with him now, now that she knew that Master Marlowe was a pot boy. She'd only seen the scholar, the flash drinker in his doublet and colleyweston cloak, the glib talker, the gambler who always won. She hadn't known he'd once done the same job that she now did, alone in the darkness of an inn's vault, dragging weights that were too heavy, straining her arms until they dislocated; her left shoulder would always hang lower than her right. 'No, he missed you,' she told him. 'Come in wild-looking, breath in his fist. Said he had to find you. You in particular, Master Marlowe.'

'Did he say why?'

She shook her head. 'I gave him a drink,' she said, 'and we ... went outside.'

Marlowe nodded and flicked his hand at her. He had no need of detail. There was more to this than a fumble with a barmaid. 'And then?'

'He went home, I suppose, said he wasn't feeling too well,' she said. 'He'll be back in college. You'll find him there.'

'Yes,' Marlowe said. 'Yes, I suppose I will.' And he moved away.

'Kit,' she said suddenly, her voice sounding too loud as she spoke his name for the first time in three years.

He half turned. 'I'm sorry,' he said, 'if I hurt you.' And he was gone, striding along Jesus Lane in the morning.

TWO

Kit Marlowe didn't allow things like hangovers to rule his mornings. While the others lay in their beds in the old storehouse converted years ago for the Parker scholars in perpetuity – on their stomachs, to save their sore backs – groaning quietly to themselves, he was back in his college grey, breakfasting and planning the rest of the day. He sat on the edge of a bench, at the end of a table in the buttery, nibbling thoughtfully on a heel of bread, and toying with a mug of small beer. Several times he was spoken to, but since he gave no reply, and in fact didn't even seem to hear the speaker, soon he was alone in a little circle of silence. Even the echo of the cavernous room seemed to stop dead at the invisible barrier around him.

'Master Marlowe?' A boy of about eleven stood in front of him, holding out a piece of paper.

'Leave him alone, lad,' one of the scholars called. 'Machiavel is deaf today. Come and talk to us instead.'

Everyone at the table guffawed and pushed each other, pointing and grinning. Some of them weren't much older than the boy, but they were

31

pretending to be men of the world.

The child turned sternly to the table of louts and raised a treble voice to be heard. 'I have a message for Master Marlowe,' he said, firmly. 'I was told to deliver it to no other.' He set his mouth firmly and stood like an ox in the furrow.

The boys at the adjoining table were starting to get up and move towards the lad when suddenly Marlowe came to life. He put down his crust of bread and looked up, identifying the ringleader immediately. 'Master Moorcock,' he said, affably. 'I would be pleased if you and your rabble would take your squawks elsewhere. I would like to read my message in peace.' He smiled pleasantly at the boy. 'Is there an answer required, do you know?'

'I believe so, Master Marlowe,' the boy replied, with much nodding of the head, most of it caused by the knowledge that he would not now have to return to his lodgings without his hose, black and blue from the buffeting of the Corpus Christi scholars. The stallholders in Petty Cury were used to sights like that.

'Then trot along to the Bursar's lodgings, there's a good lad and get me some ink and a quill. Unless you can remember it, perhaps, if I tell you what it is.'

'I could try and remember, Master Marlowe,' the boy said, standing proudly, and trying to look thoroughly reliable in every respect.

Marlowe unfolded the paper and read, as best he could, the crabbed writing. He looked up at the boy. 'This writing is appalling. Who is it from?'

'Master Tobin, the assistant organist of King's College,' the lad said. 'He said it was really important.'

'Hmm.' Marlowe held the paper to the light, trying to make sense of the message. 'Oh, wait, I think I have it.' His forehead creased with worry as he read. '"Master Marlowe, could you please come and deputize for evensong today (Thursday). Rph..." What? Oh, Ralph ... "Ralph Whitingside has absented himself these last two days and Master Thirling's leg is somewhat bad again, causing him to fall in service. Dr Falconer is poorly again with his old trouble. We need an experienced chorister, both to lead the boys and to sing for RW. Please send your answer with the boy who carries this message. W Tobin."' Marlowe looked up at the boy. 'You are a chorister, are you lad?' he asked.

'Yes, Master Marlowe. Thomas Tobin.'

Marlowe gave him a second look. 'Yes, you have a look of the Tobin family about you. Do you lodge with...?'

'My uncle, sir. Yes.'

Marlowe knew Walter Tobin to be a kindly man, surrounded by colleagues bedevilled with impediments. It didn't altogether make for a quiet life and his request was a simple one.

'Well, young Thomas, tell Master Tobin that I would be happy to deputize for Ralph.'

The boy nodded and repeated the words under his breath.

'God's breath, Tom, you don't have to tell him

word for word.' Marlowe laughed. 'But, and this is something you must remember, Tom, tell your uncle that there are two conditions.'

The boy looked eager and ready to commit things to mind.

'One is that I get paid even if Ralph turns up.'

The lad raised a finger and rummaged in his sleeve, drawing out a coin wrapped in a cloth.

'Oh.' Marlowe took it from him. 'Well, you only have one thing to remember, then. And that is that, if Ralph does not show up, then Master Tobin will help me look for him until he is found.'

Thomas looked at him with big eyes, then said, 'Do I have to remember that word for word, Master Marlowe?'

'Yes, Tom,' Marlowe said, getting up and putting the paper in his doublet. 'I rather think you do. Run along, now, and tell your uncle. Do you know the service for today?'

'We're doing a chant from Archbishop Parker's Psalter and *Gaude Gloriosa Dei Mater* for the anthem.'

'Master Thirling was in a somewhat Tallis mood when he planned today's service, I see,' Marlowe said. He'd been singing this stuff now for the best part of twelve years and could still practically do it in his sleep.

'It shows his leg is bad, Master Marlowe. He can conduct us with one hand when we do Tallis, because we know it well. It saves him from so much falling.'

'That's a shame,' Marlowe said, ushering the

34

boy ahead of him as they left the buttery and emerged into the sunshine of The Court. 'It livens up an evensong when Master Thirling falls over. Now, off you go and make sure you deliver my message properly.'

The boy ran off through the archway and down the High Ward. Marlowe, deep in thought, made his way to his rooms, dodging behind a doorway to avoid the grey shade of Gabriel Harvey. There was only so much a man could take.

Men like Marlowe didn't usually list their favourite church services, but had he been brought to the sticking place, then top of the pile would have had to be evensong. The congregation was small, but devout, the boys rather better behaved, having endured a day of lessons, practice and a little admonitory beating as required. The service itself was short, with more music of a more gentle kind, and there could be no setting more beautiful than the Chapel of King's College, with its angels, its quatrefoils and its intertwined initials of HR to remind everybody who the king once was. Master Thirling's leg appeared to be holding up well, with only a minor stumble as the choir processed in. The dusty sunshine of a June afternoon filtered through the high windows and gleamed on the wooden panels of the choir, where the Tudor greyhounds and dragons coiled round the royal arms. The soft singing of the boys, underscored by the few men, swam in the motes and, had

Marlowe believed in a God in Heaven, could almost have been heading straight for His ear. For an hour, Kit Marlowe allowed himself to be a chorister again, singing to the Lord with a clear voice that the Lord watches over the way of the righteous, but the way of the wicked will perish.

They had not yet been granted their degrees, had not yet drunk from the silver-mounted auroch horn that took pride of place in the college silver. But they were out again that night anyway, curfew or no, because Kit Marlowe had a funny feeling about Ralph Whitingside.

Henry Bromerick took the Angel and the Brazen George, weaving his way through Petty Cury and Lion Yard. Tom Colwell got the Boar's Head, the Cardinal's Cap and the Lilypot, keeping his back to Corpus Christi until he reached the all-shielding angles of Silver Street. He even dashed furtively into the Eagle, hideously close to the college and Lomas' watchful eye though it was. He covered up the pelican and lilies badge on his Corpus robe as best he could and peered through the gloom. Nothing. Matthew Parker took the Falcon, the Blue Boar and the Dolphin, beyond the Market Hall, but there was no sign of Whitingside and nobody had seen him for days. Marlowe had furthest to go. He'd hauled off his college robes and stashed them behind a bush in The Court. In his doublet, he'd get more attention from the right people in the town's inns and the prowling

Proctors would leave him alone. He crossed Magdalen Bridge as the lights twinkled double in the river's eddies and the roisterers already began to roll home, ready for the nightly battle to sneak back into their colleges. He heard the watery rattle of the skiff oars as the punters and wherrymen strained at their boats under the dripping archway.

Somebody remembered Whitingside at the Falcon in Petty Cury, but that was probably last week. The innkeeper at the Black Boy swore the man still owed him for the ham and cheese supper he'd laid on after the Lenten feast. Come to think of it, he still owed him for a feast he'd put on for the Lord of Misrule back in the bleak midwinter, but by the time he'd remembered that, Marlowe had gone to the Devil.

The Devil's Inn was as far north as Cambridge scholars chose to walk. It was uphill all the way, past the cherry orchard and the river meadows, under the shadow of the rotting castle with its black earthworks and its ghosts. Marlowe sauntered in on tired legs under the leering gargoyle of Beelzebub that looked about to vomit into the street below. For a while, his eyes failed to acclimatize. It was surprisingly chill in the hall where he stood, the huge fireplace dark and empty in its summer repose. But this was Cambridge and even in high summer the chills crept from the reeded river and the winds, men said, blew straight from Muscovy in the desolate east with no mountain range to block them and only the flat fens of the Low Countries for company.

Marlowe's eyes narrowed as he found his quarry and he sat down heavily on a wooden stool alongside him.

'Master Marlowe.' The man looked up, surprised, clutching a hand of cards tightly to his chest.

'Latimer?' The scholar nodded. 'Where's your master?'

The servant blinked. He had the look of a pet dog caught with the family's suckling pig in his mouth. 'What's o'clock?' he asked. Will Latimer wasn't the brightest apple in the barrel, but he'd been Whitingside's man throughout his time in Cambridge and could place the man by the ticking of time.

'Near midnight,' Marlowe told him.

'You've tried the George?'

Marlowe had not. That was Bromerick's beat and of course Ralph Whitingside could be there as they spoke, holding court on the perils of Puritanism and debating all that was unholy. Somebody else would be buying the drinks. 'No one has seen him for two days,' Marlowe told him. 'Why are you here, man?' Marlowe had never had a servant in his life and couldn't comprehend the fetch-and-carry way of life. Ralph Whitingside was born to it. All he did for himself was eat, drink and fondle whores. And gentlemen like him were increasing in the colleges these days.

'Ah,' Latimer blustered. His face was red and he'd sunk a few tonight. He glanced across at his companions and laid his cards carefully face

38

down on the battered table in front of him. 'A bereavement, I fear.' He looked solemn and hung his head.

'I'm sorry,' Marlowe said. 'Anybody close?'

'My dear old dad.' Latimer shook his head.

Marlowe leaned closer to him, nodding sadly. 'Latimer,' he said quietly, 'if there is one thing I'm sure of, it is that you have no idea who your father was. So let's try again, shall we?'

Latimer looked at the man, blinking. Bugger! The dark, clear eyes, the firm mouth; you didn't get much past this man. The servant's shoulders fell. He was pretty good at this sort of thing usually, but against a man like Marlowe? Well, best not to mess. And he had had a few. 'All right,' he said. 'But you won't say anything to the Master, will you, sir?'

When men called him 'sir', Marlowe knew the battle was as good as won. 'Now, William–' he spread his arms wide – 'would I?'

Latimer took a chance. By now he had little choice, really. 'There *was* a bereavement. But that was my mother's cousin and it was five months ago. It's summer, Master Marlowe. I just wanted some time off. You know what it's like in the colleges – morning prayers at five, Aristotle, Aristotle and more bloody Aristotle until midday. Homer or Demosthenes or some other -thenes all afternoon. And that's the good days. And what am I doing? Writing it all down for the Master. Like I understand a word of it. And that's apart from the usual cleaning, scouring, velvet-primping and mucking out the

39

stables. I just wanted a few days to myself. That's not asking too much, is it?'

Marlowe ignored him. 'So when did you see your master last?'

'Three days ago. I felt a bit of a shit, really. He gave me an angel and wished me every condolence. Nice man. Nice man.' Latimer seemed lost in contemplation of the dregs of his drink, then suddenly looked up. 'But he'd have been at evensong tonight, Master Marlowe. You could have caught him then.'

'I could have,' Marlowe agreed. 'But I didn't. He wasn't there.'

Latimer frowned. 'Now that *is* peculiar,' he said. 'Likes a good sing song, does the Master.'

Marlowe stood up, taking in Latimer's fellow card players. They wore rough linen and leather – stallholders, grooms. They were Town, not Gown. Even so, he crouched close to Latimer as he said, 'How do I reach Ralph's rooms?'

Latimer hesitated, his little piggy eyes swivelling around the room, just in case. 'Fourth staircase to the west,' he hissed. 'Your best bet is the Tit Lane entrance. And you didn't hear it from me.' He patted the side of his nose.

Marlowe nodded and turned to the door. At the steps he paused as Latimer resumed his game. 'I wouldn't play that king, Will,' he said. 'Not with your luck.' He winked and had gone before Latimer hurled down his hand among a cacophony of laughter and the servant gave vent to a string of profanities that would make a cardinal blush.

Trinity Lane was deserted at that time of night. This was not the best way into King's for roisterers. There were too many angles and sharp drops for a man who'd downed a few. Better to take your chances via the shrubbery and the Proctors; on the balance of things, a striped back was preferable to a broken neck.

Marlowe knew that Ralph Whitingside had changed his quarters recently. Whitingside was no man's ward now, but a gentleman pensioner in his own right, and that gave him a new status with which the Fellows of King's and the Provost had to live. The man's old rooms were in the farthest corner from the Chapel, but now, in the new scheme of things, the fourth staircase was behind the great Gothic masterpiece of Harry VI, quieter and more secluded. All to Marlowe's good.

He'd toyed briefly with doubling back to Corpus to collect his robe and see if the lads had had any luck, but that would have brought him into the lair of Lomas and Darryl again and he knew they'd be doubly watchful after the events of the night before – still out to catch the man the other scholars called Machiavel, before the ceremony of the degree put him out of their reach forever. Besides, the lads knew where Marlowe would be and if they'd found Whitingside, they'd have brought him word by now.

So, he'd gone, capless and doubletted, rising on his toes and trying not to clatter on the cobbles in the lane. The black angles of King's

reared up above him, but he'd stayed sober all
night and he'd done this before. He grabbed the
ledge above his head and hauled himself
upwards. There was no moon tonight, no Heavenly lantern to shine God's eye on the ungodly.
And anyway, for once, all Christopher Marlowe
was doing was trying to find a friend. It was the
rank stupidity of the university that you couldn't
just walk in and say 'hello'. A formal visit
would mean paperwork, questions asked and
answered, snooping. And there were too many
men in Cambridge recently who had stood up to
be counted, filled in the paperwork, answered
questions. Some of them were dead now,
screaming hymns of hopelessness as the flames
seared the skin from their writhing bodies.

He caught the next parapet, slipping once as a
piece of masonry chipped off under his boot-
sole. Hand over hand he crossed the wall's face,
checking each window to make sure the shutters
were closed.

The sizars, poor miserable sods, would be
asleep now, huddled together for warmth in the
Great Hall, dreading the clang and scrape of the
Chapel bell. But these rooms, whose walls he
clung to now were the gentlemen pensioners'
quarters, large and well-appointed. He hoped
none of them had dogs that would catch his
shadow and bay the lack of moon.

In the angle of the roof, he hauled himself
upright and lay for a moment on the damp cold-
ness of the tiles. Some June this, with autumn
already coating the stonework in the small

42

hours. Dominus or not, could he really stand another winter in Cambridge before his own warm south beckoned him? He crawled along the eaves, feeling the bird droppings, hard and crusty under his fingers. A sleeping pigeon woke, startled and flapped frantically to the sky.

Now, Marlowe was on the leads, the little attic windows of the servants' quarters standing sentinel over the sleeping town. A small studded door crouched to his left, half-hidden by the ivy that grew there. He tried it gently with his shoulder and it creaked open. Good old Latimer; Marlowe felt vaguely guilty now about exposing the man's hand at the Devil.

He ducked inside and crept along a corridor, wincing as his groin collided with a table. One door, two, and then in the dim half-light from the nearest window he found the staircase. The banister was like polished glass under his hand, the ancient oak worn smooth by generations of scholars. On the first floor, he stopped. He couldn't risk lighting a candle, although they stood unlit at intervals on the furniture in the hall. He peered at the name beside the door, but it was too dark to see. He felt with his fingers. An 'F', definitely. A tall letter in the middle ... Firebrace. Damn. He padded on, checking left and right. The next was easy. Hartland. Where *was* the man's room?

It was the light that stopped him. The growing glimmer of a candle from the floor below, illuminating the plaster ceiling, pargeted with its knots and heraldry. Then, the sound. A rattle of keys, a low, almost tuneless humming. Not a King's scholar, certainly. Not with a voice like that.

Marlowe flattened himself against the wall. He just had time to catch the name by the door as the candle's glow lit it – Whitingside – before he slid round the corner, not daring to breathe. He had not graduated yet. And breaking into another college would mean he never would. Not even the kindly Dr Norgate could save him and those bastards Harvey, Lomas and Darryl would have a field day.

He heard the whisper of skirts along the passageway, the rattle of a key and the squeak of a door being opened. He popped his head round at an awkward angle to see the bedder disappearing into Ralph's rooms.

Eliza Laurence had been a bedder since before Christopher Marlowe was born. She'd come all the way from Royston as a girl, walking barefoot with her father who got an ostler's job, courtesy of the university. She knew these stairs like the back of her hand, every twist and turn. She bobbed before all the scholars, whatever their rank and had never spoken to the Master or the Fellows in her life. But then, she'd never drunk a pint of beer, or missed the Sabbath or seen the sea. And she'd never seen anything like what she saw lying in the guttering candle flame on the bed in Ralph Whitingside's room. She would have screamed, but couldn't.

And that was because Christopher Marlowe had placed his hand tightly over her mouth.

THREE

Marlowe closed the door with the hand that wasn't steadying Eliza Laurence. He led her, weeping, into the next chamber and sat her down.

'I am a friend,' he said quietly. 'I mean you no harm.'

She blinked up at him through her tears. 'Oh, sir, what can have happened? Is it the plague?'

He shook his head.

'The sweating sickness?' she suggested, trying to make sense of what she'd seen in the next room. 'My old mother went of that years ago. It strikes you down like God's own hand.'

A hand had struck down Ralph Whitingside, certainly, but Marlowe wasn't sure God had much to do with it. 'What's your name?' he asked her.

'Eliza, sir.'

'You're a college bedder?'

'Yessir.' Her eyes were wet in the guttering light of her candle, still wobbling in the clasped hands in her lap.

'Do you usually go into scholar's rooms in the early hours?'

'No, sir!' The woman, for all her shock, was

outraged. 'I had my instructions.'

'From Master Whitingside?'

She nodded. 'He told me to clean his rooms this morning, sir. He was to be away, sudden like, but would be back by today. Well, I've got three staircases to do, sir, so I had to start early. It'll be breakfast for the scholars soon.'

Marlowe looked at the sky through Whitingside's leaded panes. There was just a blush of pink on the horizon. Eliza was right. 'When did he tell you this?' he asked her. 'When did you see Master Whitingside last?'

'Oooh.' She pursed her lips, secretly glad that she had something to think about other than the corpse beyond the oak-clad wall. 'Tuesday, sir. It was Tuesday, because that was the day Dr Falconer was took funny.'

'Took funny?' Marlowe repeated. 'That would be Dr Falconer, the organist?'

'That's right, sir. He has these turns. Master Whitingside, he laughs ... laughed at him, saying it's God striking the wicked.' Eliza suddenly went rigid and pale in the candlelight. 'Should he have done that, sir?' she asked Marlowe. 'Master Whitingside, should he have taken the Lord's name in vain?'

Marlowe patted her arm. 'We don't know these things, Eliza,' he said. 'I must look to Master Whitingside. Will you be all right here for a while? You'll wait for me?'

'Let me keep the candle, sir,' she blurted out, suddenly afraid of the dark.

'Of course,' he said and fumbled in the half

46

light until he found another one and leant to her, to touch its wick to her trembling flame.

Ralph Whitingside lay in his own filth on the bed, the candle flames dancing on the hollows of his cheeks and eyes. Kit Marlowe had seen dead men before, but none like this. Whitingside was half-dressed, his hose and boots in place, the points of his shirt tied but his doublet open, one sleeve dangling on the floor, as if he had died putting it on. There were dark stains over his chest and shirt, pooling in the tumbled bed covers. The smell was overpowering, sickly and sweet, like Death itself.

Marlowe steeled himself and held the candle to the dead man's face. Whitingside's mouth was open, his sunken eyes dull and dried out with sightlessly staring at the ceiling above him. The pupils were tiny and dark circles were spreading outwards over his cheeks. A bubble of saliva across his mouth flashed silver in Marlowe's flame, then burst and was gone in a second, dried up by its slight heat. For all the world, it seemed as though the dead man spoke. But there was no sound, no breath. The time for talking with Ralph Whitingside was truly past.

The Corpus man felt the King's man's chest, arms and legs. The body was cold as the grave. Nothing seemed broken and there was no blood. Yet when he stood back and widened the candle's all-seeing arc, he realized that the room showed signs of a struggle. A chair had been overturned, the rugs on the floor had been kicked into untidy folds and the contents of the

47

chamber pot, dark like the stains on the bed, had been spilled on the boards.

He knew he would not be allowed in these rooms again, so he must act fast. He checked Whitingside's wardrobe, his travelling chest, his presses. Clothes that befitted a man who was about to take his place on life's stage – starched linen, pomandered velvet, pattens for his brocaded shoes. In the corner stood a swept-hilt rapier of Spanish design, its quillons curling like quicksilver in the candle's flame. That alone would have paid some poor sizar to stay in Cambridge half a lifetime – and given him the run of the buttery in any college in the university.

Marlowe went back to the parlour where Mistress Laurence still sat, trembling, welded to her seat more by shock than Marlowe's injunction. She barely noticed as he swept past and only came to as she heard him rummaging through Whitingside's shelves of books.

'What are you looking for, sir?' she asked.

Aristotle and Ramus? Marlowe mused to himself as he read the spines of the dead man's library. No. Virgil and Ovid. Better, but hardly anything incriminating. 'I wish I knew,' he muttered without looking at her. A bundle of papers caught his eye, wrapped in scarlet ribbon. He tucked them into his doublet in one deft movement, careful to keep his back to the woman and was just turning over Whitingside's Geneva Bible when something fell from inside it. It was a slim volume, parchment, much

48

written on in his old friend's handwriting, crossed this way and that, now vertical, now diagonal. Some of it was in Greek, some in Latin, but it was the single inscription on the front that gripped Marlowe most. *Quod me Nutruit me Destruit*. That which feeds me destroys me. He frowned. He couldn't remember reading that anywhere. Pliny, perhaps? Not Cicero, surely? The volume followed the other papers into his doublet.

He glanced out of the window. Against the black tracery of Gonville's rooftops, the dawn was creeping over Cambridge. Soon the solemn bell of King's would call the faithful to breakfast, then to Chapel. And with the finding of Ralph Whitingside, all Hell would break loose.

Marlowe squatted in front of the bedder, snuffing out his candle and relying on hers. He helped her to her feet. 'Eliza,' he said, 'you must go to the Proctor. Tell him about Master Whitingside. The authorities will know what to do.'

'Yessir,' she said, still numb in the chill of the morning. Marlowe nodded and swept to the door. He took one last look at the dead man on his bed. Time was he would have crossed himself, knelt in prayer; perhaps, since this was dear old Ralph, cried. But not now. Those days were past, gone forever.

'Sir—' Eliza's voice held him for a moment longer – 'when they ask me, sir, I shall have to tell them, about you, I mean.'

'Of course.' He nodded briskly.

'May I know your name, sir?' her voice

49

trembled.

He smiled in a way that frightened her. 'Know that I am Machiavel,' he said. And he was gone, to the stairs and the leads and the light.

'Machiavel?' Dr Goad strained to catch the word. 'Did she say "Machiavel"?'

'She did, Provost.' Benjamin Steane nodded, alarmed. 'I've been fearing this for a while.'

'Have you?'

Steane looked with contempt at the old man. He'd been waiting for his shoes now for more years than he cared to remember and the old duffer was getting dottier and deafer by the day. The exasperating truth was that old provosts didn't die and they didn't fade away, either.

'You can walk into any study in this university,' Steane told him, 'and ten to one you'll find a copy of the most pernicious book ever written – *The Prince* by Nicolo Machiavelli. The man was the Devil himself, Provost, and yet today's scholars think nothing of reading him.' He shook his head. 'There's sore decline.'

'There always was, Benjamin.' The Provost's memory went further back than Steane's. Under his predecessor, scholars had failed to doff their caps to their betters, or to make way for them in the street. Goad intended, as a young new broom, to do something about that. One of his first acts as Provost was to ban attendance at bear-baiting, bull-baiting and playing football in the street.

'And bathing,' he suddenly blurted out, as

50

though he'd been talking all along. 'You remember the incident?'

Steane didn't, but he'd heard it so often from the Provost he felt he had witnessed the thing personally.

'Young Dick Hadden.' Goad was shaking his white-haired head. 'Drowned in the Cam in the prime of his youth. Oh, he could have gone a long, long way. Why do you suppose the scholars call that place Paradise, Benjamin?'

'Boys will be boys, Provost,' Steane observed, 'the careless cruelty of youth.' For years in Cambridge the sick joke had run that Dick Hadden had found Paradise earlier than he'd expected. Steane cleared his throat and nodded to the bedder standing, head bowed, before them in the lodge hall. 'Now, perhaps, to the matter in hand?'

'Hmm? Oh, yes, of course. This stranger–' his old eyes focused on the woman – 'the one who called himself Machiavel, where did he come from?'

'I don't know, sir,' Eliza Laurence mumbled. She was walking through a nightmare from which she couldn't wake up. She, who had never spoken to the Provost or any of the Fellows before, was now facing the most powerful man in her life. It was the day of judgement for her and Dr Goad might have been St Peter himself. 'One moment I was alone in the room ... well, alone save for the Master ... then he clamped a hand over my mouth so I shouldn't scream.'

51

Steane nodded. 'Clear guilt, Provost.'

'The door was locked, Benjamin,' Goad said. 'This woman used her key – and Whitingside was dead in his bed. Are we sure that foul play was involved? A sudden seizure, surely? Apoplexy. Perhaps the sleeping sickness?'

The Provost looked hopeful. His college had come in for its share of knocks under his hand, scurrilous notices about him pinned to the Lodge door and the main gate. Getting on as he was, he was too old for all that now and wanted a quiet life. That said, there had not been a reported case of the sleeping sickness in the college for a quarter of a century.

'Perhaps.' Steane nodded. 'Provost, may I have a quiet word?'

'Hmm?' Goad looked up at him. 'Ah, of course. Er ... leave us, Mistress ... ah ... But prepare yourself.'

'Sir?' Eliza Laurence's eyes widened.

'There will have to be an inquest, my good woman. Late tomorrow, I shouldn't wonder – such is the way of things. I'll try to arrange it here, in the Great Hall. You are First Finder. You will have to be there.'

'Yessir.' She bobbed and made her exit as quickly as she could.

Benjamin Steane relaxed, the minion having gone, and he sat next to Arthur Goad. 'Provost, you don't seriously believe this is God's will, do you? Natural causes?'

Goad stared at him, gnawing his lip. They were different generations, these men, but they had the common bond of fellowship between them. 'Either way, Benjamin, we must play this down. Scholars do not die every day at King's without there is plague in the town and if we are talking about murder, I want this Machiavel caught, now. You know the coroner?'

'Sir Edmund Winterton? Yes, I do.'

'Go and see him. Get him ... er ... on our side.'

Steane sat upright. 'Provost,' he said, levelly. 'I hope you're not suggesting I interfere with the majesty of the law.'

'Tsk, tsk,' Goad said waspishly. 'In Cambridge, dear boy, we *are* the law. I'm not asking you to do anything underhand. Just ... finesse. A little delicacy. The right, non-committal verdict, quiet burial. What do we know about Whitingside? Pushy parents?'

'No parents at all as far as I can gather,' Steane said. 'He was a ward of court until his eighteenth birthday. He's Lord of some scabrous little manor somewhere in Kent.'

'Good, good. With a bit of luck, nobody'll make too much of a fuss, then. Get along to Winterton. Have a crate or two of college beer sent round to him – the good stuff. And, Benjamin?'

Steane turned in the doorway. 'Yes, Provost?' he said on a sigh.

'Softly, softly, for God's sake!'

If the lads had been gloomy at the Swan the night before, tonight at the Brazen George was positively sepulchral. They had all drunk too

53

many toasts to good old Ralph in their host's finest Dutch brandy and they sat staring into their cups or the middle distance.

'Suicide,' Henry Bromerick was mumbling. 'Who'd have thought it? Ralph Whitingside, suicide. I can't get over it.' He looked up at the others as if to find some explanation in their faces.

'You can't get over it because it isn't true, Henry,' Marlowe said. 'If Ralph killed himself, how did he do it?'

'Poison,' said Tom, always the sharpest of the bunch. 'You said yourself, Kit, stains on his clothing, his bedding. He'd have been sick.'

'Where was the cup?' Marlowe asked him.

'The what?' Matthew Parker frowned.

'If Ralph took poison, what did he do? Swig something from a bottle? I saw no bottle in his rooms. Did he drink from a goblet, carefully wash and dry it and put it back on the sideboard? Does a man so miserable he wants to end his own life do that?'

'There are more things in Heaven and earth...' Bromerick ventured, with his vast experience of life in the King's School, Canterbury and Corpus Christi College, Cambridge.

'And one of them is murder,' Marlowe said, nodding.

'Wait. Wait a minute.' Colwell held up a hand, wrestling with all that Marlowe had told them in the brief snatches of free time during the day, before Dr Lyler hit them with everything the Civil Law course had to offer. 'You said Ralph's

54

door was locked. The bedder unlocked it.'

'That's right,' Marlowe said.

'So...'

'So if someone killed him, they had to have a key,' Parker chimed in. 'So it has to be someone at King's.'

'It has to be someone who killed Ralph, took *his* key and locked the door, that's all,' Marlowe pointed out.

Silence.

'Still,' Colwell said. 'To get access to Ralph's rooms at all, you'd need to have the right connections. Christ, Kit, you had to get in by the roof.'

'Point taken,' Marlowe said. 'But it was Will Latimer who told me how, in his cups at the Devil. How many more people has he told? I wouldn't trust that man further than I could throw him. How many other college servants blab indiscreetly over their ale or on street corners? And who–' he leaned forward so that their heads were together – 'wanted to see Ralph Whitingside dead?'

The heads moved back and all four of them sat upright, stock still for a moment and looked at the others. Marlowe clicked his fingers for the cups to be refilled. 'I've written to Roger Manwood,' he said.

'The scourge of the night-prowlers?' Parker whispered. Bromerick let out a whistle through his teeth. Back in Canterbury, exhausted mothers quietened their fractious children with threats of Roger Manwood.

55

'Yes,' Colwell crowed, a look of triumph on his face already. 'He'll know what to do!'

Robert Greene stood cap in hand at Gabriel Harvey's door at Corpus that Saturday morning. All Cambridge was buzzing with the story of Ralph Whitingside's death and Greene was not the sort of man to let rumour and innuendo pass him by. He needed to be in the thick of it.

'Dr Harvey?' The great man had appeared at long last from behind the buttresses in The Court.

'Who are you?' Harvey looked him up and down. The Fellow was wearing the robes of St John's College but his skin was dark and he appeared to be wearing an earring.

'Robert Greene, sir. St John's, lately back from Italy.'

'Italy? Really. Nowhere near Rome, I trust.'

'No, no, sir. Verona. Lucca. There was plague in Florence. We were turned back.'

Harvey was already walking. 'Your travels are fascinating, Dominus Greene, but I am rather busy.'

'Yes, sir, I know. On your way to the inquest on Ralph Whitingside.'

Harvey stopped in his tracks, waiting for a couple of sizars to slink past, doffing their caps to him. 'You seem remarkably well-informed for a man–' he pinged Greene's earring with a fingernail – 'so lately come from Italy.' And he strode on.

'But I have information, sir,' Greene called

56

after him. 'About Christopher Marlowe...'

Sir Edward Winterton sat in the Provost's chair in the Great Hall of King's College. Around him clucked his clerks, carrying ink, quills, parchment and boxes of sand, to write down, in Latin, all that transpired that morning. To his left, on the hard oak benches normally reserved for the King's scholars, sat the sixteen men and true who would decide the issue in question – whatever happened to Ralph Whitingside?

Winterton was a fierce-looking old man at first sight, but closer to, his mild eyes gave the game away; his bark was worse than his bite. He wore his coroner's robes today and sat beneath a furled banner of Her Majesty, the *Semper Eadem* bright in gold lettering on the blue of the scroll. He wore his collar of office with its roses and portcullises to remind everyone that he spoke for the Queen. And he wore his sword to remind everyone that he had once ridden with Lord Dudley at Pinkie, where they'd both trounced the Scots back in the days of the boy-king, Edward.

A single chair, carved, upright, lonely, stood in front of the coroner's dais. A long way behind it, a large crowd had squeezed itself into the Hall – the Provost and Fellows of King's, a handful of their servants and as many interested parties and ghouls as Harry VI's great building could hold.

'Inquisition indented,' intoned the clerk of the court, 'taken this day in the County of Cambridge on the second day of July in the year of

57

Elizabeth by the grace of God of England, France and Ireland, Queen, defender of the faith etcetera twenty fifth, the year of our Lord 1583...'

After the preliminaries were over, the fanfare blown and the coughing subsided, Winterton barked in his hoarse voice, 'First witness. First Finder.'

Nobody stepped forward. People looked right and left, frowning, muttering and wondering what the delay was. In the corner, Dr Steane pushed Eliza Laurence forward, gently shooing her into that vast space around the witness chair.

'Who is the First Finder of the body?' Winterton roared.

'I am,' a clear voice called from the back.

Everybody turned and there was a babble of voices. Gabriel Harvey's mouth fell open involuntarily as Kit Marlowe strode through the Hall and bowed to the court.

'Who are you, sir?' Winterton asked.

'Christopher Marlowe, sir, Secundus Convictus of Corpus Christi College, University of Cambridge.'

Winterton waved him to the chair. Marlowe looked across at Eliza and smiled. She bobbed and doubled back, grateful to slide back into anonymity again, if only for a short while.

'You found the body, Master Marlowe?' Winterton asked. The clerks scratched away.

'I did, sir,' he said. Then, to the clerks: 'Can you spell the name? Only, my own college seems to have difficulty with...'

58

'Marlowe!' Another voice ended his sentence. All eyes turned to the back of the Hall.

Winterton slammed the tip of his staff of office down on the floor by his feet to order silence. 'Who are you, sir?' he asked.

'I am Dr Gabriel Harvey,' the voice called, 'formerly Fellow of Pembroke Hall, now of Corpus Christi. What was he doing there? How did an undergraduate come to have access to the rooms of a graduate – and from a different college?'

There was hubbub in the room, until Winterton's staff of office thudded on the woodwork again. 'Enough!' he thundered. 'In my courtroom, sir, *I* ask the questions.' He waited until the murmurings had died down. 'Well, Master Marlowe,' he said, fixing the man with his terrible stare. 'Explain yourself.'

'If I may, my lord?' Another voice, gentler than Harvey's and in its gentleness compelling, came from the back and a slender, robed figure emerged from the crowd.

Winterton looked exasperated. If he'd known he was in for a day like this, he'd have rolled over in bed and given the job to his deputy. 'And who might you be, sir?' He did his best to keep his voice under control.

'I am Professor Michael Johns, of Corpus Christi College. I hate to call what my learned colleague Dr Harvey has to say into question, but technically, according to college statute, Master Marlowe was, as of two days ago, Dominus Marlowe.'

59

'There has been no ceremony!' Harvey countered, stung by the man's interference.

'Indeed not,' Johns said quickly, 'namely because Dominus Marlowe elected to wait until such time as he was able to go through said ceremony with his fellow Parker scholars. The statutes are on his side, Dr Harvey.'

'Are they?' Harvey rasped. He was standing nose to nose with Johns now, his eyes burning and his jaw flexing.

'Apparently so.' Winterton was determined to end this wrangling then and there. 'And I will have the law observed, sir!'

For a long moment, Harvey hovered. From the tension twanging through his body like a bowstring, he looked for all the world as if he were about to strike Johns down. Then he looked at Marlowe, sitting quietly with his back to them both. 'You, sir,' he snapped at him, 'are a disgrace to Corpus Christi and to this university. Not even in your robes.'

'Indeed not.' Marlowe stood up, spinning on his heel to face Harvey. 'Any more than I was when I found Ralph Whitingside's body. I had no wish to dishonour the name of Corpus Christi then and I have no wish to dishonour it now.' He smiled and that smile made Harvey spin away, striding for the door.

'Make a note of that man's name,' Winterton instructed his clerks, still pointing at Harvey's retreating figure. 'Contempt of court. He shall be fined five shillings. Now–' he cleared his throat as Johns bowed to him before resuming his seat and Marlowe took the witness chair again – 'for the benefit of the court' – he nodded to the jury – 'some of you gentlemen are not of the University, so it behoves me to explain. As an undergraduate, this witness had no automatic right of entry to another scholar's rooms. As a graduate, that is different...' The coroner leaned forward in his seat. 'Although I fail to see, Dominus Marlowe, why you didn't just walk in through the front door...'

Marlowe smiled. 'Old habits, my lord,' he said, 'and the front gates were locked.'

There was a ripple of laughter from the younger members of the crowd, which Winterton chose to let go for the moment.

'You went to Ralph Whitingside's rooms,' the coroner established. 'Why?'

'Ralph Whitingside was an old friend of mine, my lord. We met regularly, for academic discussion and contemplation.'

Henry Bromerick, several rows back, nudged Tom Colwell, who in turn hushed him.

'I had not seen Ralph for three days and had expected him to help my friends and me celebrate our graduation.'

'I see,' Winterton said. 'And where was this celebration to take place?'

'Oh, forgive me, sir.' Marlowe opened his dark eyes wide. 'I am much afraid I am unacquainted with the hostelries of the town.'

It was Tom Colwell's turn to stifle a guffaw, stuffing part of his sleeve in his mouth.

'Very well.' Winterton was prepared to take

this young man at face value for the moment. 'What did you find, First Finder?'

Marlowe told it all. Or at least the all he wanted the court to know. What he could not do, or would not do, in that house of strangers, was to talk of the smell in the chamber, the dead eyes of his friend. Neither would he tell them of the reason for a reckoning in a small room because, as yet, he didn't know it. And the letters and the curious little book. Eliza Laurence hadn't seen him take them and there was no one else to know they had gone.

There were no other witnesses who had seen anything. Eliza was dragged back out to that lonely place to sit in that accursed chair. She took the oath with a trembling hand and a shaking voice and swore on the Bible that she acknowledged was her crutch and comfort; but she could not look Sir Edward Winterton in the face and in the end, the kindly Dr Steane spoke for her, annoying though the coroner found it.

'Mistress Laurence is a simple soul, my lord,' Steane said. 'I have talked to her at some length and she is in awe of your honour's greatness...'

Winterton rolled his eyes.

'...she was told by Master Whitingside that he would be away and that she was to clean his room against his return on the day that she – and Master Marlowe – found him.'

'Except that he had been nowhere?' the coroner asked.

'Who is to say, my lord?' Steane replied. The question was rhetorical.

62

'Quite so. The man who called himself Machiavel.' Winterton threw one last question at her, bypassing Steane in the process. 'Do you see him in this court?'

Eliza Laurence shrank back in the chair, tucking her chin as far into her coif as it would go. Her hands were knotted in her lap but somehow she wrenched her sweating fingers apart and pointed to the far wall where Marlowe lolled with his arms folded. Murmurs filled the court.

The rest was mere formality, demanded by Sir Edward Winterton who was a stickler for such things. Dr Goad, the Provost, confirmed that Ralph Whitingside had presented himself at the college shortly after Christmas Day in the year of our Lord 1578. He offered to show the Court the ledgers if it so wished. Whitingside had matriculated Bachelor of Arts three years later and was now studying for his Masters degree. It was generally assumed that he would enter the church, but on receiving his inheritance some two years ago, that seemed less likely. His interests? Hebrew, obviously; Rhetoric; the Discourses. The old man had frowned as he recited this – what a curious question for the coroner to ask. Had the man no academic leanings at all?

'He sang fairly,' Goad suddenly remembered, 'had a fine tenor voice when he joined us, from the King's School, Canterbury. Er ... you'd have to ask Richard Thirling, my choirmaster, for more.'

Winterton pursed his lips. He'd never heard of

a man killed for his voice before. This whole thing was an irrelevance. It was mid-afternoon before the procedure came to an end. The coroner outlined the evidence for the benefit of the jury and asked them if they needed to retire. They didn't.

'Your task,' Winterton told them in time-honoured fashion, 'is to decide how, when, where and by what means the deceased came to his death.' He paused, secretly enjoying, as he always did, his moment in God's light. 'But if you'll take my advice, you will find that, in a moment of madness, Ralph Whitingside took his own life.'

The murmurs in the hall grew to a mutinous rumble. There was nothing in anything anyone had heard to lead to such a conclusion. The Parker scholars looked at Winterton, at each other. They hadn't known Whitingside like Marlowe had, such was the age gap among former schoolboys. But Kit didn't believe it. And if Kit didn't believe it, it wasn't so. There was so much shouting that the jury's foreman could barely agree with the coroner that that was, indeed, the verdict of them all.

Winterton rammed his staff down for silence and the usher proclaimed, with all solemnity, that the business of the court was over. He commended Ralph Whitingside's lost soul to God and called for three cheers for Her Majesty. Everybody responded lustily. Everybody except Christopher Marlowe.

'Machiavel,' Winterton called to him as the

crowd shuffled out into the sunlight of King's quadrangle.

Marlowe turned to him. 'Sir?'

The coroner stepped down from the dais, slowly passing his staff and chain of office to his clerks. Now, he was stripped of his role and stood toe to toe with Marlowe, man to man.

'You don't approve of the Court's findings?' he asked.

'You were wrong,' Marlowe told him.

'The Court was wrong,' Winterton said.

Marlowe half turned, as if to leave. 'You are Sir Edward Winterton,' he said softly. 'A Queen's Coroner, knight of the shire. You own half of Cambridgeshire–' he pointed to where the jury had sat – 'and half those men, too, I shouldn't wonder.'

Winterton started. 'You insolent young puppy,' he snarled. 'Do you accuse me of jury tampering?'

Marlowe looked at him. 'They are serving men, tapsters, petty bookkeepers and Bible readers. If you told them the moon was made of cheese, they'd believe it. They'd walk into the fire for people like you. It's the way of it and it always has been. But it still doesn't make it right.'

'And what of you, Master Machiavel?' Winterton asked, calmer now. 'Who will you walk into the fire for?'

Marlowe smiled. 'When I know that, Master Coroner,' he said, tapping the man lightly on his fur-edged robe, 'I shall be sure to let you know.'

65

FOUR

There is no good time to bury a man of just twenty-two summers, but that night, in its moonless dark, was as good as any other. The lingering warmth of the summer day had gone, but the dew had not yet come as the flickering lights of the dark lanterns began to gather in the lee of the wrong side of the churchyard wall. Whispered voices greeted each other as Ralph Whitingside's friends came together to say goodbye.

The gravedigger's cleared throat sounded as loud as a trumpet blast in the sibilant near silence. Then, he spoke, in the normal voice of one to whom death and decay is a normal stock in trade. 'I'll just leave you gentlemen to your business, then.'

'Thank you, my man.' Dr Steane, also no stranger to gravesides, was dismissive.

'I'll have my payment before I go,' the man said, not unkindly, but merely speaking as someone who had often had trouble, after his necessary deed was done, in extracting the coins from the suddenly parsimonious bereaved. There was too much work in digging the body back up, and what other recourse did a man in his line of work who had not been paid have?

Marlowe's voice sounded, low and respectful to Whitingside, a reminder to the others. 'Thank you for your work, Master Harkness. Here is your fee, and a little for a drink to warm you tonight.'

The man mumbled his thanks. It wasn't many men who would bother to find out his name, to treat him like a human being. His was not a trade that brought him many friends; in a crowded churchyard, he was often digging among the bones of the not long dead, and this grave had been no different. In the unconsecrated ground on the wrong side of the churchyard wall, reserved for suicides and babies who died unbaptised or perhaps even before they breathed, space was short and the graves unmarked. Only the unevenness of the ground bore silent testimony to their number, the Granta dead. The gravedigger was glad of the dark. That way, the mourners wouldn't see the little flecks of bone in the mound of earth off to one side. He'd found a skull once, whole and grinning; even he had needed his extra drink that night. He touched his cap to Marlowe and melted away. By morning, the grave would be level again and after a few weeks of summer growing, the weeds would have masked the place where Ralph Whitingside lay, one among many.

Steane looked around at the knot of mourners, each face lit dimly from below by their lanterns. No one had come from King's apart from him, no friends, no Fellows, no Provost. Pitching his

67

voice low now that the gravedigger had gone, he said, 'Thank you for coming, gentlemen. I am only sorry that this service has to take place in these circumstances.'

Marlowe spoke for them all. 'Thank you for offering to conduct it for us, Dr Steane. It's not every churchman...'

Steane held up a hand. 'Think nothing of it, Dominus Marlowe,' he said. 'Ralph Whitingside was a devout member of the choir of King's College and I think I owe him this much.'

'Or any man who is not a suicide,' said Henry Bromerick bitterly. 'This should be happening in the light of day, with a proper ceremony.' He stifled a sob.

'This should not be happening at all,' Marlowe corrected him. 'But as it is, shall we continue, Dr Steane?' He glanced over his shoulder into the dark under the trees. 'Some of us need to get to our beds. It will get chilly soon, towards dawn.'

Steane nodded and bowed his head, waiting a while as the others adopted their chosen attitude of prayer. By an unspoken common consent, they had all put out their lanterns and so Steane's voice spoke from total darkness. 'I know that my Redeemer liveth, and that he shall stand at the latter day upon the earth; and though this body be destroyed, yet shall I see God; whom I shall see for myself and mine eyes shall behold, and not as a stranger.' The familiar words rolled out and brought some comfort to the friends gathered around the grave. 'The Lord be with you.'

'And with thy spirit.' The words echoed off the wall and trees, giving the impression of other mourners grouped behind in the dark. Tom Colwell pressed closer to the others; he was at the back of the group and felt chill mortality laying a hand on his shoulder.

'Let us pray.' Steane didn't need to see the prayer book to say the words. He had been saying them now for thirty years and more and sometimes hardly heard himself speaking them. The circumstances of this burial were not something he was familiar with – churchmen were seldom at the burial of a suicide – but he had offered to do this, and he would do it properly, or not at all. But even so, part of his mind was jumping on ahead. There would be no reading, that much was clear. But he didn't feel it was a funeral service without a psalm. He needn't have worried. As he concluded the opening prayer for the dead man, two sweet voices lifted up to his left.

'Out of the deep have I called unto thee, O Lord; O Lord, hear my voice.' Marlowe and Colwell intoned the words of the one hundred and thirtieth psalm, known as *De Profundis*.

Old habits die hard and Parker and Bromerick took up the decani response. 'Oh let thine ears consider well; the voice of my complaint.'

Steane felt a tremor pass through him. These voices, raised to God in this bleak place where no organ wheezed and groaned reminded him of how he had felt when he first entered the

69

Church; before the whole thing had become something to organize and manipulate. He was brought back to the dark present by a shuffling noise over to his left and he remembered why they were here. Two parish paupers, earning a sorely-needed farthing, carried the linen-wrapped body of Ralph Whitingside on a hurdle, the bier stored in the church being beyond the pale for him, and placed it on the ground at the side of the grave. The last verse of the psalm died away into silence and then, loud enough so everyone could hear it, there was the sound of weeping from the trees. Only Marlowe knew for sure who it was and, taking their lead from him, no one moved towards the noise, but let the poor soul mourn alone.

Making the sign of the cross as so few men did these days, Steane bowed his head and spoke the words of committal over the dead man's body. The paupers, with minimal ceremony, heaved the body into the grave, which, being shallow, took him with hardly a sound. Then, to Marlowe's surprise, Steane spoke again.

'O God, whose blessed Son was buried in a Sepulchre in the garden, bless, we pray, this grave and grant that he whose body is to be buried here may dwell with Christ in Paradise, and may come to thy Heavenly Kingdom, through thy Son, Jesus Christ our Lord, Amen.'

There was a muttered 'amen' from the small congregation. The paupers, standing off to one side, pushed back their ragged hoods and exchanged puzzled looks in the dark. They had stood here often enough, but had never heard that bit before. Nor had Marlowe.

'I didn't know that it was normal to consecrate a suicide's grave,' he said quietly to Steane as they walked away from the graveside, trying not to hear the gritty sound of the spades cutting into the pile of earth beside Ralph Whitingside's last bed.

Steane picked his way in the dark over the tussocky grass and took a moment to reply and to compose his voice. He had been unusually moved by this service, by the voices singing the psalm, by the crying in the trees. He cleared his throat. 'It seemed the least I could do,' he said, and forged ahead, to where his horse cropped the grass at the edge of the lane.

Marlowe was thoughtful. So someone else didn't believe Whitingside was a suicide. He was now more determined than ever to solve this mystery; as friend and First Finder (or near enough) it could almost be said to be his duty. He turned and waited for his friends, who were fiddling with their lanterns, passing the flame from one to the other, trying to banish the dark as Steane's horse clattered into the distance.

'Come on, my lads,' he said, with what sounded for all the world like genuine enthusiasm. 'Let's go and see if we can find an inn with a light showing. I think we all need a drink, in Ralph's memory, don't you?'

And, arm in arm, the Parker scholars moved off into the dark, taking a little world of flickering light with them.

At the grave, the paupers had done their job, patting down the earth with the flat of their spades and had gone. A pale shape detached itself from the trees and crept close to the churchyard wall. Meg Hawley stood, wrapped in her dusty summer cloak, looking down at the bare earth for a moment then, with a low moan, sank to the ground and lay, as though alongside the man beneath the soil, with her arm outstretched above him as though, too late, to protect him from his enemies.

The Cam winds on for ever. It twists, dark and green, with its clawing weed through the mellow stone of the colleges, gliding past the wherries and fondling the trailing willows that added their tears to the water.

Beyond Magdelene Bridge, where the flat lands to the east gave way to Sturminster Common, it widens and shallows and thick sedge hangs over it, shielding the banks from the noonday sun. It was here that Nicholas Drew dozed that scorching Sunday. He'd never been much of a church goer, but to avoid the recusancy fees, he'd gone along to St Bene't's as usual, resenting anew that those stuck up bastards from Corpus Christi College used *his* church as if it were their own. Along with most of the Town, he despised the poll-shaven scholars with their books and their serious frowns. Most of all, he hated their hypocrisy. The same men who cut him dead in *his* church of a Sunday morning, shoulder barged him off *his* pavements on Sunday night and drank in *his* inn, talking loudly in Latin with some private joke at his expense.

But the cloudless blue consoled him. All his life he'd known this river, making his meagre living by ferrying the University from one side to the other or punting them up stream and down. He knew the river's moods, the dark waters of winter where the rain pitted the surface, the stagnant hollows where the ice lay under the bitter wind. And this time of year was Drew's favourite, when the water was warming up and the fish flew slick and silver in the flickering lights and shadows of the shallows.

His line trailed in the water and his rod was wedged in his usual niche on the bank. He lay back on the soft moss, chewing the end of a newly pulled grass stalk, sweet as honey. He tilted his ferryman's cap over his eyes. No more work today. No more church. You're nearer to God by a river than anywhere...

There was a tug on the line and before Drew could scramble up to haul in his wriggling, terrified catch, the line and rod jerked out of the bank and splashed into the river. Shit! Had old Nick hooked a Leviathan here in the sparkling waters of the Cam?

His line had tangled in something floating by the far bank. Whatever it was had been meandering midstream and now veered away from him. No surprises there. The current did that along this stretch, the river-bit everybody called Paradise. The surprise was the bundle itself. At first, as he scrambled to his feet and followed it, it looked like a pile of rags, waterlogged cloth tossed from a market stall in Petty Cury. But Drew's line was still caught in it and his rod was floating faster now, out of his reach. He knew the currents here. They were fickle and unpredictable, the river bed uneven and shelved. Men had died here, reaching Paradise twice as their lives came to an end.

Bugger! Nicholas Drew was running now, stumbling over the clods of turf as he raced the bundle. There was no bridge until Anglesey Abbey and that was nearly two miles away. He'd have to risk the water if he wanted to get his rod back and he'd have to do it before the deeps he knew lay downstream. If he got into difficulties there, he'd never get out.

He tried it as best he could, hauling off his pattens and his jerkin, crashing into the river's turbulence. The water that had felt so warm to his fisherman's fingers earlier was now, suddenly, very cold and it hit him like a wall. Sheep grazing on the bank, startled by the sudden noise, skitted away, bleating in their fear. Then they stopped to look at him, stupid, passive, unhelpful.

Drew was a strong swimmer and he reached the bundle quickly. No time to disentangle the line before he was in the deeps, so he dragged the bundle to the far bank and caught an overhanging willow branch, bracing his feet on the sedge to stop himself being carried on by the

74

river's pull. Damn, this thing was heavy. He swung both hands upwards, gripping the bundle between his legs and jerked backwards, pulling the thing out of the water. It nearly slid back as he let go, but he just had time to grab it and roll it over. Then he screamed and fell back into the long grass.

It was late afternoon before Coroner Winterton reached the spot. He left his carriage on the north bank and plodded with his servant through the tufted grass to where the little knot of people stood on the banks of the Cam.

At his approach, they doffed their caps or curtsied according to their sex and stood looking as deferential as the sheep across the river.

'Who found her?' Winterton asked.

'I did, sir. Nicholas Drew, ferryman.'

The coroner took in the man. No need to invoke the Sumptuary Laws here. He was dressed as a ferryman should be. 'What were you doing here?'

'Fishing, sir.'

'Well, Master Drew.' Winterton knelt with as much dignity as his age and his Venetian breeches would let him. 'Today you have become a fisher of men. Or should I say woman?' He peered at the sad bundle on the bank. What was she? Forty? Fifty? It was difficult to say. The water had done its work and she had been in the water for some time. He checked the hands. The skin was wrinkled, loose, as it was on the scalp where the once-auburn hair was partially

75

detached and wrapped in her dress.

'Any of you women–' Winterton glanced up at the little crowd – 'used to laying out?'

They hesitated. 'I am, sir,' one of them said, and a thin, angular woman bobbed to him.

'Mrs Drew, sir,' the First Finder said. 'My wife.'

'Good.' Winterton got up. 'We can keep this in the family, then. Both of you will accompany me to the Dead House. Knowles–' he clicked his fingers to a servant – 'rig something up, will you? We haven't time to send for a cart and I don't want ... that ... inside my carriage.'

Mrs Drew had done her work by candlelight in the Charnel House by the Grey Friars. She had peeled the sodden dress and chemise off the corpse, floppy and slippery as it was. She had washed the body carefully and dried it, combing what hair was left and she had placed the dead woman's arms across her breasts, for modesty's sake. Then she spread a folded shroud across her hips. Men should not look on such things.

Edward Winterton waited until the layer-out left the room and he went to work. He was a husband, father and grandfather, too, and he had the same sensibilities as the next man. But he had a job to do. He looked at each hand. Despite the wrinkled skin, he noticed the mark left by a wedding ring, but the ring itself had gone. Was this the mark of a robbery? He peeled back the cloth and looked at the abdomen. Had she ever borne a child, this child of the river? He didn't

76

know. He prised open her eyelids. The eyes were sunk, the sockets almost empty and he couldn't tell the colour the irises had once had. The breasts were small and well-formed, but the skin was blackened now with exposure to the air. He checked her feet. The soles were thick and pale. She had been in the water, he'd wager, for four days, perhaps five. She had been found at Paradise, but where had she gone in? And who was she when she walked upright, talking and laughing, dancing and loving? Perhaps only God knew now.

Time and again he was drawn to the dead woman's throat. The lips were tight and pursed and around her neck, embedded deep into the purple skin, was a crucifix. Whatever else she had been, the woman was a Papist.

That was the year when the carpenter, Joseph Fludd, was Constable of the Watch. In fact, it was rather more than a year because nobody else wanted the job. His cottage, with its adjoining workshop, lay off the road which ran from the south into Cambridge, a little below the ancient church of St Michael and St Mary, Trumpington.

And it was here, wading through fragrant wood-shavings and decidedly un-fragrant chicken droppings, that Jeremiah Butler and his wife came that Monday morning, a little after nine of the clock. They knocked on the little door below the thatch.

'Are you the one they call Trumpy Joe?' Butler asked as the door opened.

'I am Joseph Fludd, carpenter and Constable,' the cottager said, standing as tall as the doorway would let him. Each man eyed the other, assessing status. Butler was clearly a yeoman, well dressed but unarmed and his wife wore a French hood of intricate design over her coif. Fludd was still in his leather apron, splinters in his fingers and polish under his nails.

'Jeremiah Butler, of Royston. My wife, Jane.'

There were nods all round.

'Did you want a table, sir?' Fludd asked. 'A press, perhaps? Or a settle?' He had no idea his reputation had reached as far south as Royston.

Butler looked at him with disdain. 'I was looking for the High Constable,' he said, 'but it looks as though I've been misdirected.'

'Love you, sir,' Fludd chuckled. 'We haven't had a High Constable in Cambridge since Edward was king. Old Master Hipkiss went of the plague when I was a lad. Nobody's replaced him since.'

'Who do you report to, then?' Butler wanted to know.

'The Justice, sir, for most things. The Coroner if the crime's severe.'

'Who is the Coroner here? Still Edward Winterton?'

'The same, sir. As good a man who ever drew breath.'

'I'm glad to hear it.' The yeoman turned on his heel. 'Come, Jane; we're wasting our time.'

'If it's a crime, sir, I can help.' Fludd stepped out from under the eaves of thatch. He was a well-built fellow, with an earnest look about him and an air of dependability.

'Can you?' Butler asked.

'Come this way, sir.' Fludd ushered the couple into his humble abode, kicking chickens off the furniture. He pointed to a wall at the back of the parlour, from which scraps of paper floated in the breeze from the open casement. Fludd touched them one by one. 'Not mending the bridge at Magdalene,' he read. 'Not hanging a lantern in Petty Cury; cutting turf off Parker's Piece in the night time; not having a licence to sell ale; the nuisance of muck...'

'How are you on missing persons?' Jane Butler suddenly asked. She had had enough of her husband's dithering and for all this Constable could clearly read, she was not at all convinced he was the man for job.

'Er ... yes,' Fludd said. 'I've had a few of those in my time.'

'How long have you been a Constable?' Butler asked, frowning. Fludd couldn't have been more than thirty.

'On this occasion, sir, fifteen ... no, sixteen months. Before that, twice, for a period totalling three years.'

'And in that time,' Butler pressed him, 'how many missing persons?'

'Um ... one. Well, two if you count the Master of Trinity. But he wasn't so much missing as didn't want to be found.'

'I believe my sister wants to be found, Constable,' Jane Butler said.

79

Fludd looked at her. She was of indeterminate years, but her hair which showed from under her coif showed only a light sprinkling of grey. Fludd judged her to be in her late thirties. Her eyes were at once calm and worried.

'Could you give me some details, Madame?' he asked. 'A description of your sister. When she went missing. Any distinguishing marks. Anything you can tell me will be of use.'

The woman looked nervously at her husband and then spoke. 'Master Fludd, I wonder if I could sit? I am feeling quite unwell with the worry and...'

Fludd was immediately contrite. 'Of course,' he said. 'Would you like something to drink? Some ale, perhaps. Some water. I have my own well and the water is very sweet.' He tried to keep the touch of pride out of his voice.

'No, no, I will be quite all right if only I could sit.'

Fludd ushered her to a window seat and plumped a cushion for her. The men sat on hard chairs, ranged in front of her, as if in homage. Sitting with the dusty sunlight behind her the years dropped away as she began her story. The Constable had ink and parchment beside him and dipped occasionally as he made quick strokes with the quill.

'I feel, Master Fludd, that I must begin by telling you that I don't know whether my sister has any marks, distinguishing or otherwise. Until I saw her a week ago yesterday, that would be Sunday sennight, I had not seen her since she left our parents' house thirty years ago, when I was just seven years old.'

The Constable gave himself an invisible pat on the back – his guess at her age had been remarkably accurate.

'She had married young,' Jane Butler went on, 'and I remember the fuss for the wedding; she was our parents' eldest daughter and the sewing and the cooking and everyone rushing to and fro – it was great fun for a little girl.'

'Who did she marry?' the Constable asked. 'Just for the notes.' And he waved his hand to the fluttering wall.

The woman looked at her husband, who waved his hand at her to carry on. 'I don't know.' She caught the expression on the Constable's face and grimaced back at him, ruefully. 'I know that that may sound strange, but I only remember the wedding preparations. The wedding day was confusing for a little girl, so many new people, so much music, dancing.' She smiled at Fludd and an excited seven year old looked out of her eyes. 'I know I made myself sick eating all the marchpane animals the cooks had decorated the table with. I have never been able to eat it since. But as to who she married, I can't remember him at all.'

'But surely,' the Constable asked, 'other people in the family must have known who he was. Must have spoken of him since. Did something happen? Did he die young?'

'I don't know what happened to him,' she said, simply. 'I remember...' she furrowed her brow,

81

trying to work out how to tell this stranger about an event thirty years ago which had rocked her family to its foundations. 'I remember her coming home, late one night. My mother was crying. I was excited, because I had missed my sister, and I thought she was home for a visit. But in the morning, she wasn't there. People told me I had imagined it.'

'And had you?'

'No. Later, when I was older, my mother told me that my sister – her name is Eleanor, Eleanor Peacock – had married a man who had turned out to be a bad lot. He had abandoned her and she had come home with only the clothes on her back. To avoid a scandal, my parents sent her to our aunt in France. She had joined a convent there when King Henry...' her voice tailed away. Especially in this day and age, it paid to be circumspect with strangers. There were plots everywhere, Jesuits roaming the roads and planning God knew what.

The Constable understood. Every family had a Catholic somewhere in its closet. 'Your aunt is a nun?'

'Was a nun, yes. Of the poor Clares, I believe. She went to France when her convent was dissolved.' Jane Butler drew a deep sigh. 'She did well there, and when Eleanor's shame came on the family, mother said, it seemed the right thing to do to send her to live with her sister, who was known as Sister Bernard. After the Saint, you know.'

Fludd was a man who found he had enough to

do with the constabulary job and the carpentry that he didn't need to spend hours poring over the calendar of Saints' days. However, he was as kind as he was busy and so nodded understandingly.

'So Eleanor went to France. She never took her vows, she remained a Lay Sister, but she became very devout. She wore a wedding ring as a bride of Christ, adopted the habit and was, to all intents and purposes, I suppose, a nun.'

'Why did she come home?' Fludd asked.

Jeremiah Butler spoke up now. 'My wife's mother died,' he said. 'Her father couldn't manage his home. The servants were running wild, the farm was in rack and ruin. We brought him to live with us, but' – he stole a covert look at his wife – 'it was not successful. Then we had word that Jane and Eleanor's aunt had died in France. It seemed the perfect solution. Eleanor could come home to nurse her father. I have taken on the farmlands to run with my own.'

Fludd almost added aloud 'And my mad old father-in-law will not be in my house morning, noon and night.' But in fact he said, simply, 'That seems an ideal solution.' He turned to Jane Butler. 'So, she got back on the Sunday. When did you see her last?'

'A week ago today.'

The Constable was amazed and showed it. 'So she was in your house for just one day?'

'Yes,' the woman said. 'Just one day.' She foraged in her sleeve for a cloth and blew her nose noisily. 'Not even that, really. She got home at about nine at night, it was quite dark, so that must have been around the time. Then, on the Monday morning, Jeremiah–' she flicked a hand at him and blew her nose again – 'Jeremiah gave her some money to go and get some new clothes. She looked very...'

Jeremiah Butler took over. 'She looked like a French nun's idea of how a fashionable lady dresses, Fludd. Perhaps I should say a French nun's idea of how a not very fashionable lady dressed thirty years ago. She had on a drab coloured dress, and a head ... thing...' he waved a hand distractedly in the air, sketching a scarf wrapped round the head and neck. 'She had a cross, on a rosary, which she wore outside her clothes. She was very ... noticeable.' He sat back and gestured to his wife to carry on her story.

But she had little more to add. 'That is the story, Master Fludd. She went out to go marketing, and I have not seen her since.'

'And you're sure she came to Cambridge?' the Constable checked.

The Butlers stared at him. 'Have you been to Royston lately?' the yeoman asked. The point was made.

Fludd scratched his head and looked out of the window over Jane Butler's shoulder. He was trying to frame a way of asking his next question without upsetting the woman. 'And yet you only come to me today?' he said.

She immediately burst into tears. He gave himself a mental kick – he hadn't managed to avoid upsetting her after all.

84

Her husband answered for her. 'We thought she had ... well, she'd been in a convent for thirty years, man. We thought she might have...'

Incredulous, Fludd suddenly understood his meaning. Tentatively, he checked that his facts were straight. 'You–' and here he pointed at each of the Butlers in turn – 'assumed that because she had been celibate for thirty years she had ... gone ... off ... in order to...'

Butler blustered. 'Yes. Well, that's what *I* would do!' This was pronounced with an air that suggested that that was what *any* sane person would do.

Jane Butler shook her head and whispered, 'No. I knew she hadn't done that, but Jeremiah...' again, she could only flap her hand at her husband and then blow her nose.

Fludd put down the quill, got up and paced across the room, thinking. Then, he spoke to Jane Butler. 'Madame, is your sister of about your build, perhaps a little slighter, with auburn hair? She has the mark of a wedding ring, perhaps?'

Jane Butler leapt to her feet and grabbed his hands. 'Yes! That is Eleanor. She took off her ring as Christ's bride when she left the convent, but there was still a mark.' She turned to her husband. 'Jeremiah! Do you hear? Master Fludd has found Eleanor!'

Joseph Fludd held both her hands firmly in his. 'Mistress Butler,' he said, in a calm, low voice. 'I fear that the news may not be good. No, do not get distressed, but I fear we must pay a

85

visit to the Dead House.'

Jane Butler turned white and fainted dead away, crashing to the sawdust-coated floor in a less-than-ceremonious heap. Her husband looked on as Joseph Fludd laid her more comfortably, instinctively loosening her lace collar and hoping the yeoman would understand. 'So, my wife's sister is dead, then?' he said.

Fludd nodded. 'I fear so,' he said.

The man buried his face in his hands. 'Who will look after her blasted father now?' he asked.

It was only with an effort that Joseph Fludd did not strike the man. But he had no time for such behaviour. He was Constable of the Watch and he had a coroner to inform.

FIVE

Constable Fludd hated the Sturbridge Fair. In some ways it was the highlight of the Cambridge year and made more money than all the fairs in England. The problem was – who did it make money for? For all Fludd's life there was wrangling between Town and Gown about who owned the fair and who creamed off the profits.

People like Fludd weren't included in discussions like this. Rumour had it that the great and good of the Town met behind locked doors in the church of St Bene't and they were called the

Black Company and that they all had cloven hoofs under their merchants' robes. All Trumpy Joe Fludd knew was that while other people were making money or making merry or both, he was going to get his head cracked keeping Town and Gown apart.

The sun was already high by the time Kit Marlowe arrived. The first day of the fair was a holiday for the whole university, so most scholars who had a second suit of clothes wore them now, welcoming the chance to shed the fustian of their calling for a while. Only the sizars still wore their clerical greys and browns and they counted their coppers to see how far their meagre purses would go in terms of beer and pies.

'Get your beer and pies here!' the cries echoed and re-echoed in the cacophony of noise across the Common, the discordant lutes and pipes of the minstrels vying with each other and bouncing off the walls of the old leper church by the river.

Fludd, his staff with its gilded Cambridge arms in hand, walked the river bank. The Cam here was crowded with punts and skiffs, brightly fluttering with carnival ribbons, bobbing on the busy water. The smell of roasting pig and frying eels wafted from the fires in the centre of the field and roars went up from the crowd as two brawny wrestlers tussled with each other in the long grass.

Kit Marlowe was wearing his black and scarlet doublet today, his dagger at his back.

Actually, he'd had to buy a new one after Proctor Lomas had had the temerity to confiscate his on the night before graduation. He took in the crowd: the flirting village girls from Cherry Hinton, Babraham and Dry Drayton; the shepherds from the Bedford levels in their smocks; and the children scampering and laughing around the clowns and running shrieking from the dancing bear, which swayed and snarled on its length of chain. For a brief moment, Marlowe met the gaze of the bear-ward, a surly-looking fellow with only one eye. Had he lost the other, the scholar wondered, to a short-tempered paw from his dancing partner?

Marlowe recognized, as he combed the booths of the fire-eaters and sword-swallowers, one or two Corpus men. Henry Bromerick wouldn't have strayed far from the roasting pig, he could be sure of that. Tom Colwell would be browsing in the bookstall, looking for a bargain or something racy and prohibited he could suddenly whip out in college just to annoy Gabriel Harvey.

It was the foreigners Fludd was watching. The Sturbridge Fair of the Feast of the Holy Cross was four centuries old and word had got around. Flemish weavers had set up their jacquard looms on the flat ground near the leper church and were haggling in their curious broken English for their exotic silks and brocades. A large German woman, festooned with trashy ribbons was haranguing the crowd with the exquisite workmanship of her husband, a tiny man with thickened glass spectacles who was carving a cuckoo clock at his stall behind her.

The Constable noted the reaction of the fair-goers who sampled the slimy cheese on the French stall.

'You want to try English cheese, mate!' a labourer grunted, reaching for an ale mug to rinse away the taste of the Brie. 'You froggies'd be all the better for a bit of Stilton.'

It was as well perhaps that neither the labourer nor Fludd understood the flick of the thumbnail on incisor that the French stallholder flashed back.

At the butts, a couple of sizars, all of fourteen in their freshman fustian, were making fools of themselves aiming at the targets. Scholars were exempt from the law that insisted on regular archery practice and against the village lads it was no contest. One of the sizars took aim as he had just watched the others do and the bow-string twanged painfully, stripping a layer of skin off his left forearm, while the arrow dropped uselessly to the grass at his feet. The watching lads jeered as the sizar writhed, holding his arm to his side and hopping from foot to foot with the pain.

'Never mind, son,' one of the villagers was saying. 'You'll get better at it. Care to put some money on the next one?'

But if the sizar had missed his mark, Kit Marlowe had found his. Against the trunk of one of the huge elms that ringed the field, Meg Hawley was talking to someone. Her head was thrown back with laughter and her golden curls flashed in the sunlight. Marlowe groaned inwardly. It was the person with her that was the problem.

'Cut along now, Dominus Parker,' he said, as he reached the pair.

'Kit!' Matthew Parker darted backwards in surprise, away from the girl he'd been trying to kiss.

'Fumbles in the Swan after dark are one thing–' Marlowe wagged a finger at him, smiling for all the world like Dr Norgate in one of his more indulgent moments – 'but this is the Sturbridge Fair, man. Remember where you are. Look – ladies, gentlemen, children present. One or two churchmen, I shouldn't wonder.'

Matt Parker decided to take umbrage. 'Are you implying that Meg isn't a lady?' he asked.

Marlowe was half a head taller than his old friend and had sent him sprawling more often than either of them had attended the buttery. He smiled at Meg, then reached across and took her hand. 'Certainly not.' He bowed and kissed her fingers, with their pot-carrier's callouses. 'Mistress Hawley,' he said. 'You look radiant today.'

For all Meg Hawley never knew how to play this man, she curtsied deeply. 'Why, thank you, Master Marlowe.'

'Master Marlowe?' A voice made them all turn. A solid-looking fellow stood there with curly russet hair and cold blue eyes. He wore the leather studded jerkin of a labourer and there

90

were three men with him.

Meg broke away from the scholars and held the newcomer's arm. 'Hello, Harry.' She smiled up at him. 'I was looking for you.' She patted his shoulder.

'Yes,' he grunted, not taking his eyes off Marlowe. 'I can see you were.' He glanced down at her. 'You know this man?' he asked.

'He's ... he's a customer,' she trilled. 'At the Swan, you know.'

'Yes.' The stranger looked Marlowe up and down. 'I know.' He passed Meg back to the clutches of the men behind him and stepped forward. 'What I want to know is why a roisterer like you is kissing the hand of my betrothed.'

Marlowe frowned for a moment, then smiled. 'I'm sorry,' he said. 'I had no idea.'

'No,' the villager said. 'That sounds about right.' He flashed defiance at Matthew Parker. 'And you, you're another of these quill-scratchers, I suppose.'

'Dominus Parker is a scholar of the University of Cambridge.' Marlowe spoke for the man.

'University of Cambridge, my arse!' the man spat and turned to go.

Marlowe let him get three or four paces. 'Hire your arse out a lot, do you, clod?'

The man stopped, squaring his shoulders, eyes widening. He spun back to Marlowe. 'What did you say?'

Marlowe threw his arms wide. 'Deaf as well as stupid,' he tutted, shaking his head.

It all happened in a second. The villager's

knife was in his hand, the blade glinting in the midday sun. Meg cried out, but neither man heard it. Marlowe slowly and deliberately drew the dagger from the sheath in the small of his back. The villager blinked at it and at the smouldering, dark eyes of its owner.

'That's not fair.' It came out as a school-yard whine. 'That dagger against my whittle. It's twice the length.'

'I don't like to boast,' Marlowe said, 'but before we start, might I have your name? I hate to kill a man I haven't been introduced to. Such bad breeding, don't you think?'

'This is my intended, Master Marlowe.' Meg dashed forward, wriggling away from the churl who held her. 'Harry Rushe. He lives with us all on the farm, remember, I told you. He didn't mean any harm, Master Marlowe.'

'Is that true, Rushe?' Marlowe asked. 'You don't mean any harm?'

'Dickie,' Rushe called to one of his confederates. 'Give him your whittle. If you'll fight man to man with me, Marlowe, we'll settle this once and for all.'

Dickie produced his knife, hilt-first to Marlowe who shook his head. 'If it's an advantage you're after, Master Rushe,' he said, and slapped the hilt of his dagger into Parker's hand. 'Look after this, dear boy.' Then he turned to face Rushe, open-handed and beckoning him forward.

Meg gasped. She'd seen her man in a knife fight before. It wasn't pretty. But before she could intervene, talk some sense into the thick idiots, Rushe had lunged at Marlowe. The blade missed and the Corpus man grabbed the labourer's wrist and, using his body as a pivot, twisted the arm backwards. The blade fell from his grip and there was a sickening dull crack as his forearm snapped. Rushe dangled there, on his knees and in agony, as Marlowe hauled him upright.

'Stop!' a voice boomed across the noises of the fair. Even before much of a crowd had gathered, Constable Fludd was standing by the duellists, his staff with its lead-weight end under Marlowe's chin, prodding his ruff. 'Let him go,' he growled.

Marlowe looked at the Constable and smiled. 'Certainly,' he said and let the man go. Rushe fell with his full weight on his broken arm, gave one grunt of pain and passed out.

The midsummer sun never shone in the gatehouse of Cambridge castle. The tower stood below the old Norman motte, shaded by a copse of birch on one side and a cherry orchard on the other. The castle itself had long ago collapsed, as furtive Cambridge men, at dead of night, had silently lifted the building apart, stone by ancient stone, and carried it away to shore up their tenements in Jesus Lane, Market Hill and Slaughter Yard. Eventually, they had abandoned the night altogether and brazenly quarried the flint and chalk from the motte itself, often under the disinterested gaze of Joseph Fludd's forebears, constables of the watch who didn't do much more than that.

They had reinforced the gatehouse in the days of King Harry, adding bars to the windows and the various college Proctors took regular advantage of the brew house in the old barbican. So, despite the rats and the damp, mould-black patches on the Medieval walls, Cambridge gaol had something of a lived-in look.

An ancient man with pale, red-rimmed eyes stared at the young men striding past outside his cell. One was the Constable – the old man knew him well. He was a shit, but you knew where you stood with Trumpy Joe. The other was a well-dressed bastard, a roisterer by his cut. But the old man knew that a week or so in this place would pluck his feathers.

Kit Marlowe waited while Joe Fludd unlocked the charge room. Across the dimly lit passage from him, a harlot called out to him and hauled down her kirtle, waggling her ample breasts at him. Marlowe just smiled as Fludd shepherded him inside and slammed the door. He opened a heavy, leather-bound ledger on the table in front of him and spun it round, dipping a quill into an inkwell and holding it out to Marlowe.

'I would say "make your mark",' Fludd said. 'But I think you can do better.'

Marlowe took the quill and wrote with a flourish.

'Machiavel?' Fludd frowned. 'Is that really your name?'

Marlowe looked up. The man could not only

94

read, he could read upside down. Impressive. 'No,' he said, crossed out the dangerous nickname and wrote again.

'Christopher Morley?' Fludd read aloud. Not so good this time.

'Marlowe,' Marlowe said. 'The name's *Marlowe*. I think it must be my handwriting. Shocking.' And he wrote something else alongside.

'Corpus Christi,' Fludd read. 'I shall have to inform the College authorities.'

'I wouldn't have it any other way,' Marlowe said. 'What are the charges, Master Constable?'

Fludd looked at him. 'Sit down, Master Marlowe,' he said.

A little surprised, the Corpus man slid the heavy chair towards him and faced his inquisitor.

'Tell me,' Fludd said. 'How well do you know Harry Rushe?'

'Well enough to break his arm,' Marlowe shrugged.

Fludd looked at him. He had looked at many men in his years as Constable. Cutpurses, nippers, foisters, coney-catchers, whores, he'd seen them all. Toothless old ladies who'd rob you blind; cripples who swore they'd lost their legs in France or Scotland and begged a penny to show their stumps; little girls who'd lift their skirts for a farthing; little boys who could slide a silver dagger from its sheath with no noise at all. And Fludd prided himself he could read men's faces. But he couldn't read Kit Marlowe's.

'Have you met him before today?' he asked.

'No,' Marlowe said flatly. 'Never.'

'I have.' Fludd leaned back in his chair. 'He's a troublemaker, Harry Rushe. Lives out by Fen Ditton with the rest of his ungodly brood. He's broken more heads than I've fitted mortices.' He smiled. 'Looks like he met his match today, though.'

'Are you going to lock me up or give me a gold purse?' Marlowe folded his arms.

'Neither,' Fludd suddenly decided and the heavy bunch of keys he'd been toying with were scooped up and hung on a rack near his head. 'God knows how much mayhem's been going on at the fair while we've been walking here. I will be informing your master...'

'Dr Norgate,' Marlowe said, helping him. 'Be my guest.'

'Stay away from Rushe,' Fludd told him, *'and* from the fair if you'll take my advice. If I have to arrest you again, I won't be so lenient.'

He rattled a wooden box in Marlowe's direction. 'For the retired constables' benevolent fund,' Fludd said.

Marlowe smiled and popped a handful of coins into the slot. It wasn't very well-worn so presumably not many people looked on constables in a benevolent way. Then he held out his right hand.

'Hmm?' Fludd frowned. 'Oh, yes.' He rummaged in his Constable's coat and hauled out the dagger. 'Nice piece,' he said. 'You know if you'd killed that lout, this would have been the

96

deodand, don't you?'

'I know how the law works, Master Constable. And yes, this dagger–' he slid it back into its sheath – 'is the most valuable possession I have. It cost more than all my books put together. That tells us a lot about the world, doesn't it?'

'Think yourself lucky,' Fludd told him. 'You chose a good day to transgress. If I hadn't got bodies everywhere I look, I'd have shackled you tonight.'

'Bodies?' Marlowe asked.

'Yes. Well, one body, to tell God's truth. Woman. Fished out of the river yesterday.'

'Accident?' Marlowe knew Paradise and the Cam's little ways. All the same, in his experience, women didn't swim for pleasure. That was something stupid scholars did, in their cups and egging each other on. Fludd looked at him. This was official business and it was not the Corpus man's. But *something* made him confide.

'Who's to say? She was found with a rosary tight around her neck. Of course, it *could* have got tangled with her clothing or the river weeds. But...'

'But you don't think so?'

'No.' Fludd shook his head. 'No, I don't.'

'Tell me, Constable,' Marlowe spoke softly. 'Were there any signs on this woman's body to show that she had been poisoned?'

'Poisoned?' Fludd repeated. This was really beyond his experience, but he wasn't going to let Marlowe know that. 'No. Why? Should there be?'

'No reason.' Marlowe shrugged. 'It's just that sudden deaths seem to be in vogue in this fair town of ours these days.'

'Fair!' Fludd clicked his fingers. 'See yourself out, Master Marlowe. I have to get back,' he said, and he dashed past, out into the dark corridor, making for the sunlight.

Marlowe clicked the heavy door to behind him and stood facing the harlot with a quizzical expression on his face. She grinned and tugged down her kirtle again, letting her ample breasts bounce free once more. Marlowe peered closer, first at one, then the other. He pulled a face. 'No thanks,' he said and strode away with her 'Bastard!' still ringing in his ears.

'Ah, Michael.' Dr Norgate was sipping the mulled wine he liked to take after supper in Hall, when the shadows lengthened across the Lodge in The Court. 'Thank you for coming.'

'Marlowe,' Johns said.

'I fear so. Do you have a moment?'

'Of course, Master.' The professor took the proffered chair and unlaced his cap, helping himself as of old to Norgate's claret. 'Some trouble at the fair, I understand?'

Norgate nodded. 'I had a note from the Constable not an hour ago. Pleasant fellow. Rather more conscientious than they normally are. It seems Marley broke a man's arm.'

Johns was appalled. 'On what cause?' he asked. If it was Marlowe, there had to be a cause.

'You know what these village oafs are like,

Michael.' Norgate sighed, resting his head against the soft leather of his chair, worn to the shape of his cranium from years of pondering the Gospels. 'It would have been a look, a word ... a girl, even.'

Johns frowned. No, it wouldn't have been a girl.

'The Constable seems to think it is a Gown matter. He has passed it to me.'

'And what do you intend to do about it?'

'The man hasn't actually taken his degree yet, Michael. He's a chancer, this Marley. An over-reacher, if ever I saw one.'

'He has a fine brain, Master.' The loyal Johns always backed his scholars if he could. 'One of the finest I've come across.'

'Yes, yes,' Norgate said, nodding. 'No doubt, no doubt. But there's something ... some madness about him. I can't define it.'

Johns chuckled. 'No one can. I gave up trying to do that three years ago.'

Norgate's indulgent smile vanished. 'If you hope one day to sit in this chair, Michael,' he said coldly, 'you'll have to develop more of an inner steel. Doesn't do to get too close to the boys.'

Johns looked suitably chastened.

'There will be a financial implication in all this. If Constable Fludd has passed the matter to us, we must act as Justice of the Peace. Marlowe's behaviour has brought the college into disrepute. And for the second time this week.' He peered at Johns over his spectacle rims. 'You know, I'm not sure you should have spoken for him at that poor chap's inquest. Gabriel told me all about it and he's furious. It's as well Fellows of colleges don't duel.'

There was a silence. Michael Johns had worked at the great man's side for years now. He knew when silence spoke volumes. 'I'll have to put it to the Society,' Norgate said. 'You'll be Marlowe's advocate again, I assume.'

'If I feel it necessary, Master,' Johns told him.

'Oh, it will be,' Norgate said. 'When do we meet next?'

'Friday, Master. After supper.'

'Good. Oh, and get me the buttery accounts, will you? I want to see if Dominus Marley can afford the fine the Society will have to impose on him.'

A few hundred yards away from the Master's Lodge, as the sun sank over the tracery of the colleges and a quiet darkness settled over Corpus Christi, two scholars sat in their shared room with sheaves of paper spread out on the table in front of them.

'So there's nothing in the letters, then, Kit?' Tom Colwell wanted to know, lighting some candles as the daylight began to fade.

Marlowe sighed and threw the last sheet down. In the last few days, he'd gone over these again and again, hoping for some clue from the letters to a dead man.

'This one–' he waved the letter in the air with one hand, while reaching across for more wine

– 'is from his bailiff at Blean, whingeing about the woodland.' He dropped the letter and rummaged for another, peering sideways over the rim of the cup, as he slurped some of Colwell's tokay. 'This one ... is a final demand from his tailor, Tate of Canterbury. The others–' and he flicked some randomly into the air, sitting back in his chair as they settled back on to Colwell's ink-stained table top – 'routine stuff, mostly months old. What about that?'

He was pointing to the document in front of Colwell. The scholar slumped across the strewn papers. 'Kit,' he said, 'if truth be told, I'm not getting very far. It's a sort of journal, I think. Not very flattering about any of the King's people. Listen to this – it's all in Latin, of course, as you'd expect from dear old Ralphie. I don't want to speak ill of the dead, but did you ever meet a bigger snob?'

Marlowe laughed. Already Ralph Whitingside was levelling. The plaster saint whose life had been suddenly snatched from him was acquiring the reputation of an ordinary man, with foibles of his own.

'He says,' Colwell went on, 'if I've got this right, "Goad is older than God".' They both guffawed. 'And what about this – "Falconer doesn't know his *contra fagotto* from his *posaune*." And it's not just King's men, either. This is quite recent, I think. It's nearly the last thing he wrote, judging by its position in the book. "Saw that harslet Greene the other day. Sporting an earring. Has he gone over to the other side?"

What do you make of that?'

'Greene?' Marlowe frowned. 'Not Robyn Greene? St John's?'

Colwell shrugged. 'Don't know,' he said. 'Who's he?'

'Can't be the one I'm thinking of,' Marlowe said. 'Harslet's too mild a word. Insufferable little shit would be nearer the mark, but I'm well known for my charity. But, no, it can't be. He went on his travels when he graduated on account of me telling him if I saw him in Cambridge again, I'd rearrange his face.'

'Charity indeed!' Colwell chuckled. 'The rest of it is pretty cryptic Latin, some Greek, even a little Hebrew, but it's odd. Upside down? I can't make it out.' He threw the book down. 'Fancy an ale at the Cap, Kit? I'm parched.'

'Not tonight, Tom,' Marlowe said, reaching across for the diary. 'I'm going to curl up with a not-very-good book. How are your stripes now, by the way?'

'Mending.' Colwell winced as he stood up. 'You shouldn't have reminded me.'

'If you see that tow-rag Bromerick on your travels–' Marlowe threw himself back on his bed, arranging the candle so he could read – 'you might remind him he owes me last week's buttery bill. And as for Parker...' He was suddenly serious. 'Well, watch out for Matty Parker, Tom. You know his ways.'

'I do!' Colwell nodded and made for the passageway and another near nightly game of cat and mouse with Lomas and Darryl. When would these bloody stripes heal? Once they had, everybody would take a quaff from the college silver, thank the Master, the Chancellor, the college cat and actually get a degree. After that ... well, what Tom Colwell assumed Lomas and Darryl could do was certainly illegal and probably anatomically impossible.

SIX

The next morning Kit Marlowe woke with the superior feeling of being the only person in the room who had not drunk too much cheap ale. The other Parker scholars were whimpering in their cubicles as the reality of morning began to bite. The dawn chorus which had awoken Marlowe had not been the light twittering of the swallows returning to the eaves above his window; it had been the internal rumblings and crashings of his room-mates' bowels and he had the choice of getting out into God's fresh air, or stifling in second-hand alcohol and the shrimp pie sold by an unscrupulous pieman on the corner of Slaughter Yard.

Full of new milk and stewed apple from the buttery, he went humming a catch under his breath, up the stair to his room. As he turned the second corner, he sensed rather than heard the presence of someone on the landing. For one of the other scholars to be abroad and moving would have been a miracle by St Bibiana of a high level. Foxe's *Book of Martyrs* was no longer required reading, but Marlowe read by instinct anything no longer smiled upon by authority and was familiar with the saints' areas of expertise from the toes to the top of the head. No one who knew the Parker boys would have come up so early.

He reached the landing in two more bounds and, as he turned the final bend, saw Benjamin Steane, standing quietly outside the door, a rough bag at his feet and, leaning against the wall, a swept-hilt rapier, looking somehow lonely without a belt and body to support it.

'Dr Steane,' Marlowe said. 'What brings you here so early?'

The Fellow of King's jumped and put a hand to his chest. 'Master Marlowe,' he said, gasping. 'I didn't hear you come up the stairs. You must walk like a cat.'

Marlowe lifted each foot in turn, showing Steane his hob nails. 'I don't think so, Dr Steane,' he said. 'Perhaps your mind was elsewhere.'

'Perhaps, perhaps. But, to the reason I am here; I came to give you such things of Master Whitingside's which I thought his friends might like to have. Some books, some clothes. His sword. It was all I could find worth removing. Except the bed, perhaps, which anyway is college property.'

'That's very kind of you,' Marlowe said,

opening the bag and peering in. 'But, can we move away from the door? My friends are inside ... sleeping.' He looked at the man, still standing almost pressed against the door. 'Dr Steane? Are you feeling quite well? I must have badly startled you – I am so sorry. I'm sure the lads wouldn't mind if you come in and sit down for a while.'

The clergyman gave him a wan smile. 'I do feel a little faint, Master Marlowe. If I could come and sit down, that would be kind.'

Marlowe took out his key and, turning it with a dry shriek that must have been torture to the ears and heads inside, pushed the door open, calling, 'Lads, we have a visitor. Make yourselves decent, if you please.'

He looked back over his shoulder at Steane, who looked paler than ever in the effluvium that oozed round the door.

Marlowe sniffed and grimaced. 'I'm sorry, Dr Steane. It's the shrimp pie. We all know not to buy it, but somehow...'

'I understand, Master Marlowe. It is a favourite with King's scholars too, I fear. Early service can be very trying in the choir stalls.' With another smile and a slight push with his foot at the sack on the floor, Steane turned for the stairs. 'I will leave the scholars to their ... to their...' Try though he might, he remained completely lost for words and settled for changing the subject. 'There didn't seem to be much in Master Whitingside's rooms.'

'It was good of you to look,' Marlowe said,

from the doorway. 'It can't have been pleasant in there.'

'Indeed not, Master Marlowe, as you know only too well. But his bedder, Mistress Laurence, did the job for me. A sterling woman.'

'Indeed,' Marlowe said, turning to go into the room, swinging the bag with some difficulty over one shoulder and picking up the sword by the hilt. 'Nice sword, Dr Steane. Are you sure this—' he shrugged the shoulder under the sack and lifted the sword higher – 'should not be going back to his estate?'

From halfway down the stairs, Steane said, 'His estate is big enough, Master Marlowe. As it is, I believe there is some confusion over who inherits. Master Whitingside was a ward himself before he was eighteen, I understand, and there is only a very distant cousin who is still to be contacted. So, please—' Steane pointed to the sack – 'divide the books, read and enjoy them and wear the clothes. I am sure that is what Master Whitingside would have wanted.' And he disappeared around the turn in the stairs and was gone.

Marlowe was in the buttery again later that day. It was between lectures and he was still wrestling with the intricacies of Ralph Whitingside's journal. Against that the Civil Law as droned about by Dr Lyler had few attractions. But if Marlowe would not go to the law, the law would come to him.

He heard the clatter of hoofs in The Court and

saw through the wobbling distortion of the glass two horses, lathered with sweat, one rider helping the other out of the saddle. He recognized them at once and throwing his buttered crust to Henry Bromerick, who looked at it with still-queasy distaste, he dashed outside.

'Sir Roger!' he shouted, bowing extravagantly in front of the older of the riders. Roger Manwood was a great bear of a man with heavy jowls and a broken nose – no one dared ask him how he got it.

'Christopher, my boy!' Roger Manwood held out his arms and clasped the scholar to him. 'Let me look at you.' He held him at arms' length. 'You've lost weight.' He patted Marlowe's chest. 'They're not feeding you properly.'

'I get by, sir.' Marlowe laughed.

'You know Nicholson.' It was a statement of fact.

Marlowe nodded to Manwood's servant. 'William,' he said.

'Master Marlowe.' Nicholson grinned. He had the surly scowl of many Kentishmen, but he'd go to the rack for Sir Roger Manwood. He liked the lad well enough, but he liked his sister Ann even better and wasn't sure how young Christopher would take to that bit of information. Better keep it under his codpiece for the moment.

'Have you ridden through the day?' Marlowe asked Manwood.

'And half the bloody night,' Manwood said. 'The roads up here are appalling, Christopher.'

Marlowe laughed. 'Wait till you try the beer.'

'I'm staying with Francis Hynde at Madingley Hall tonight, and perhaps for a day or two. Unless he's lost his impeccable taste since I saw him last, his cellar's the best in Cambridge, if not all the Fenlands.' he looked around him, struggling to adjust his belt and rapier. 'So, this is Bene't College.'

'We call it Corpus Christi nowadays, sir,' Marlowe said. 'I'd show you my room, but it's probably full of people like Colwell and Parker by now and I fear we won't all get in.'

Manwood had vague memories of the boys from back home, but, seen one Parker scholar, seen them all, really. 'Is there an ordinary nearby? I'm famished.'

'The Copper Kettle does a very good pastry, Sir Roger. Unfortunately...'

'Yes?'

'Well, it's quite expensive. We poor scholars...'

'Nonsense. This is on me. Er...' he felt his purse. 'Well, not *me* exactly. I seem to have left my other purse at home. Nicholson?'

The servant sighed. He'd been here before.

'Hoo-hoo, Sir Roger!' A voice called from the buttery doorway.

Manwood dipped his head away from the sound and scowled. 'Oh, Lord. Tell me that's not the Bromerick boy.' Not *all* Parker scholars looked the same, he suddenly realized.

'Henry, sir,' Marlowe said. 'Salt of the earth.'

'Sod of the earth,' Manwood muttered. 'How

108

he ever got a Parker scholarship, I'll never know. Get me out of here, Christopher. I feel my old trouble coming on.' He waved to Bromerick with as much bonhomie as he could muster. 'Hello. Must dash, Henry. I'm sure I will see you later.'

Bromerick nodded, waving enthusiastically.

'And hopefully, that will be a full ten minutes before you see me,' Manwood muttered, hurrying for the main gate with Marlowe. 'So,' he said, as they strode through the archway and on to the High Ward, 'you call it Corpus Christi, eh? Bit Papist, isn't it?'

'A shade,' Marlowe agreed.

'Sorry.' Manwood tapped his arm. 'We're all a bit on edge at the moment. Secret Jesuits everywhere. Kent's full of 'em. I burnt two only last week.'

'Good crowd?' Marlowe asked.

'Tolerable. Look ... er...' He took in Marlowe's college robes. 'I feel rather underdressed now. But I thought my Exchequer robes a little flashy for this place, leaving aside the uncomfortable bunching if one tries to ride in them. Even in Canterbury, somebody mistook me for Lord Burghley the other day.'

'Never!' Marlowe was mock-outraged on his patron's behalf. You couldn't help but love Sir Roger Manwood. Yes, he was the scourge of the night-prowler. Yes, he took bribes for England. Yes, he burnt heretics. But he wasn't a bigot – Catholics and Puritans both fried on his command. They were all the same to him. But he lived at Hawe, not two miles from Marlowe's home at the West Gate in Canterbury and he'd put the boy forward for the King's School. The rest was history.

'Nicholson.' Mister Justice Manwood clicked his fingers and pointed to the horses. 'Find somewhere to put those, will you? Then join us. Christopher'll get the drinks in.'

That was how they'd first met, in fact. Kit Marlowe was only eight when he'd tipped half a flagon of ale over the great man's boots in the Star. He'd expected a cuff round the ear but instead he got kindness and a lifelong friend in the passageways of power.

Soon they were all three tucking in to cakes and ale at the Kettle. Roger Manwood looked around him vaguely. 'Nicholson. Did we not have some parcels when we set out? For Christopher.'

Nicholson reached under the table and brought out two objects, wrapped in rough cloth. He gave the larger to Marlowe. 'Shoes, Kit,' he said. 'From your father. Made on your old last, so I hope your feet haven't grown.'

'I think not.' Marlowe smiled. 'What's in the other parcel?' He reached out for it.

'Hmm.' Nicholson was in a quandary. He knew from Ann that it contained hand-knitted stockings from Katherine Marlowe, Kit's beloved mother. He also knew that Mistress Marlowe was no great fist with the needles, so from the outside there was no way to tell. Best to keep counsel. 'Could be anything, Kit. It's from your mother.'

'Ah.' Marlowe pressed it, and then shook it, holding it up to his ear. 'Well,' he said, thoughtfully. 'It is quite hard in places and soft in others. It is a very odd shape.' He shook it again and then smelt it. 'It isn't food,' he said and gave it one last squeeze. He looked up at the two with a broad smile. 'It's stockings! Look–' and he held the parcel out – 'that thick bit is where she turned the heel.' He loved his mother, but with her stockings on his feet, he had no need of shoes. He tucked the parcels behind his chair. 'Thank you for bringing these.'

Manwood had sat patiently through the procedure, a fond smile on his face. Now it was his turn. 'Tell me about dear old Ralph...'

By the time the tale was told, the afternoon sun was gilding the worn oak trestles and glinting dully on the pewter ware. Marlowe had missed three lectures and Sir Roger's gout had pinned his left leg in one position, around which the Kettle's serving woman had to tread warily.

'So what's your best guess?' the Justice asked.

Marlowe bent his head lower, staring into the dregs of his tankard. 'Ralph Whitingside was murdered, Sir Roger. I'd stake my degree on that. The question is, how? And the next question is, who?'

Manwood sighed. 'Indeed,' he said, nodding. 'The lad was my ward. Under my roof at Hawe for four years.' He brushed away a tear, he who never dealt in sentiment. 'I owe him.'

111

'I'm glad to hear you say that, sir,' Marlowe said.

But Manwood held up his hand. 'Don't pin your hopes on me, boy,' he growled. 'I'm an old man and I have no jurisdiction here. I'd do more harm than good. You, on the other hand...'

'Sir Roger,' Marlowe explained. 'I'm a scholar, sir. Still on the cusp of graduation. I have no skill, no money, no power.'

Manwood looked at him and frowned. 'I've heard it said the others call you Machiavel.'

'Where did you hear that?' Marlowe asked.

'Never mind.' Manwood chuckled ruefully. 'Is it true?'

Marlowe shrugged.

'Then live up to the bastard's name. If I'd had Nicolo Machiavelli in my ward in Canterbury, I'd have nailed his ears to a post, cut out his entrails and fed them to my dogs in front of him. But I concede his ideas got results. You must do the same.'

Marlowe shook his head. 'I don't...' and he felt Manwood's iron grip on his forearm.

'It's July,' the Justice said. 'As it was some ... what ... eight years ago, I remember two boys playing in the river at Hawe.'

'Sir Roger...'

'One of them took a tumble, landed in the current. And the current carried him away.'

'Sir Roger...'

'The other jumped in, without a second's thought for his own safety and dragged him from certain death. Now, what were their

112

names? Ah, how the memory plays tricks.'

'Sir Roger...'

'What, sir?' Manwood snapped. 'Would you deny your Lord three times, blasphemer? Ralph Whitingside saved your life, Christopher Marlowe. Find out who ended his. You owe him that much, at least.'

The silence lay heavy between them.

'Two questions, Christopher,' Manwood grated. 'How? And who?' He took a draught from his tankard. 'The who is your responsibility. But the how ... I can't help you myself, but I know a man who can. If anyone can explain Ralph's death to you, it's my old friend John Dee.'

'The Queen's Magus?' Marlowe looked up.

Manwood nodded. 'The same. You'll find him at Mortlake, along the Thames. Nicholson here will get you a horse. And William?' Manwood half turned to his man, smiling and laying a hand on his sleeve. 'Something decent, please; not just four legs and a hole to put the hay.'

In the event, William Nicholson did Christopher Marlowe proud and Friday morning saw him trotting south over the hard-rutted road past Constable Fludd's carpenter's shop through Trumpington on the highway to Royston. The rains of the early summer had gone and the hemlock and bryony alongside the road bore a creamy frill from the thick dust thrown up with the passing traffic.

Marlowe's bay gelding moved easily, hoofs

113

raising dust at his high-carried tail. He travelled light, his blanket cloak wrapped round Ralph Whitingside's rapier bouncing on the saddle cantle behind him. He had not ridden in a while and when he dismounted to pee behind a gorse bush, felt the muscles in his thighs like lead.

It was nearly noon as he neared the town and saw before him, plodding on the road, a funeral procession winding down the gentle hill. They had rigged a makeshift bier to a cart harness and a shaggy-coated pony plodded ahead of its sad load. A black cloth wafted occasionally in the breeze and every few yards an outrider rang a handbell for any slower traveller to clear the way. This was clearly not a cortège bound immediately for the grave and by the dust on the sombre pall Marlowe knew the party had been on the road for more than a day.

A grim-faced yeoman and his wife sat inside a carriage in front of the bier and nodded to Marlowe as he trotted past, doffing his cap in respect. This was no plague victim, he knew, since no plague victim could leave the town in which they died. And he never knew their names. It was Jeremiah and Jane Butler bringing their drowned kinswoman home for burial.

Marlowe reined in his horse at the market house and pressed a coin into a scruffy boy's hand to hold the animal for him. He downed a pasty and some ale before finding the midden in the yard, and rode on, thudding under the ruined wall of the ancient priory of the Austin Friars, demolished and despoiled and taken away to provide new buildings for Royston town.

The sun was already low over the harvest fields as he clattered across the meandering Lea into the high street of Ware. Again, the ruined grey, this time of a Franciscan priory, sitting like a rotten tooth beside the town. Dogs barked, snapping at his horse's heels as he took the rise. He dismounted in the cobbled yard of the Saracen's Head and found the innkeeper, a surly individual who would have turned away Joseph and Mary themselves.

He ate alone in a corner of the inn, tucked away from the nightly roisterers loud with their ale and their women and retired to bed early, battling with the straw palliasse and scratching in response to the bugs that were the bane of any traveller's life.

The Black Society met that night as a sudden storm broke over the scholastic turrets of Cambridge. The rain fell like arrows, bouncing on the cobbles of Bene't's Lane as cloaked and hooded figures made their way in twos and threes down the steps and under the dark Norman arch of St Bene't's. The great and good of the ancient town of Grantabridge were meeting as their fathers and grandfathers had for generations, discussing the great civic issues of the day.

'Have you the faintest idea what a conduit would cost?' an exasperated voice almost screamed from inside.

'Flemish weavers? I wouldn't give you two

groats for 'em.'

'Well, what's the University doing about it?'

It was this last question that reached Michael Johns' ears. He was feeling guilty already. As the man with fewest paces to walk from Corpus Christi next door, he was virtually the last to arrive. He entered as quickly and unobtrusively as he could through the linking door on to the narrow darkness of St Bene't's ambulatory and padded down the twisting stone stairs.

He was not only the nearest, he was the driest. Even the Master had had to cross The Court in the sudden downpour and the old man sat, dripping, on the left of the Mayor along with the other representatives of the university in their gowns and hoods. Doctors Goad and Steane from King's nodded to him, Gabriel Harvey of his own college cut him dead. A few of the others he knew vaguely – Rymer of Trinity, de la Pole of Jesus, the two-seat-filling bulk of Evans of Pembroke Hall. The burgesses of the town were, to a man, wringing wet, sitting steaming in their civic finery. Johns only ever saw these men at meetings of the Society. For all he knew, they lived in little presses under the stairs and only appeared for the twice-yearly slanging match that was the meeting of the Magnum Congregatio, the official Latin tag of the Black Society.

'Good of you to call, Michael,' Dr Norgate whispered out of the corner of his mouth.

'Sorry, Master,' Johns whispered back. 'Henry Bromerick wanted a word. It was vital, he said.

116

Wouldn't wait.'

'It never can with Bromerick,' Norgate observed.

'Gentlemen!' the Mayor banged his gavel. 'Can we get on with the business in hand?'

And they did.

There was no mention of the incident the day before when Dominus Marlowe of Corpus Christi College had broken the arm of Harry Rushe, labourer. Time was on Marlowe's side as Constable Fludd, up to his eyes in the fair as he was, had not had time to put quill to parchment and process the necessary paperwork. And so Professor Johns did not, after all, have to speak for him.

Even so, the bickering went on long into the small hours of Saturday as the bickering had gone on for generations. If the university was making money out of the fair, why didn't the university protect the town's craftsmen from the invasion of foreigners? When were they going to provide Proctors to police the ground? And if the townspeople wanted a fair, why must it run on the Lord's day, which was to be kept holy, the university wanted to know. The same old questions, the same old arguments echoed through the thick old walls of St Bene't's and down the creeping passageways of time.

Provost Goad had done well to reach the gate of King's unaided, especially as the puddles still stood in the dimples of the gateway pavement.

'Benjamin,' he wheezed, pausing and stooping

to catch his breath, 'your arm a while.'

Benjamin Steane came to the rescue as he had so often before and held out a rigid arm on which the grateful provost leant. 'Tell me,' the old man said, 'what you made of tonight.'

'The usual,' Steane said. 'Everybody on their dignity. Everybody trying to score points off everybody else.'

'One day–' Goad padded forward again, refreshed – 'we'll rid ourselves of this Town nonsense for ever and only the University will reign supreme.'

'Amen to that,' Steane said.

They reached the stairs and a Proctor handed Steane a guttering candle. 'Evening, Provost,' he chirped, touching his cap. 'Dr Steane.'

'All quiet?' Goad asked. 'Nothing untoward?'

'All's well, sir.'

King's, it had to be said, was on a knife edge after the death of Ralph Whitingside. Scholars stood whispering in clusters, Fellows eyed each other suspiciously. Sizars, without the experience of age or the cash that comes with breeding, had to be hushed for their bursts of outspokenness. No one felt safe. The Proctors themselves felt guiltiest of all. No one believed that nonsense about suicide at the inquest. Someone had sneaked into the college and murdered Ralph Whitingside. And what about the roisterer who called himself Machiavel? He could get in and out of the place like a spider. And if he could, who else might have been there before him? So the Proctors had doubled

118

their guard, checked everybody, patrolled the grounds. They carried their cudgels now, untucked from their belts and they stopped everybody, friend and stranger.

Steane took the Provost to his rooms on the first floor, the little annexe that stretched out over the Lodge proper where Goad entertained his guests. At the door, the old man looked left and right before he said softly, 'How was Winterton, by the way? I assume since his preposterous verdict at the inquest, he saw our point of view?'

'Our point of view, Provost?' Steane repeated. For so brilliant an intellectual, Benjamin Steane could be positively obtuse.

'That nothing must sully the honour of the college, Provost-elect.'

Steane took a step backwards.

Goad chuckled. 'Don't tell me you still think Whitingside was murdered?'

'I don't know, sir,' Steane told him, 'but I just don't see him as a suicide. It wasn't that that surprised me.'

Goad peered at his second-in-command in the candle's half-light. 'Oh,' he said. 'The Provost-elect bit. Well, I haven't spoken to the Fellows or Convocation yet, but I think you can assume that all that is a mere formality.'

'Well, I am flattered, Provost, nay, touched even. But...'

'But?' Goad's face contorted. He could think of a dozen men, half of them now dead, who would have killed for a chair at King's, let alone

119

the Provost's.

'Sir, I think I should tell you that I have been called to the purple.'

Goad's eyes widened. 'A bishopric?' he mouthed. 'Where?'

'Bath and Wells, probably. Winchester if I'm lucky.'

'My dear boy.' Goad's smile was frozen. 'I had no idea.'

'You know the Archbishop, Provost?' Steane said.

'John Whitgift?' Goad almost spat. 'Yes, I do. Jonian, wasn't he?'

'No. He was a Fellow of Peterhouse. But I mean he's the sort who plays his cards close to his chest. Should he ever play cards, of course, as I'm sure he doesn't. So I was not allowed to divulge.'

'Even to me?' Goad gave his lieutenant his most withering look.

Steane spread out his arms and shrugged. 'I'm sorry,' he said and was left in the pitch blackness as the Provost took the candle from him and slammed the door. Waiting there while his eyes acclimatized to the dark, he decided that in the circumstances, it was probably best if he saved the news of his impending marriage for another day.

It was a mind-numbed Professor Johns who bid the Master goodnight a little before the old Corpus clock clanged the hour of two. The roisterers were home and even Lomas and

120

Darryl had shambled off to their beds to be ready for the Chapel bell and the advent of another Corpus day.

The rain had stopped as suddenly as it had started and the warm night air had dried the grass and emptied the puddles. Johns watched as Dr Norgate's tired old frame vanished into the shadows of the Master's Lodge. He saw his candle light flicker halfway up the stairs, then at the top and across the landing. He half turned and collided with a shrouded figure lurking in the shrubbery.

'Bromerick!' Johns shouted, then in a whisper, 'God's Teeth, Henry. What are you doing there?'

'Waiting for you, sir,' the lad told him.

Johns led the boy into the dim light of his own staircase. Bromerick was still dressed, wearing his college robes. They had been soaked to his skin when he'd talked to Johns earlier, on the professor's way to his meeting. They had dried out as he'd paced The Court and gone back to his rooms to check the papers again.

'Go to bed, man.' Johns said. 'No amount of Greek can be so pressing.'

'Ah, but this is different, Professor,' Bromerick told him. 'It's like no other Greek I've ever read.'

It had to be said that there was a great deal of Greek Henry Bromerick had never read, but Johns had known this young man for three years now, ever since he came as a red-faced fourteen year old from Canterbury, clutching his Parker

121

scholarship in his hand and had lodged his name in the buttery ledger. Like all Corpus students, Bromerick had run up and down on the crisp mornings of winter, trying to get warm before the morning's lectures in the Schools. He'd watched him praying 'fervently' in Chapel, with one eye open to smirk at the others, seen him grow into a man with half his heart on his sleeve.

'How's the back now?' Johns asked.

'Getting better, sir, thank you. The Master will be able to award our degrees any day now.'

Johns smiled. 'Good. Come into the decent light and show me this Greek.'

Under the arch of the stairwell, the professor and the scholar stood head to head, reading by the candlelight guttering in the sconce on the wall. It was a slip of paper, in Bromerick's hand-writing.

'I transcribed it,' Bromerick said. 'I just hope I got it right.'

'Transcribed it from where?' Johns asked. 'Something obscure in the library?'

'Not exactly, Professor.' Bromerick looked furtively from side to side. 'Can I trust you?'

Johns smiled. 'You've attended enough logic lectures to know, Henry,' he said, 'that only you can answer that.'

The scholar dithered for a second. 'Then I can,' he decided. 'This came from Ralph Whitingside's rooms in King's. The original is part of a journal of some kind. Written in Latin, Greek and Hebrew.'

'I'm impressed,' Johns said. 'Glad they're teaching them something at King's. How did you come by it?'

Nothing.

'Henry?' Johns looked at the man, the kindly eyes boring into him.

'Kit,' Bromerick said.

'Ah.' For Johns, that said it all. 'And what does Kit make of it? I didn't see him at supper, now I think of it.'

'Kit hasn't seen it, at least not this bit. Tom ... er ... Dominus Colwell is working on the rest, but he's drowning in it so he passed this page to me.'

'Well, you're right, Henry,' the professor said, tilting the paper this way and that. 'It isn't like any Greek you've ever read. That's because it's not Greek. It's a code of some kind, a cypher. Beyond me, I'm afraid.'

Bromerick looked crestfallen.

'It's important to you, isn't it?' Johns asked.

'Kit thinks it might help explain why Ralph died,' the scholar said.

Johns nodded. 'All right,' he said. 'Leave it with me. I know someone who may be able to shed some light ... no promises, mind.'

'No, sir, of course not.' Bromerick brightened.

'Now,' Johns said with a sigh, 'go to bed, Henry. You have to be up again in four hours time and I not long after.'

'Thank you, sir. Good night, sir.' And the scholar was gone.

* * *

123

Marlowe was already saddled before the sun had crept over the rickety rooftops of Ware and took the road south-west. The carts increased now that he was in the south of Hertfordshire, creaking and rumbling their way to London and the Thames. By midday he was walking his gelding over the rough marsh ground near Barnet, edging his way past ponies, asses and palfreys being led to the great horse fair. Here, he knew, in his great-grandfather's day, Yorkist and Lancastrian had killed each other in the thick fog of an April morning and the great kingmaker, Earl of Warwick, had gone down to the merciless halberd blade of some anonymous foot soldier. His ghost, men said, still wandered the misty hollows near the road, looking in vain for his lost soul.

He followed the road through the boggy ground, getting ever lower and wetter until he came to the pontoon ferry, tied up at an unstable-looking quay. The ferryman was sleeping, curled up in the middle of the raft, looking in his dung-coloured clothing like something left behind by his last passenger. Marlowe coughed extravagantly and the man leapt to his feet, almost overturning his craft which, being low in the water, shipped quantities of the Thames and rocked and rolled before regaining its equilibrium.

'Take yer somewhere, sir?' he asked Marlowe, shading his eyes against the sunset.

Marlowe was a little nonplussed. Here he stood at the bank of a river, served by a ferry pulled across that river on a rope to one destination: the other side. And yet the ferryman seemed to be giving him an option. Marlowe could only applaud his hubris in assuming he still had freedom of choice. However, there was also a chance that the man was completely barking mad. So he kept things simple. 'Just across to the south bank, if you would,' he said and eased his nervous horse on to the pontoon, the animal slithering and clattering on the planks, whinnying softly in mild panic.

The ferryman reached up to take the penny which was his fee. He derived a lot of innocent amusement from these foreigners; come out of the north they did, knew nothing of the ways of London and her river. Sat up there, they did, on their horses, skitting and shying across the flow. If they just got down and stood at the animal's head, they wouldn't keep falling in and drowning. He sighed. He bore them no ill will and there was a lot of fuss with a drowning, but it broke the tedium of an otherwise uneventful day. He'd been First Finder eight times now; must be a record west of the Vintry.

The church of St Mary was gilded by the dying sun as Marlowe rode into Mortlake. The sleepy little town on the banks of the rushing Thames was the end of his journey and he was glad of it. His legs ached, his back ached, his shoulders ached. In fact, he was hard put to it to find any part of him that didn't ache. He asked directions from a man at work on the riverbank with his hurdles and nets.

'Dee?' the man repeated in an accent Marlowe had never heard before. 'Dr John Dee?' And he spat volubly into the river.

'Not a friend of yours, then?' Marlowe sat upright in the saddle.

'Not a friend of anybody's,' the eel-fisherman told him. 'What d'you want him for?'

'I rather think that's my business,' Marlowe said. 'Will you help me or not?'

The fisherman looked Marlowe up and down, taking him in. The man was riding a good horse and he couldn't help noticing the rapier-hilt, cold and chiselled under the horse-blanket. Then there were the eyes – dark and deep like the waters he fished every day. Best not to mess with this man.

'A mile yonder.' He pointed. 'There's a depiction of the world on his gatepost.'

Marlowe nodded and swung the horse away.

'I hope you're a friend of his,' he heard the fisherman call. But he didn't catch the rest. ''Cause if you are, you're a rare breed, but it might save your life.'

SEVEN

Marlowe allowed his horse to amble from then on. The fisherman had seemed to know his geography, but Marlowe had no confidence in the distance-judging skills of someone who made his living up to his waist in water most of the time. But, a mile down the road, give or take a gnat's whisker, he came upon a high yew hedge, pierced by a gate. The posts on either side of it carried wooden spheres, roughly hacked by an uncertain hand into depictions of the coastlines of the known world. Frobisher's new islands were most freshly incised, and someone had tried hard to show a man being eaten by a large bear. Since this was only some three inches high and seemed to have been done with a large chisel, Marlowe had to use all of his imagination and a great deal of his acquired knowledge to guess this correctly.

He swung his leg over the horse's back with difficulty as his muscles had now ceased all communication with his skeleton or brain and he looped the bridle around the gatepost. With a friendly admonition to the creature not to eat the hedge for the good of its health, he pushed open the gate and walked into the world of the magus,

John Dee.

The house seemed to squat in a slight dip in the ground ahead of him. The brick glowed in the last rays of the sun creeping over the hedge and reflecting in the many panes of the windows, giving the building an air of looking out from its garden with blind eyes that could see right into the onlooker's head. Marlowe shivered, but resolutely approached the door and raised his hand to the knocker, which was shaped like a Gorgon's head, its mouth ever-open to hold the clapper.

Before he could raise it, the door creaked inwards and a voice intoned, 'You are here to see my master.'

Marlowe was almost speechless with shock. In the last few miles with the sun rapidly sinking, he had tried to imagine what this house and its occupant would be like and so far, nothing had been a disappointment. He licked his lips and cleared his throat before speaking. 'Yes.' Not exactly his usual level of witty riposte, perhaps, but it served its purpose. 'How did you know?' He addressed the fresh air of the entrance hall, as he had yet to see another human being in the vicinity.

A small, wizened man stepped from behind the door and looked Marlowe up and down with the air of one who didn't much like what he saw. 'You were about to knock on the door. It gave me a clue.' Again the disparaging glance and then, 'Follow me.' He paused to light a candle from a guttering stub near the door. The candle grease had been dripping from it for so long that it had reached the floor and so the candle end was perched on top of a greasy cone. Bits of wick studded the wax and looked like insects encased in a morbid amber. The little old man turned in a doorway and spoke again.

'This way. The Master's time is precious and not to be wasted by the likes of you.' The door opened and swung shut behind him, catching Marlowe, who had stepped lively, a smart one on the shoulder. Pushing open the door, he was just in time to see the candle flame disappear around a corner. He was in a corridor with no windows, curving to the left and slightly downward. The echoing steps of the manservant came back triple to him and the man's shadow danced with grotesquely elongated legs behind him.

'This way,' Marlowe heard him say. 'It doesn't do to get lost in the Master's house.' The scholar felt his bowels loosen ever so slightly and wondered if, in all its wonders, Dee's house included a privy. Then, suddenly, he was in a blaze of light. The room they had entered was twice the normal height, with a mezzanine floor clinging halfway up the wall and reached by rickety-looking ladders at intervals. The far wall was floor to ceiling windows, with pane upon pane of glass far purer than Marlowe had ever seen in a window, with just a strip down the middle etched with gold and precious dyes in the shapes of mermen, dragons and un-nameable creatures. It faced west and the red glow that flooded in seemed to be straight from Hell.

There was so much to see that Marlowe could at first see nothing; the scene was just a mass of colour and flickering shadows. But after a few seconds, shapes emerged from the chaos and he could see that on almost every surface were crowded bottles and jars in which, suspended in the death of alcohol, floated every conceivable abomination of nature: two-headed kittens; a baby with no arms; a calf with six legs. These jostled mutely with preserved body parts which made Marlowe look away, suddenly queasy. He had buried his best friend too recently to be comfortable in the company of such charnel house horrors.

From the middle of the kaleidoscope a voice spoke. This voice was not like the manservant's, harsh and slightly mocking. This voice crept like treacle in at the ears and didn't stop until it wound its fingers into the depths of the brain and foraged there to find what it would. 'Welcome to my house,' the voice said and Marlowe's eyes were able, with the clues from his ears, to pick out the man who spoke. He had seen depictions of John Dee, of course, in the chap books sold in Cambridge marketplace. He was wearing his picadil cap and his long, sparse beard spread over his chest, as in the pictures. But his eyes were beyond the skill of any chapbook illustrator. From beneath a broad brow and finely drawn eyebrows, they gazed out as if from another world, bringing the wisdom of the ancients to bear on the follies of the now. Marlowe met his gaze for as long as he could and Dee nodded. 'Well done, Master ... Marley?'

'Marlowe!' he snapped. Could no one get his name right? Then, a tiny trickle of ice water ran down his spine. How did this man get any part of his name right? He had not given it to the manservant on the door.

Dee read his expression and smiled. 'A parlour trick, Master Marlowe, nothing more.' He waved a piece of paper in the air. 'This was in your saddle roll, with a pair of what I believe must be stockings.'

Marlowe smiled. A note from his mother, whose writing, like her knitting, had never been very accurate. He was disappointed and relieved in almost equal measure. 'I see,' he said. 'Christopher Marlowe, at your service.' He bowed. 'My friends call me Kit. My enemies call me Machiavel.'

Dee stood up and walked towards Marlowe, brushing aside the paperwork which littered the floor. 'Then I shall call you Master Marlowe, I think,' he said. 'Why are you here? Not many people call unexpectedly, especially at sunset.' He put an arm round Marlowe's shoulders and propelled him towards a door hidden in the gathering shadows under the mezzanine floor. 'That's when the grooms release the owls and the bats.' He bent round to look into Marlowe's startled eyes and laughed. 'You must learn not to take me too seriously, Master Marlowe,' he said, giving the scholar a friendly shake. 'The owls and the bats come with the scenery. It is the hounds the grooms release.' As though on cue, a baying rose outside in the grounds, followed by a nervous whicker from a horse, sounding very nearby.

'My horse,' Marlowe said, pulling away from Dee's guiding arm. 'I left him outside.'

'Don't worry, Master Marlowe,' Dee said. 'My grooms stable as well as release. Your horse is rubbed down and comfortable with a nosebag of oats by now, if I know my men. Come.' He pulled Marlowe's sleeve. 'Come and meet my wife. She doesn't see enough people and it is dull living with an old fool like me. Come.'

He led Marlowe through corridors which twisted and turned on each other, some with windows looking out on grounds which stretched away to the river, trim box hedges leading the eye to the distant bridge, others with no windows, but with enigmatic doors, their keyholes sealed with dusty cobwebs, punctuating their length. Just as Marlowe was beginning to fear that he would never see the end of this maze, Dee reached a door and, pushing it open, revealed a cosy drawing room, complete with a beautiful woman sitting at the window, looking out on to the darkening garden. At the sight of the two men, she rose gracefully to her feet and walked towards them, seeming almost to skim across the rushes on the floor. As she reached the men, she sketched a curtsy to Marlowe who replied with a deep bow. Her beauty was almost unreal, every feature perfect, her skin like alabaster under snow.

Dee watched them fondly and then reached out and put an arm tenderly around her waist. 'Master Marlowe, I would like to introduce my wife, Helene. Helene, this is Master Christopher Marlowe, who has come to see me. I don't yet know why.' He smiled at Marlowe. 'Are we to be put out of our suspense, Master Marlowe?'

Marlowe looked at Helene Dee and then at her husband. He didn't really want to tell his sorry and rather gory story in front of this exquisite creature. Dee seemed to read his mind.

'Please, don't feel at all unsure of telling your tale in front of Mistress Dee.' He gave her waist an extra squeeze and she kissed him fondly on the ear. 'She has been used to horrors of all kinds ever since she came to this house. And before, I fancy.' Helene gave a small and rather theatrical shudder and closed her eyes briefly, but continued to smile.

Marlowe looked concerned and bowed his head. 'Where did Mistress Dee live before?' he asked. 'That she saw horrors.'

Dee answered briskly, 'Here and there, Master Marlowe. Here and there. But, wait. I can see that you are diffident about sharing your tale.' He turned to his wife. 'Run along now, my dear. We will see you later perhaps, at dinner, when Master Marlowe has shared his troubles with me.'

Helene Dee bowed her head politely to Marlowe and left the room. It was only later that Marlowe was to remember that she had not spoken a single word.

* * *

Down in the kitchen in the bowels of Dee's house, the cook was toasting bread. Her hair hung in elf locks on either side of her face. Dee had chosen her specifically because of her unspeakable ugliness, much as he had chosen Helene for her beauty and little more. The manservant was sitting on the other side of the fire, his nose in a tankard. He looked up as the woman entered.

'Oh, Nell,' he said, in a friendly way. 'Pull up a chair. Drink?' He reached down and picked up the jug.

'Ooh, ta,' the girl said. 'I'm parched. Got any more toast?' The cook tossed her a piece, which she dunked in her ale.

'Woss going on upstairs, then?' the manservant asked, around a mouthful of bread.

'Oh, he's in the old mystery mode,' the girl said. 'I come from here and there, horrors, that sort of thing. The usual.'

'Love him,' said the cook. 'He's bored, that's what it is. He ain't had nothing in the showstone for so long, he's wond'rin if he ain't lost the skill for it.'

'No, no,' said the girl. 'Only yesterday, he saw a black man cutting a woman's head off.'

'And what does that mean, then?' the cook asked, turning another piece of bread.

'I don't know,' the girl replied. 'That's the thing with telling the future, innit? It's the future.'

'He didn't predict this Marley bloke, though,

did he?' the manservant observed, with blunt accuracy.

'No,' Nell said. 'That's true. But he's just a wandering scholar, I think. He is a bit handsome to be much of a thinker. In my experience, most people are one or the other.'

The cook and the manservant looked at each other. Nell had, for once, hit the nail right on the head.

John Dee sat back in his chair, rereading the letter which Manwood had sent, by hand with Master Marlowe, of Corpus Christi College, Cambridge. It seemed quite straightforward, just an introduction really, wrapped around an invitation to stay at Madingley while Manwood was there, but the mention of a horrible murder had piqued his interest.

'So, Master Marlowe,' he said. 'Your friend, one–' he looked down at the letter – 'Ralph Whitingside, has died, murdered, you think. And that's why you have ridden for two days to come to me?'

'Sir Roger Manwood was sure that you would be able to help me,' Marlowe said, although what he had experienced in this house so far was beginning to make him wonder.

'I'm sure I will,' Dee said. There was an unhealthy gleam in his eye. 'I haven't done this for a while, but I think we could have a crack at raising Master Whitingside and asking him what happened.'

For a moment, Marlowe thought that perhaps

his two days riding and then the rather bizarre setting had upset his hearing, or his understanding, or even both. 'I beg your pardon, Doctor Dee,' he said. 'Did you say "raising"?'

'Yes.' Dee looked at Marlowe as if nothing untoward had been said, except perhaps his questioning of it. 'I have had some success in raising the dead, you know, Master Marlowe. Indeed, I am quite well known for it. In the right circles.'

Marlowe suddenly felt it was quite important to keep this man happy. Who knew how a madman might react if crossed? He smiled accordingly and nodded, whilst looking covertly for ways of escape.

Dee was going on. 'The Queen consults me regularly and wouldn't dream of doing anything important without speaking to me first. My spirits tell me whether a proposed course of action will be successful or not. If they say not, then the Queen would not dream of carrying it through.'

'Are they ever wrong?' Marlowe ventured to ask.

'No, never!' Dee shut his mouth with a snap. 'Although of course, sometimes evil spirits speak as friends and give false advice.'

'So the Queen does the wrong thing,' Marlowe said.

Dee leaned forward. 'Never say such a thing,' he said. 'And especially not in front of him.' He pointed to a large toad that appeared to be dozing on the hearthstone. It reminded Marlowe of the portraits he had seen of Cardinal Wolsey. 'He misses nothing.'

Marlowe's smile was by now a complete rictus. Had Manwood gone mad, to send him to this place?

'But I can see that you are doubting, Master Marlowe. Test me this way. Tell me one thing about your friend's death and I will tell you the cause of it.' He sat back, with his hands clasped on his chest and his head thrown back, so he appeared to be examining the ceiling. Stuffed birds hung there, an owl in full flight, a goshawk plunging on its prey.

Marlowe thought through what he had seen in the flickering candle flame that early dawn in Whitingside's rooms. It was hard to revisit, but he forced himself. If by describing what he saw he could make Dee forget his plans to raise the dead, then he would rack his brain until it hurt. 'He ... he had ... his back was arched, his fingers were clenched and...'

Dee held up a hand. 'No, no. That is ample. Now, let me think...' His head snapped back up so that his amazing eyes bored into Marlowe's. 'I will ask you some questions. Answer me truthfully. Try no tricks, now, Master Marlowe. Now, then ... he had vomited?'

Marlowe nodded. Not too clever a guess, when all was said and done.

'The vomit was green–' Dee was getting into his stride now – 'like grass. His bed was dis-ordered. The room looked as though there had been a fight. Umm ... let me think ... no one had

137

seen him for a few days. Tell me, did Master Whitingside have a wife?'

Marlowe shook his head.

'A woman of any kind in his life?'

He thought of Meg, not the purest woman who ever lived perhaps, but certainly in love with Ralph. He nodded. 'A girl loved him, yes.'

Dee narrowed his eyes. 'Then he had something some of us never have,' he said. 'Do you know this wench?' he said. On Marlowe's nod, he continued, 'Could you find out whether Master Whitingside could ... perform in his last days?'

'Perf ... oh, I see. Yes, I dare say she would tell me if I asked her.'

'Because if it was found that he could not ... perform ... then that would make the diagnosis certain.'

'Diagnosis of what?'

Dee looked smug. 'That your friend was poisoned by a tincture of foxglove. Easily obtained and deadly.'

'Would he have taken it himself? Do people do such things?' Marlowe suddenly had a sickening feeling that he was chasing the wrong hare.

Dee reached forward to a pestle on the table in front of him and began to grind something inside it with a brass mortar. 'The Scots,' he said, 'call the foxglove bloody fingers or dead man's bells.' His eyes flicked upwards to glance at Marlowe, who was watching him, fascinated. 'Apt, eh, in the case of your friend? The Welsh–'

he carried on with his dark stirring, leaning in to his task and twisting the mortar widdershins – 'always of a gentler disposition, know it as fairy-folks' fingers or lambs-tongue leaves. Quite poetic, don't you think?'

The poet-to-be did.

'Dr Fuchs, late of Tubingen gave the plant its real name – digitabulum.'

'A thimble?' Marlowe frowned.

Dee smiled. Cambridge was still turning out scholars after all. 'Dr Dodoens prescribed it boiled in wine to relieve the chest.'

'Does it?'

'No, Master Marlowe,' Dee said coldly. 'It kills you.' He sniffed the contents of the pestle. 'My old friend John Gerard finds it useful for those who have fallen from high places.'

'Not that either?' Marlowe was beginning to follow the drift of all this.

'Most assuredly not,' Dee said, 'but since the man is Lord Burghley's gardener, only time will tell.' He closed to Marlowe in the deepest confidence. 'They don't come much more highly placed than Lord Burghley.'

'Unless you include yourself, Dr Dee,' Marlowe said, but Dee chose to ignore it.

'You asked me whether people take the foxglove to poison themselves. I don't doubt that people have taken the tincture for that purpose, but it is quite slow to act and if they changed their mind, there would be nothing that could be done, save watch them die in agony. And of course–' he chuckled – 'should they

139

recover, they would be guilty of the sin of suicide. Attempted, that is.'

'So it is murder, then?' Marlowe said.

Dee rubbed his hands together. 'Now we need to find out who did this horrible deed. And there is a complication, which might work for or against us.'

'Oh?' Marlowe was all ears.

'Cambridge is in the eastern counties, Master Marlowe, the Fenlands. The foxglove is rarely found there.'

'So, you're saying...'

'The man – or woman – who gave your friend the tincture may be an outsider, someone who is not native to Cambridge but bought the deadly thimble-full from elsewhere ... Canterbury, perhaps.'

Marlowe nodded. He couldn't wait to get back to Cambridge and start digging into Ralph's last hours. He got up. 'Thank you, sir,' he said. 'If I could perhaps sleep in one of your stables for the night, I will be away in the morning.'

'My dear fellow,' Dee said. 'You will do no such thing. I will come with you to Cambridge and we will start at first light. We must find out your friend's murderer and to do that there is but one course of action.'

'What is that?' Marlowe asked.

Dee rubbed his hands together again. 'We must raise Master Whitingside and ask him to his face.'

EIGHT

It seemed only hours since Marlowe had last stood here in the dark, the wrong side of the churchyard wall. The moon was different; even Dee could do nothing about that and he had been rather testy about it. Apparently his raising spell worked better at certain phases of the moon, and this wasn't it. But it seemed to Marlowe that time was of the essence. Ralph Whitingside would not be any deader if they waited, that was true, but on the other hand, his murderer could be putting miles between himself and Cambridge, especially if he got wind of Dee's presence and his errand there.

They had crossed the river at Putney, where Marlowe saw the great grey towers of the abbey at Westminster far to the east, and had ridden across country to Highgate and Enfield before spending the night in the shadow of St Mary the Virgin at Chelmsford.

Dee could have been Marlowe's father in terms of years, but he stood the pace well, his tough little chestnut cantering alongside Marlowe's bay as they took the slope into timbered Lavenham, still prosperous in its heritage of wool. It was late afternoon as they rode through

141

Saffron Walden, the sun casting shadows on the pargetted walls they cantered past. Marlowe could not believe this route was shorter than the one he had taken south – the detour to Lavenham alone should have added half a day. Yet they had trotted past the church of St Michael in Trumpington as the sun set over the tomb of the great crusader knight who lay there.

Marlowe turned to Dee, with a question in his brain which would not take shape on his lips. How could he ask a question which requested an explanation for the bending of time and distance to the magus' will? He chose, in the end, to remain silent. The smile playing on Dee's face told him all he needed to know; that he had no need to know, that as long as the end justified the means, the means were unimportant.

In the graveyard, the preparations were long and involved, Dee muttering to himself as he unpacked the many canvas sacks at his feet. Carrying them from the horses to the church, trying to look casual as the weight slewed them from side to side on the narrow pavements had been tricky. But tricky was meat and drink to Dee. Then there had been the problem of finding first the candle and then the flint and tinder. Then lighting the candle without setting fire to the hedge. But finally, all was ready.

Dee was seriously missing his usual helpmeets, either Helene or his manservant. Even Edward Kelly, co-magus and con-artist, long gone to the University of Cracow would have been of some help, as once Dee began his raising ceremony he was often so deep in thought, concentrating on the job in hand, that he needed help in sticking to the ritual. The results when everything went right were spectacular and dangerous enough, God Himself knew well. What might go wrong if a herb was wrongly placed, an incantation wrongly pronounced, was probably in the Devil's keeping.

So Dee muttered and muttered, placing candles at precise angles to one another, making lines between them over the uneven ground of Whitingside's grave in salt, in powdered roots of arcane cultivation, in blood from his own pricked finger. He swirled his way around the graves in an arc, a circle of fire from the brand he carried, before plunging it suddenly into the earth.

Eventually, all was in place and Dee stepped back. Marlowe had expected the angel Uriel, or at the very least fireworks and incandescence and was leaning, disappointed, bored and yet not a little relieved, against the still warm stones of the churchyard wall. Surely, this mix of mathematics and herbalism could not bring a soul back from wherever it had gone. And Marlowe was increasingly of the belief that the soul, should there be such a thing, went out with not so much as a whimper as soon as breathing stopped.

In a low voice, Dee gestured to Marlowe to light the candles in a specific order, starting at the top left and going widdershins around the circle, lighting the one in the middle last. The candles were short and black and as each wick flared a smell which Marlowe was loath to identify began to permeate the air. Dee was speaking more clearly, words now in Latin, now Hebrew, now in a language with which Marlowe felt himself familiar, in a dark, visceral way. It sounded like the first words ever spoken; it could be foretelling the end of the world when all the stars would go out one by one, and God would rule a clean new universe again. He shivered. Then, like the foretold stars, one by one the candles went out, left to right, widdershins.

The silence was palpable, thick and dark. Marlowe had stared into the blackness for so long that he had started to see little sparkles on the edge of his vision. Everywhere he looked, he could see will o' the wisps dancing. When he moved his head, they moved too with long tails behind their infinitesimal bright bodies. Dee's muttering now was so fast that the Latin words which Marlowe had understood at the beginning were now just a slur of sound, rising and falling in a hypnotic cadence and filling the space around the two men in a spiral of hopeful magick.

Dee leaned down and was almost touching the grave with his forehead. He grabbed Marlowe's sleeve and pulled him down with him. They could smell the new growth of weed and flower in the soil, the dampness from a summer shower releasing the smells of dead foliage and tin from the earth. Dee's breath was loud in Marlowe's ear, and on the breath the endless chant, dulling the senses until it filled the world. In front of Marlowe's dilated pupils, even in the dense black night, he thought he saw the soil begin to stir, as though the earth itself drew in its breath, waiting to exhale and give Ralph Whitingside back to the living, if only for a while.

Dee sprang back, pulling Marlowe with him. 'Give him room!' he said, his eyes bright even in the near-darkness. 'Let the dead speak!'

Marlowe jumped a mile as a voice in his ear shouted loudly enough to break the drums. Dee was expecting a reply, but nonetheless gave a small start.

'Let the dead speak? Not in my parish!' The priest of St Stephen's, who had turned a deaf ear and a blind eye in compassion for Ralph Whitingside's friends at the illicit burial, was having no truck with necromancy or any other -mancy, for that matter. The Reverend John Springer was of the new persuasion. He allowed no rings at his wedding ceremonies and there were no pews in his church. He had personally painted over the Garden of Eden on his vestry wall and was happy to throw the thigh bone of St Stephen into his rose garden, where it might do some good.

He had been watching these two for some time and, whilst a little gentle grieving by candlelight was all very well, although a little morbid for his own personal taste, he had been alerted by his serving girl as she turned down their bed, that there were dark doings in the churchyard. Not quite in the churchyard, but near enough and, dragging on his cassock, Springer had sprinted out of his house hard by the church wall and done his work.

Springer was built like an ox and toyed with banging the heads of these black magicians together before having them burned. The old man would be a walkover, but the younger one looked as if he might be able to handle himself and Springer's Christianity was not as muscular as all that.

'Get out of my parish and don't let me see either of you again!' he bellowed. The pitchfork he had leaned against the wall for extra emphasis decided the pair when in the hands of a religious maniac and they ran for it.

From what he judged to be a safe distance, Dee shouted back at the man. 'Do you know who I am, hedge priest? I am John Dee, Magus to the Queen of England.'

'Well done!' Springer said. 'I hope she would be proud, to know you were conjuring up spirits who should be allowed to sleep in peace. Go on with you, both of you, and do your nasty conjuring somewhere else. If I see you again, it'll be the Consistory Court and then the stake.' He shook the pitchfork for emphasis and Marlowe and Dee thought it best to resume their headlong flight, not really slowing down until they turned the corner of Bene't's Lane and cannoned into Constable Fludd.

'I didn't finish it,' Dee hissed to Marlowe before the introductions were made. 'God only knows what will happen in the Potter's Field

146

from now on. The banishing rite!' He was shaking his head. 'My God! My God!'

Back at the wrong side of the churchyard wall, the ground settled back into place with an almost inaudible sigh. For now.

Henry Bromerick lay pale and ghastly on the bier in the little room in St Bene't's, the temporary resting place of Corpus scholars before they were carried with cap and bells to the little graveyard that nestled next to The Court. Sometimes families claimed their dead and took them away to their homes, to bury them in their own churchyards with the yews and the mouldering stones for company.

No one was thinking that far ahead in the case of Henry Bromerick, certainly not Dr Norgate who stood bareheaded by the boy's corpse. And certainly not Professor Johns who stood with him.

There was an unceremonious crash as the little door that linked the church to the college swung back and the sound of boots clattered on the stone outside. Kit Marlowe stood in the doorway, his cloak and hat gone, his doublet unlaced. He barely noticed Norgate and Johns and acknowledged neither of them, striding across the room and taking Bromerick's cold hand. The boy's thatch of brown hair was swept back from his face where the woman-who-does had brushed it for him. The face itself had been washed and the eyelids closed. Only the stains on the Corpus robe remained, a darkness spread over

147

the pelican and lilies.

Bromerick's jaw was set fast, the mouth slightly open, the scar of Lomas' whip darker than the skin around it. His fingers felt like iron in Marlowe's grasp.

'Kit,' Johns said softly, touching his arm. 'We are so sorry.'

'Yes.' Norgate nodded, having forgotten his manners in the events of the last couple of hours. 'Yes, Dominus Morley. Please accept our condolences.'

Marlowe looked up at them both, the soft kindliness of Michael Johns, the aloof, studied sophistication of Norgate. 'I'd like someone else to see this,' he said.

'Someone...?'

But before Norgate had finished his question, Marlowe had dashed back to the door and ushered in the man with whom he had tried to raise the dead. Dee nodded, but no more to the men in the room, Bromerick among them. Then he took the dead man's hand, as Marlowe had done, and checked his fingernails. He placed his palm on Bromerick's forehead and lifted an eyelid.

'Sir...' Norgate was outraged but Marlowe lifted a finger to stop him and it worked.

Dee frowned when he saw the stained robe front. 'This man has been dead for some hours,' he said in the treacly voice that fascinated Marlowe. 'See, the stiffness of death is in his fingers, his jaw.' He looked up to the little oriel window where the first light of dawn was creeping through the shadows. 'He will be stiff as a board by breakfast time. By tonight he will be soft again, malleable – and we'll know more. If I may have the body then?' he asked the assembly. 'On my own.'

'Have the body?' Norgate finally exploded. 'Sir, this is Corpus Christi College...'

'We must ask who you are, sir.' Johns felt the need to support the Master.

'This is Dr John Dee of Mortlake,' Marlowe answered. 'Doctor Norgate, Master of Corpus Christi and Professor Johns.'

'The Queen's Magus?' Johns whispered in awe.

Norgate was less impressed. 'Her Majesty may confide in you, sir. I do not. And I am the law here in Corpus Christi and I'll have no truck with fairground charlatans. You will kindly leave the college precincts or I will have you removed.'

'Master...' Johns began, but Marlowe cut him short.

'Two friends of mine have died in the last twelve days, Dr Norgate,' he said, levelly. 'You'll forgive me if I find this fact seriously disturbing and not a little odd. If you defy Dr Dee, sir, you're treading on dangerous ground.'

'Dangerous...' Norgate was speechless.

'Master Marlowe.' Dee smiled. He had been in these situations before. 'We must not presume on the good Doctor's time. I remember my days at Trinity. The Master is God, even on this hallowed ground. Is there somewhere you could

149

buy me breakfast? I always think better on a full stomach.'

Dee tucked into his new milk, hot bread and frumenty like there was no tomorrow – as of course for Harry Bromerick there wasn't.

Joseph Fludd was no slouch either, waving at the serving wench in the Kettle to top up his milk. Only Marlowe didn't eat. He sat nursing a pitcher of water and left it undrunk.

'Tell me again,' Marlowe said to the Constable, even though he had heard it twice over as the pair had jogged back along the darkened Cambridge streets, Dee stumbling behind them as best he could. Even leading the horses, Fludd and Marlowe easily outpaced the man and had reached St Bene't's ahead of him.

'Master Bromerick was found here.' Fludd placed a fruit bowl in the centre of the table. 'This is Lion Yard.' He looked up at Dee, as though explaining to a savage from the Frozen Sea. 'Off Petty Cury.'

'I know where it is, Master Constable.' Dee raised a deadly eyebrow. 'I was a Fellow of Trinity at its foundation. There are not many holes-in-corners of this town of yours I don't know. Tell me, do the roisterers still warm their arses on the stools of Little Germany, or is the Cardinal's Cap the place to be? Or perhaps–' he nudged Kit – 'I should ask Master Marlowe that.'

Marlowe smiled despite himself. 'I understand from the more idle of my fellows that it's the

150

Blue Boar these days,' he said.

Dee closed to Fludd. 'There was a nest of Papists in Kettles Yard,' he said, 'and another on the Lammas Land south of the Causeway. You've wiped them out, I suppose?'

Fludd was uncomfortable. 'I believe the university has, sir. Church matters. I only deal with the town, what happens in the street.'

'And what happened in the street,' Marlowe said, bringing the conversation back, 'was Henry Bromerick.'

'Yes.' The Constable nodded grimly. 'This was yesterday, a little after six of the clock. Witnesses told me he was took funny, went rigid sudden like and fell over. Hit his head against a handcart on the way down. There was some blood.'

'What about the front of his robes, man?' Dee asked. 'You saw the body, I presume, where it lay?'

'I did, sir. He'd been sick. Thrown up all down himself. Not a nice thing to see. A woman fainted dead away, apparently. By the time I got there, they'd picked her up.'

'And moved the body?' Dee checked.

'I should imagine so, sir. They'd put him on a cart, in Gonville Alley, away from the crowds, as it were. It's not every day a man drops dead in Cambridge. What was it, sir? Ague? Sweating sickness?'

'Murder,' said Dee, munching into a newly baked loaf he had liberally spread with honey.

'Two in twelve days,' Marlowe said. 'And

151

both friends of mine.'

Fludd sat upright with hands raised, not a little bewildered. 'Sirs,' he said. 'I'll be the first to admit I haven't a clue what you're talking about.'

'Ralph Whitingside,' Marlowe said, swilling his water listlessly in the pewter pitcher. 'King's man. I found him dead in his college bed two weeks ago come Friday. He had stains on his shirt, over his bedclothes.'

'And now,' Dee said, taking up the tale, 'Henry Bromerick, Corpus Christi man. You, Constable, found him dead, yesterday. He had stains on his robes. A mirror of the soul, Master Fludd, two men dead in the same manner.'

Fludd nodded. 'It's the sweating sickness. Can't be anything else.'

'It can be *anything* else,' Dee assured him, 'but it's not. How long would you say, Constable, Master Bromerick had been dead?'

'Er ... I was up at the Castle when they called me, sir,' he said. 'I came straight away, so perhaps twenty minutes, half an hour.'

'And Ralph Whitingside, Master Marlowe?' Dee turned to him.

'Hours? A day? Who knows.'

'If that hedge priest had not come to drive off his demons, we might all know,' Dee said ruefully. Fludd, even more confused, looked from one to the other, but no details were forthcoming. 'What colour, Fludd, was the staining on the dead man's robes?'

'Green, sir. Bright green.'

152

'Remind me, Master Marlowe, for Master Fludd's information. How was it with Whitingside?'

Marlowe shrugged. 'Green. As far as I could tell in the dark.'

Dee nodded. 'It would have darkened with exposure to air and light anyway.' He took a deep draught of milk and wiped his moustache free of it before he went on. 'If I remember rightly, Master Marlowe, you told me Whitingside's room was overturned as if there had been a fight.'

'Yes.' Marlowe nodded, frowning to recapture the scene. 'A chair overturned, papers strewn, rugs kicked on the floor.'

'And Henry Bromerick, Master Fludd, was "took funny", you said.'

'That's right, sir,' the Constable agreed, seeing a sort of pattern in the magus's reasoning. 'If there'd been any furniture to hand, he'd have kicked it over, I'm sure of that. He hit a cart as it was.'

'And I am sure too, gentlemen,' Dee said, untucking the kerchief from his collar and folding it neatly on the trestle, 'Ralph Whitingside and Henry Bromerick were both poisoned with, unless I miss my guess, the common foxglove. The plant is frequently found near rabbit warrens, but you've none growing wild in Cambridge, gentlemen.' He stood up. 'I wish you luck in your searches.'

'Wait, Dr Dee.' Marlowe was on his feet too, gripping the great man's sleeve. 'Where are you

153

going?'

'To Madingley,' he said. 'To see my old friend Roger Manwood. I can't stand Francis Hynde, but into every life a little rain must pour.' He closed confidentially to Marlowe. 'You'll think me an appalling snob,' he murmured, 'but Hynde's father was an apprentice bookbinder. Now, his lad's lord of the bloody manor. It's a mad world, my masters.'

'But...'

Dee held up his hand. 'Master Marlowe. You have a road to walk, sir, and you must walk it alone. These men were friends of yours. You owe them your keenest wit, your sharpest dagger. Someone killed them.' He looked at Fludd and sighed. 'Only you, Master Marlowe can solve this conundrum.'

He tossed a gold coin on to the table and strode for the door where a boy held his horse.

'What about the showstone?' Marlowe called to him. 'Can you look into it for me?'

Dee could look into the showstone. Had looked into it on numerous occasions, the polished crystal of smoky quartz that foretold the future. But each time Dee used it, he felt afraid. And each time, he felt a little piece of himself vanish into it. He beckoned Marlowe over, clamped a hand on his shoulder and spread his other arm wide. Before him ran the turreted outer wall of St Catherine's and beyond that the Gothic splendour of King's. 'Here's your showstone, Kit,' he whispered, 'and you must look into it for yourself.'

154

Tom Colwell didn't get much out of the Discourses that afternoon. Neither did Matthew Parker. It was a hot, sticky day, the sun burning on the thick panes of Corpus Christi and beyond them the hoi polloi of Cambridge went about their business. It was market day and the roads in and out of the square were jammed with sheep, cattle and geese, the whole town like some mad Babel with its cacophony of street cries.

Neither man had slept. And both men were turning things over in their minds when they should have been concentrating on their lessons. A sizar had brought them the news a little after seven as the pair sprawled on their hard beds, wondering where Henry Bromerick was and when Kit Marlowe would be back. The sizar had been hysterical, white and shaking and Tom Colwell had sat him down and had held his shoulders, telling him to breathe deeply and to focus. By the time the lad had finished his tale, it had been Colwell who was shaking. He couldn't look at Parker, not at first. Then they'd both run the gauntlet of the Proctors and clattered round to Bene't's Lane, cutting through St Edward's Passage and on into Lion Yard. A knot of ghoulish bystanders had clustered at the entrance to Gonville Alley. The Parker scholars had hauled them away and stood looking at the remains of their friend. The Constable had been there too, peering at the dead man's face.

'Leave him alone!' Matt Parker had shouted,

suddenly overwhelmed by it all. He couldn't stand the thought of some stranger handling Henry like a side of mutton in the market. He'd known this man since he was a boy, since they were babies together in fact. As long as he could remember, Henry Bromerick had been there, wrestling in the long grass, throwing stones at the weavers' houses along the river Stour, rivalling each other in the choir stalls of the cathedral and daring each other to walk the whole frightening length of the Dark Entry.

Now, all that was gone. All that life, all that youth, all that hope. There was no one in Cambridge now who knew him like Bromerick had. He felt the space at his back, the lack of his friend in a way that he had never felt his presence.

The Constable had asked them their names, their business there and how they knew the dead man. One of them, and it may have been Parker, had mentioned Kit Marlowe to the Constable. And the Constable had stood upright on hearing the name and, telling them to take the corpse to the college, he had gone, shooing away the crowd at the alley's end.

Men along the road had doffed their caps, women had bowed their heads. Here and there people had furtively crossed themselves as the sorry load creaked past them. Colwell with an iron lump in his throat, Parker convulsed with crying. Their dead friend on the bier between them.

At the end of the interminable Discourses,

with the sun still high and the market only now winding down, the lads packed up their books and made for the buttery. A welcome sight met them in the entrance – Kit Marlowe. The three hugged each other silently, Parker weeping all over Marlowe's doublet.

'Kit...' he began.

'I know,' the older scholar said. 'We need to talk.' He caught the eye of Gabriel Harvey sweeping the hall in gown and cap. 'But not here.'

Benjamin Steane was annoyed. Very annoyed, in fact. His main aim in life was to ensure that everything ran on oiled wheels, that everything that happened happened both *when* and *how* he planned it. But, Goad, the old fool, had inadvertently pushed him down a path too soon. He had been forced to tell him of his impending elevation to a See of his own and then, the next day, of his marriage. He had taken the coward's road in sharing his second secret and had sent a note. He had instructed his Mercury, an unfortunate sizar too slow to get away, to wait for a reply, but there was none. He wasn't sure when he wrote his note, and now never would be, but he thought that of the two, his marriage plans would have shocked the Provost most.

During Steane's time as priest and Fellow, priests and celibacy had been very much a moveable feast, depending on who was currently occupying the throne and most of his calling had found it easier to stay celibate for public

157

consumption at least. The maelstrom that was faith in England over the last few years had left the clergy, as well as the laity, shocked and bewildered. Under the boy-king, Edward, some priests had been allowed to marry. Under his sister, Mary, they could not. Some had taken 'housekeepers', who kept all parts of the household warm and comfortable, including the bed. Others frequented ale houses of a certain sort, in heavy if often inept disguise. Fellows were always celibate, no matter who wore the crown and Steane doubted that Goad even noticed women. After all, the only ones he ever came across were serving girls and bedders and as such they were probably not even visible to him.

Steane had no vanity and didn't really know whether he was attractive to the opposite sex or not. His Fellow's robe more or less ruled it out. But he had met his future wife at the house of his sponsor for higher office and he had no doubt that purple was a very attractive colour to a certain woman. That she was a widow with lands and money of her own but no real status had suited him. A Bishop's Palace could be a cold and lonely place without some serious gold to line the walls and keep out the draughts.

The wedding was to take place very soon, in the Church of St Mary Magdalene at Madingley. His wife-to-be was Ursula, a sister-in-law of Francis Hynde and had been married for the first time there and was eager to repeat the experience. Steane hoped that the marriage venue would be the only thing this union had in common; his beloved's husband had dropped dead of an apoplexy within the first year of their marriage. Since then, she had been hunting for a replacement and she had found Steane just in time. The desperation was only written on her face for an experienced man to read; Steane had missed the signs completely.

He stumped crossly over cobbles towards the choir school. His dearest had asked, or some may say insisted, that the full panoply of King's College Chapel be brought to Madingley, choir and all. Francis Hynde's social climbing father, the bookbinder, had installed a small pipe organ and in Ursula's ignorance she assumed that Dr Falconer, the King's organist, would delight in playing it. Thomas Tallis and William Byrd, already approached, had sadly been busy on her wedding day. In fact, they were sure they would be busy on every day for the next few years, such was the pressure on the Masters of the Queen's Musick. She had fetched Tallis a playful whack around the ear and told him he should rest more. The temporary deafness certainly slowed him up for a while.

So now, Steane was on his way to try and persuade Falconer and Thirling to provide some music for his nuptials. Steane was not a sensitive man by most people's standards, but he was beginning to feel a slight snarl of unease deep in his gut. It was as if a buried thought were tugging lightly at some deep sinew, trying to remind him of something which he had once promised himself but had now forgotten. Fortunately for his beloved, though, Steane's ambition was stronger and stifled the little niggle before it could be properly heard.

As he entered the choir school, the ringing silence echoed through his head. Falconer and Thirling were together in one corner, heads together and the ghost of Thirling's laugh hung in the air. The boys and men of the choir were sitting, all leaning towards them as if in a high wind, trying to hear the gossip, as had been the way of choristers since a voice was first raised to praise God. Steane knew that he had been the subject, but was senior enough and fierce enough to stamp out any ribaldry at his expense.

He raked the room with his eyes and the choristers all fell to studying their anthem for the day with a will. 'Dr Falconer, Dr Thirling. If I may have a word with you outside for a moment?' He stood in the doorway of the School and waited for them to cross the room. Just as they were about to go through the door, he swept in front of them, leaving Thirling quite literally wrong-footed. 'I would like to ask you a great favour,' he said, in tones that said that they had no choice but to comply.

Thirling, leaning heavily on his cane, was the first to recover his poise. 'Of course, Doctor. What would you like us to do?' His smirk was well-hidden.

Steane studied their faces and decided that if he watched for every nuance, he would be here all day and he had other fish to fry. 'As you may know, I am shortly to be married...'

Falconer and Thirling proved themselves to be a loss to any troupe of players one cared to name. Innocence spread across their faces, arms were outstretched in mute amazement. Falconer went so far as to pat the Fellow lightly on the back.

'You may wonder how I am to do this, as a Fellow of this College?' Steane felt the conversation would be incomplete without this rhetorical question. They raised their eyebrows and smiled in unison. 'I am to become a Bishop,' Steane said. 'I have not shared this with the College Convocation as it has only just been confirmed. Upon that confirmation, I asked Mistress Ursula Hynde to become my wife and she has graciously accepted.'

Falconer raised a quizzical eyebrow, hastily lowered before Steane could see. He himself had been the unwilling recipient of Mistress Hynde's attentions one summer's afternoon in the organ loft and had been lucky to escape virgo intacta. It had brought on an extra virulent visitation of his old trouble. She could block a lot of exits, could Steane's intended, most of them at one and the same time. He patted the man on the back again, in overt congratulation, in covert sympathy.

'So, to my request. My intended bride would like there to be music at Madingley, where we are to marry. I wondered if you gentlemen and the choir could provide something. An anthem, perhaps. A psalm, always nicer sung, I think.' He smiled encouragingly.

Falconer didn't hesitate. He knew the organ at Madingley would fit nicely in the ophicleide of the King's organ, but the sight of Benjamin Steane being joined in holy matrimony to Ursula Hynde was not something he would willingly forego. 'I would be delighted!' he cried. 'Richard–' he turned to the choirmaster who thought the organist had taken leave of his senses – 'it will be such fun, don't you think? A small choir, quite select, I feel, would do the Chapel at Madingley the most justice. Tobin's nephew ... he must come along.' He turned again to Steane. 'Such a sweet voice, the boy has. In fact, perhaps just trebles? Hmm, Richard?'

'Oh, no,' Steane said. 'I'm afraid my bride is set on a full choir.'

Thirling, who had lost the gist of the conversation several twists before, shook his head. 'I'm afraid I cannot provide a choir, Dr Steane.' Suddenly, he gave a cry and fell over, clutching his leg. Falconer had kicked him sharply on the ankle and it had undone his delicate equilibrium. While he scrambled back to his feet, Falconer answered for him.

'A choir *is* possible, Dr Steane,' he said. 'But we are short on men. Some are away from Cambridge – I am thinking particularly of the two who have been rusticated for ... unusual practices.'

'Ah, yes,' Steane said, nodding. 'There was nothing proved, of course. Had there been...'

'The Consistory Court?' Falconer asked.

Steane frowned at him, astonished at the

162

man's naivety. 'The rope, Master organist,' he growled. It was no more than the truth.

'Then, of course,' Falconer went on, listing his losses in the choir stalls, 'there is poor Ralph Whitingside.'

'Is that a problem?' Steane enjoyed the services at King's and, perhaps unusually among his colleagues, derived a deep satisfaction from the liturgy. But his ear for music was average at best and he didn't really see what the loss of a few voices mattered, in the scheme of things.

The two musicians were aghast. As usual, the organist was the first to recover. 'It is a very great problem, Dr Steane. The lack of men means we will be very limited in what we can sing.'

'There must be a way round it,' Steane said. His beloved could be very testy when crossed. 'Could someone from another college step in? Haven't I seen Master Marlowe singing here, for example?'

The other two faced each other, lips pursed, then Thirling nodded. 'Marlowe would do very well. And what about a couple of the other Parker boys, to take the place of ... well, of you know who?'

'That would do very well, if it could be arranged,' Steane said. 'It doesn't matter who you get, but get someone. Let me know what pieces you intend to sing and I will tell Mistress Hynde, to make sure they are something she would like.'

'With deputized parts, we may not have much

choice,' Thirling said, the whip firmly back in his hand. 'But I am sure Mistress Hynde will not be disappointed.'

Steane nodded to the men and whirled on his heel and strode out of the room. The door slammed behind him and, with his acute musician's hearing, Thirling waited until his footsteps had died away before adding, 'Not by the music, at any rate.'

And giggling like schoolboys, they joined the real ones waiting in the School beyond the wooden door.

NINE

That night the Parker scholars got drunk for a different reason. They sat in a tight circle in a corner of the Swan as the sun went down over Cambridge and the under-constables of Fludd's watch patrolled the darkling streets with their lanterns and nightsticks, crying the hour across the Fenlands.

Marlowe noticed that Meg Hawley kept her distance, always swaying away to serve other tables. Jack Wheeler himself brought their drinks and waited for payment each time. Tom Colwell did the honours; it was his turn.

'So, let's go through it again,' Marlowe said. 'When did you see Henry last?'

'Monday morning,' Parker told him, trying to clear his head to focus on the time and the place. 'Dr Lyler's class.'

'How did he seem?'

'Fine. He'd seemed fine throughout the weekend, if preoccupied.'

'Preoccupied?' Marlowe frowned. 'That doesn't sound like Henry.' The most that had usually taxed Bromerick was which end of a pasty to start on.

'Er ... perhaps I can help there.' Colwell looked a little sheepish.

The others looked at him.

'He was working on a section of Ralph's journal, or whatever those cryptic ramblings are.'

Marlowe sat upright. 'I thought you were doing that, Tom,' he said.

'Well, yes, I was. Am. But ... well, you weren't here, Kit, and Henry kept pestering me to go for a drink with him. You know what he's ... what he was like.'

Marlowe nodded, but the loss of Bromerick was too new, the wound too raw yet to indulge in fond reminiscences. That would come later, when they were all old men nodding by the kitchen fire and someone brought them their syllabub and spiced ale, kind to their toothless mouths.

'He got on my nerves!' Colwell snapped, slapping an open hand down on the table. 'There, I've said it. He got on my nerves and I said "If you've nothing better to do, help me with this,

165

for Christ's sake".'

'And he took it with him?' Marlowe asked.

'No. No, I was very careful about that. I got him to copy out a few lines. He couldn't make any more sense of it than I could. He was thinking of seeing Johns to see if he could help. Oh, he wouldn't have broken any confidences, of course.'

'And did he?' Marlowe asked.

Colwell shrugged. 'Both of us had spent days in your granddad's library, Matt, consulting every damned oracle we could find. Nothing. I know where the pillars of Hercules are now and what an elephant looks like. I even have a vague grasp of some of Euclid's nonsense, but that stuff ... I haven't a clue. Was he particularly bright, Kit? Ralph, I mean; you knew him better than we did.'

'He was bright, yes,' Marlowe said. 'Bright but devious. Brighter than you, Tom? I don't know.'

'How did you get on with Dee?' Parker asked Marlowe. 'You haven't told us.'

Nor would he. As long as he lived, Kit Marlowe would not tell anyone what happened in that churchyard.

'He thinks Henry was poisoned,' he said. 'He knows he was. As was Ralph.'

The boys looked at him. It was Colwell who found his voice first. 'What's going on, Kit?' he asked.

Marlowe leant his head towards them. 'Somebody's killing us, lads. The other Parker scholars

166

have moved on, left the university. And the new batch hasn't arrived yet. Now Henry's gone, it's just us three.'

'But Ralph,' Parker protested. 'Ralph wasn't a Parker scholar. He just happened to come from Canterbury.'

'To be precise, Matt,' Marlowe reminded him, 'he came from Chartham. We're not talking about the Parker scholarships here. We're not even talking about Canterbury.'

Matt and Tom exchanged glances. 'What, then?' Tom asked.

'The King's School,' Marlowe said. 'That's the common link. Whatever is going on, King's is at the heart of it.'

'God's teeth!' Marlowe slammed into the little room in The Court at Corpus a little after noon. The midday bell had not rung and only a few starving sizars wandered the grounds, looking longingly at the Great Hall where the cauldrons of stew were bubbling in the buttery next door.

'Kit, I should really give you this,' Parker said, almost apologizing. He passed his room-mate a note.

'What is it?' Marlowe snapped.

'A letter from Professor Johns. He says if you miss one more lecture...'

'I'll be damned to all eternity; yes, I know,' he said, and he threw the paper out of the window.

'I told him you were at Henry's inquest,' Colwell explained. 'It's not like Johns to get shitty.'

167

'He's got his job to do, I suppose,' Parker mumbled. When all was said and done, his grandfather had been Archbishop of Canterbury; you didn't get more jobsworth than that, and Matt was part-establishment already.

'Do you bastards want to hear this or not?' Marlowe hissed. He looked at them both. Were these the Parker scholars? The lads he'd gone to school with? Spent three years in lectures with? Caroused away the night? And here they were, with one of their number dead in the charnel house and they were sympathizing with the dilemma of the domini. It defied belief.

'Sorry, Kit,' Colwell muttered. 'Of course. Murder by person or persons unknown?'

Marlowe looked at him.

'Surely not death by his own hand?' Parker blurted out.

Marlowe cocked his head to one side. 'Act of God,' he said.

The lads looked at each other. 'Natural causes.' Colwell couldn't believe his own voice even as he said it.

The Chapel bell called the Scholars to luncheon and they heard the kerfuffle on the stairs outside as dozens of feet made for the Great Hall. None of the three was in a mood to eat, but Marlowe made for the door.

'I couldn't eat a damned thing,' Parker said, surprised by his friend's speed.

'Neither could I,' Marlowe told him and Colwell and Parker looked at each other as they watched Marlowe tuck his dagger under his

168

college robe before he nodded at them both and left.

Sir Edward Winterton's carriage was creaking through the busy throng over Magdalene Bridge that afternoon. Marlowe had not spoken to the coroner at Bromerick's inquest earlier in the day. He had expressed no surprise that Colwell and Parker had not been called because that was not how the law ran. A grubby stallholder, reeking of tallow, had been the First Finder and he mumbled his evidence with constant prodding to speak up from the coroner's clerk. Constable Fludd told the court what he had found and Winterton had told the jury to deliver their verdict of accidental death. Justice, along with Marlowe, had already left the building at a trot.

Marlowe estimated it would take time for Winterton to leave the inquest. He had papers to read over and sign and a jury to dismiss and thank in time-honoured tradition before he wound his way home and Marlowe knew that his home was across Magdalene Bridge. The traffic was always heavy here, with the carriers' carts rumbling south over the Cam on their way to London and the skiffs bumping each other as the river folk got on with their precarious existence. A man on foot, especially a man with a knife and a mission, could easily see what the hold-up was and could outpace the fastest wagon on the road.

Edward Winterton was just letting his eyelids droop to begin a short nap before luncheon when he felt a thud alongside him and a Corpus Christi Scholar sat there, staring at him. Winterton sat bolt upright and opened his mouth to cry out but Marlowe was faster and his dagger-blade tickled the roots of the man's beard.

'One thing I've noticed about gentlemen's carriages like yours, Sir Edward, is that the driver has no view of the interior. Your man is no doubt efficient with the reins and whip but crafty devil that I am, I nipped in on his blind side. He doesn't know I'm here. So if I were to slit your throat and hop off just over the bridge, nobody would be any the wiser, would they? Least of all Trumpy Joe Fludd. And some other idiot of a coroner would probably say it was an "Act of God". Poor old Sir Edward! He was trimming his beard in his carriage one day when he slipped. What a calamity!'

Winterton turned his head as best he could. 'I can only conclude, Master Machiavel, that you are mad.'

'Depend upon it.' Marlowe nodded. 'But only nor' by nor'west!' He slipped the knife back in its sheath in his sleeve. 'Tell me, in the name of all that's holy, how you can instruct the jury to record the death of Henry Bromerick as accidental.'

'Are you saying I don't know my job, sir? You have just pulled a dagger on one of Her Majesty's coroners, threatened his life. For that alone I could have you thrown out of the university and into a cell from which I doubt even one with your barefaced gall would ever escape.'

170

'Henry Bromerick had bright green vomit,' Marlowe said, ignoring the threat.

'Of course,' Winterton agreed. 'The man was clearly ill.'

'The man was clearly poisoned, Sir Edward. As was Ralph Whitingside.'

'Whitingside?'

'The King's man at whose inquest we first met. You remembered me as Machiavel. Why can't you remember the name of my friend?'

'I remember it perfectly well, but why does everyone always think that the inquest in which they are interested is the only inquest in the world. I have sat on more than a few since your friend's, Master Marlowe. A sad case of a drowned woman affected me deeply. Her sister was distraught. Crying. I hate a woman crying, it influences the jury. That family also were intent that it must be foul play. But I was merciful,' Winterton said smoothly. 'I decided to instruct the jury for a "found drowned". Suicide would have unhinged the poor woman entirely. But, tell me, Master Marlowe; people have a habit of dying around you. Why is that, I wonder?'

'So do I, Sir Edward. Both of these men were my friends. And both were given draughts of tincture of foxglove to drink.'

'Foxglove?' Winterton blinked. 'I heard nothing of foxgloves. How the Devil do you come up with that?'

Now was not the time to involve Dee or the Devil, so Marlowe said, 'Never mind. The fact is that that is what killed them both.'

'Whitingside was different,' Winterton said.

'In what way?' Marlowe asked as the carriage lurched forward to edge a few more paces before coming to a standstill.

'I received a ... deputation, shall we call it, on the morning of the inquest.'

'A deputation?' Marlowe frowned. 'From whom?'

'I cannot say.'

'Sir Edward...' Marlowe straightened up, his hand going to his sleeve.

'Don't try to frighten me, sir, with your all-too-ready dagger. I fought at Pinkie. Had a halberd in my ribs that still gives me gyp all these years later.'

'I am not trying to frighten you, Sir Edward,' Marlowe said softly. 'Just to remind you of your office. You speak for the Queen here, sir. And I'd like to think you speak for justice.'

Winterton paused for a moment, trying once again to see what lay behind the calm, unruffled, unfathomable face. 'Very well,' he said. 'I had a deputation from King's College. Dr Benjamin Steane, to be exact. Do you know him?'

Marlowe nodded. 'I do. What did he want?'

'He wanted to retain the honour of the college,' the coroner told him.

'He wanted you to lie for him.'

'That's rather strong,' Winterton protested. 'And he made no such request. He merely wondered whether it was possible to play the whole thing down, brush as much as possible under the

172

rushes, as it were.'

'Which led to the suicide verdict and a burial in unhallowed ground.'

Winterton looked at him. 'You don't strike me as the kind of man who cares where anyone is buried.'

'You may be right, Sir Edward,' Marlowe said. 'All places are alike and every earth is fit for burial. But I owe Ralph Whitingside more than that.' He tipped his cap. 'Many thanks for the lift, but I fear I am going in the wrong direction. Good day.' And he jumped down from the carriage, vanishing instantly into the throng of scholars and tradesmen over Magdalene Bridge.

It was a little after two on a cloudless Cambridge day that Christopher Marlowe found Benjamin Steane. He was on his way via the St Catherine's entrance, striding across the quad at King's with his robes billowing out on the breeze.

'Dr Steane?' Marlowe hailed. 'A word?' And he doffed his hat.

'Dominus Marlowe.' Steane nodded back. 'Will this take long? I have Discourses to deliver.'

'Sir Edward Winterton,' Marlowe said.

'Ah.' Steane looked a little shamefaced. 'What did he tell you?' The quad of King's College was hardly the place for a private conversation, but Marlowe was in no mood to wait for a better time or place.

'That you came to see him,' the Corpus man

173

said. 'That you leaned on him in the case of Ralph Whitingside.'

'Leaned...' Steane was outraged. 'That's rather strong, Marlowe.'

'Is it, sir? If you preferred something weaker, you should not have gone to the coroner.'

Steane stood for a moment, gnawing his lip. Then he clapped Marlowe on the shoulder. 'Look around you, lad,' he said, beaming. 'What do you see?'

Marlowe looked, as he had so often, at the huge Gothic chapel of King's, dwarfing every building in sight. He saw the midday sun dancing on the warm grey stone and the shadows of the gargoyles short on the trampled grass. 'King's,' he said.

Steane smiled. 'Ah, Master Marlowe. Where is the poet in you? I see an idea, a dream. The finest – and, saving your own dear college – the best in Cambridge. Ever been to Oxford?'

Marlowe had not and shook his head.

'An average place,' Steane said, scowling. 'A tradesman's town, full of meanness of spirit. Here in the Fens we are at the cutting edge of scholarship – and of religion. Mark my words, Marlowe, what happens in Cambridge today happens in the rest of the world tomorrow.'

'And what has this to do with Ralph Whitingside?' Marlowe was unimpressed.

Steane checked that no one was in earshot and he led Marlowe into the corner of the quad, far enough away from any staircase entrance for no one to be able to hear them. 'In this great country of ours,' he murmured, 'we are all bought and paid for. All – every one of us – somebody's man. At the moment, I am the Provost's.'

'Go on.'

'Dr Goad has lived most of his life in these hallowed halls,' he said. 'Not, like you and me, a handful of years. It would kill him if the honour of King's were to be impugned.'

'So he sent you to Winterton?' Marlowe asked.

'Let's just say, he made a ... suggestion.' Steane groped for his words. 'And before you go haring off to the Provost like the bull at a gate you are, hear me out.'

Marlowe stayed put.

'Bad enough that Whitingside died in the college. But that murder should be involved ... Better the world thinks it is self-slaughter. Less fuss. Less finger-pointing at King's and all it stands for. Everyone looking at everyone else, looking for the skull beneath the skin.'

Marlowe was still unimpressed and Steane knew that he was. 'For what it's worth,' the King's man said, 'I happen to think you're right.'

Marlowe looked at him. 'What are you saying?' he asked.

'Whitingside was murdered. But I have no idea how or by whom.'

'I have an idea how, Dr Steane,' Marlowe said. 'As to by whom...'

They were both suddenly aware of a figure hovering near them, on the flagstones to

175

Steane's left. Marlowe glanced across and recognized Will Latimer, Whitingside's servant, standing there, cap in hand.

'Beg pardon, Masters.' Latimer bowed as though to royalty.

'What is it?' Steane and Marlowe chorused.

'May I have a word with Master Marlowe, sirs?' Latimer could grovel for England when the mood took him.

Steane waved the pair aside but he had not finished with Marlowe and waited a few paces away.

'Er ... this is a little awkward, sir.' Latimer was scrunching his cap in both hands. 'Only since ... what happened to the Master ... I've been by way of being unemployed, so to speak.'

'Yes,' said Marlowe curtly. 'It's the way of the world.'

'Yes.' Latimer hopped from foot to foot. 'Yes, it may be, sir. But ... well, I have debts.'

Marlowe smiled a wintry smile. 'Ah yes, the card school at the Devil. Or was it your father's funeral? But in either of those situations, Will, as I've told you before, never lead with the king. Play the knave next time – it's more you, if you won't mind my speaking bluntly.' And he turned back to Steane.

'Sir!' Latimer blurted out. 'I am a masterless man, sir. Without my income I will have to leave Cambridge.'

Marlowe turned back to him. 'Will, I am a Parker scholar. I have four pounds a year on which to live. There are the college fees, my

176

board and lodging. I don't know whether you realize it but the Corpus buttery is the most expensive in Cambridge.' He closed to the man. 'It's tough all over,' he said.

'Latimer,' Steane interrupted. 'I couldn't help but overhear. Come to see me at cock-shut time. There are various college funds – nothing huge, mind – but I won't see a former college servant starve.'

'Thank you, sir,' Latimer blurted out, grabbing the man's hand and kissing it. 'Thank you.'

Steane laughed, pulling his hand away. 'Wait until you see what I can do for you before you are so grateful, Latimer.' He waved the man away and the servant ran in a humble crouch round the side of the building and was gone.

'That's very generous of you, sir,' said Marlowe. 'He wasn't what I would call a loyal servant to Ralph.'

Steane shrugged. 'I wonder if Dr Falconer and Dr Thirling have spoken with you yet, Marlowe?'

'They are always civil if we meet in the street,' Marlowe said. 'But if, as I assume you do, you mean about something specific, then, no, they haven't.'

Steane coughed and shuffled his feet. 'I am to be married soon, Dominus Marlowe and need a choir for the service. With Whitingside ... er...'

Marlowe inclined his head in understanding and also to hide the surprise on his face at the news of a wedding.

'And a couple of choristers rusticated for, er...'

This time, the head was raised. '...being boys?' Marlowe asked.

'We need some extra singers.' Steane chose to ignore the question. 'Your name was mentioned first, of course, as it is the length and breadth of Cambridge when any deputizing is required.' Steane smiled ingratiatingly. 'And then we wondered if a couple of the other Parker scholars would make up the numbers as well.'

Marlowe gave a bark of humourless laughter. 'A couple is all you can have, Dr Steane. Colwell and Parker are all that are left.'

Steane looked puzzled. 'But surely ... What has happened to ... umm, Bromwick, is it?'

'Bromerick, sir. Bromerick is dead. You haven't got a monopoly on murder at King's – it's happened at Corpus too.'

The afternoon drowsed along, and Kit Marlowe with it. Seated in his customary place at the back, feet up on the back of the chair in front, cap firmly over his eyes, he let Dr Lyler's golden words sink in to his brain as they may. He often infuriated his fellow scholars by appearing to sleep but then, when suddenly asked by a Fellow what the subject of the Discourse might be, through which he was apparently snoozing he would, with no discernible effort, not only repeat the last ten minutes verbatim, but also rationalize and comment on the content. It would be easy, some said, to hate Kit Marlowe. And many did.

* * *

Gabriel Harvey occasionally carried a pomander with him as he strode through Cambridge. It was not strictly necessary around the colleges, but it was around the colleges he normally strode, attracting as much attention as he could. He hobnobbed that Wednesday afternoon with a couple of his old colleagues from Pembroke Hall and was just cutting through Trinity Street when he heard his name, hissed and secret.

'Dr Harvey!'

He spun to allow his robes to billow wide and took a vicious sniff of the pomander.

'I am he,' he said.

'Robert Greene, Doctor,' the man said.

Nothing. Harvey continued walking.

'Dr Harvey.' Greene scrabbled alongside him, trying to keep up with the man's great strides. 'Don't you remember? We spoke the other day. Of Kit Marlowe.'

Suddenly Harvey was all ears. He stood still and looked the man in the face. He wore no college robes, but a roisterer's jerkin and Spanish ruff. His hair was the colour of overcooked carrots and the afternoon sun bounced off the brilliant in his left ear. Harvey's eyes narrowed. 'I remember,' he said. 'You told me he read Machiavelli, which I knew. That he paid his buttery bills with the proceeds of tavern gambling, at which I had guessed. That he translates Ovid in the most obscene way possible – all right, I didn't know that, but I wasn't too surprised. What new libel have you come up with?'

Greene was hurt. 'Forgive me, Dr Harvey,' he

179

said. 'I was under the impression that any of those offences would cost Master Marlowe his degree.'

'Remind me, sir,' Harvey snapped. 'Are you of this university?'

'I am, sir,' Greene told him, standing taller. 'A graduate of St John's.'

Harvey snorted. 'Then who are you to tell me what constitutes a sending down?' And he spun on his heel.

'There is one crime,' Greene called out, 'for which a man can be hanged in this great country of ours.'

Harvey stopped, the pomander halfway to his nose. He turned slowly. 'Name it,' he said.

Greene closed to him. 'The crime of Sodom,' he said.

Harvey's eyes widened and he positively swayed for a moment. There were over a hundred crimes for which a man could be hanged, but somehow, he knew the way Greene's wind was blowing. He grabbed the man's sleeve and pulled him around a corner, checking the lane north and south.

'Marlowe?' he muttered.

Greene nodded.

'And who?'

It was Greene's turn to check the street. 'Ralph Whitingside, late, I understand, of King's College.'

Harvey let go of the man's sleeve and brushed the cheap velvet back into place. 'I may have been hasty,' he said. 'What else do you under-

180

stand, Dominus Greene?'

'Marlowe and Whitingside were friends, back in Canterbury. Went to the King's School. Played together at that tricky age when boys become men. I'm sure I don't have to paint you a portrait, Dr Harvey.'

'There has to be evidence,' Harvey murmured, his mind racing. 'Hard fact.'

'Dig in the Potter's Field,' Greene shrugged.

Harvey frowned. 'Why there?'

'Isn't that where they buried the late Whitingside?'

'How would that help?'

Greene sighed. How could a man with Harvey's academic credentials be so dim? 'Marlowe put him there,' he explained.

'What? Killed him, you mean?'

Greene nodded. He barely knew Harvey at all, but he knew the man's reputation. He wasn't easily rattled, but the great man seemed speechless now.

'Why?' was all he could manage.

Greene became positively oily as he outlined the possibilities. 'A lover's tiff?' he suggested. 'A third party, as it were?' It didn't look as if Harvey was buying any of this so Greene tried harder. 'I understand that Dominus Whitingside tied his points in both directions, if you get my drift.'

Harvey did. 'Like Caesar,' he remembered. 'Every woman's man and every man's woman.'

Greene smiled. His work was done. But he hadn't quite reeled Harvey in yet. 'But Marlowe

181

found him,' the Fellow reasoned. 'He was First Finder. At the inquest – I was there.'

Greene shook his head, chuckling. 'The oldest ploy in the book, Dr Harvey,' he said. 'Perhaps he had a fit of conscience and the night terrors took him. Or there again, if he made enough song and dance about it, looked a bit hangdog, sobbed a bit – you know, manly stuff – who'd have suspected dear old Kit Marlowe?'

He whispered unnervingly in Harvey's ear. 'You and I, Doctor, if we wanted to see a friend in another college, would catch him in the street or write the necessary letter for admission at an appointed hour. We would not climb over walls and rooftops and sneak into a man's bedroom in the dead of night. It screams guilt.'

'Yes.' Harvey clicked his fingers. 'Put like that, it does. It does.'

Greene stepped back, his voice louder, confident. 'May I leave it in your capable hands then, Doctor?' he asked.

Harvey hesitated, then shook Greene's hands. 'Count on it,' he said.

'May I offer you gentlemen a drink?'

Such a line was music to the ears of the two Parker scholars slouching in a murky corner of the Brazen George that night. Proctors Lomas and Darryl had fallen yet again for the live-piglet-in-the-cloisters routine while Colwell and Parker had slipped out of the side gate and across the churchyard. God knew where Kit was. Like all of them, he had been hit hard by

182

the death of Henry Bromerick, but intensity was Kit Marlowe's middle name and he was probably off on some wild goose chase of his own.

'Er ... thank you,' Parker said. 'A pint of ale, please.'

The stranger looked at Colwell.

'The same,' said Tom.

Men like this didn't drift into Cambridge inns every night of the week. He wore a doublet and colleyweston cloak of deep black and his gloves were of velvet with gold thread. He placed his plumed hat on the table. Even before he'd done this, half a dozen serving wenches as well as the landlord were at his side, grovelling, curtseying, offering to do his bidding. He placed his order, having the same ale for himself and smiled at the pretty girl still hovering at his elbow.

She curtseyed, smiling. 'Will there be anything else, sir?' she asked.

'Lettice!' the landlord cut in, cuffing the girl around the ear. 'Don't be bothering the gentleman with all that. He's not interested in the likes of you.'

'On the contrary,' the gentleman said. 'Lettice, is it?' He beckoned her forward and motioned the landlord away. She stuck her tongue out at the man as he scuttled around the corner, roaring orders to his minions. 'What do you make,' the stranger asked, 'entertaining a gentleman?'

Lettice blushed. For all she did entertain gentlemen, she wasn't usually asked outright so early in the evening and in the hearing of scholars. 'Two pennies, sir,' she said. 'That's for the

183

beast with two backs. One penny for anything less.'

The stranger smiled, reaching for his purse. 'There,' he said. 'There's a month's wages so that you don't have to do anything with beasts.' Her eyes widened as she saw and felt the gold in her hand.

'Thank you, sir.' Her voice was barely audible and she dashed around the corner before biting the coin, just to be sure. She'd hate to offend such a kind gentleman.

The kind gentleman sipped the ale. 'Hmm,' he said. 'Not bad. And in a way why I'm here.' He held out a hand. 'Francis Hall,' he said.

'Tom Colwell,' Colwell said. 'This is Matthew Parker.'

'Matthew Parker,' Hall said, lingering in his handshake for a moment. 'That name's familiar.'

'My grandfather, sir,' Parker said. 'Archbishop of Canterbury, not so long ago.' It was the lad's fate to go through this ritual. He'd probably have to do it for the rest of his life.

'Of course, of course. A fine man. Endowed your college richly, I believe.'

'Our...?' Colwell did his best to look inscrutable.

Hall smiled. 'Come, gentlemen. Hide it though you might, I know the badge of the pelican and lilies. Corpus Christi College. Unique among the halls of the university, it was founded in 1350 by the Guild of Corpus Christi in response to the devastation of the Great Pestilence...'

184

'You seem very well informed,' Colwell said, drawing back. 'Do you mind telling us what brings you to Cambridge?'

The stranger closed to the scholars. 'I don't mind,' he said. 'On one condition – that you tell me how you got out of college tonight.'

The Parker scholars looked at each other. What was this? Some new ploy by Norgate? A ruse by that bastard Harvey?

'Was it the fire-in-the-library ploy?' Hall asked, wide-eyed.

Nothing.

'The hue-and-cry routine?'

Nothing.

'Not the leper-at-the-gate stuff?'

Parker and Colwell looked at each other again and then burst out laughing. 'It was the piglet-in-the-cloister,' Parker confessed. And all three of them roared.

'They never learn, do they?' Hall chuckled. 'Let me explain, gentlemen. More years ago than I care to remember, I was sitting more or less where you are.' He looked around him. 'The place was smaller then. Young Lettice over there wasn't even a gleam in her father's eye. I was at King's.'

'Oh, bad luck,' Parker blurted out. And all three roared again.

'Now it's your turn,' Colwell said, suddenly serious. 'Your reason for being in Cambridge. Not to walk down memory lane, surely?'

'Ah, no,' Hall said with a smile. 'And yet the memories do come flooding back. I remember one bitterly cold winter...' He saw the steel in Colwell's eye and changed tack. 'Very well,' he said. 'Do you know the name Walter Ralegh?'

The scholars didn't.

'Well, he is a West Country gentleman, highly thought of at Court. He's Her Majesty's Controller of Wines and he's passing through Cambridge on Friday as part of a royal commission.' He leaned forward, tapping his tankard. 'Hence my sampling of the local brew. I've been sent on ahead to plough the furrow, as it were.' He sat back upright. 'And it's not at all bad. Walter will be pleased.'

He motioned the landlord over for a second round. 'Now, gentlemen.' He smiled broadly. 'Have either of you heard of a scholar called Christopher Marlowe?'

TEN

The evening was darkling into night as Marlowe bounced up his stair to the Parker scholars' rooms. The Discourses had gone well, he had enjoyed his dinner in College, and he now looked forward to a few hours of quiet reflection on his own, as he had just seen Parker and Colwell release a piglet in preparation for an evening at the Brazen George.

He wriggled the key into the reluctant lock and

was just beginning to lose his temper with it when he realized it was already open. He would have some words to say to Colwell and Parker when he saw them next; no doubt, having taken delivery of the piglet, all other thoughts left their heads. He just hoped the piglet hadn't been in the room too long. He pushed the door open and went in, throwing his cap in the general direction of the settle in the dark and shrugging off his gown. He threw himself on to his bed and laced his fingers behind his head. He loved people and people watching. A sonnet was forming in his head as he lay there, based on the turn of a pretty neck he had been admiring over dinner. He tried a few lines, declaimed to the dark.

'Come live with me and be my love;
And we will all the pleasures prove...'

'Nice, Dominus Marlowe. Very nicely put, although I think perhaps that second line needs work – it is an eye rhyme, after all. Ovid wouldn't approve.'

The voice, quietly coming from a dark corner of the room, brought Marlowe to his feet in a second and over to the window in two more, as he tugged the curtain aside to bring the twilight's faint glow into the room. There was a candle stub on the window sill and with trembling fingers he manipulated the tinderbox to give more light.

The owner of the voice sat in silence while he did this; there was no movement, no threat of violence, no hiss of steel being drawn from a sheath. Marlowe's recent brush with John Dee had left him understandably a little more nervous than was his usual nature, but even so his hand only trembled a little as he turned to see who had spoken.

'Professor Johns?' He was amazed to see his tutor sitting there. But more amazing still was the state of the room. Clothes were strewn everywhere, papers lay in drifts over the scholars' beds. The ashes of the last fire of spring had been raked from the grate and had mixed with the rushes on the floor to give, with the careless addition of some stale small beer, an unlovely mat of grey slurry in front of the fire.

'Hello, Dominus Marlowe. I see you are surprised to see me,' the Fellow said, smiling. 'I, on the other hand, am surprised to see how you live.' His fastidious fingers picked up a pad of soggy paper and let it drop with a small thunk.

'I am also surprised, Michael,' Marlowe said. 'I would never say we were tidy, in fact the bedders have complained often, especially about poor Bromerick's personal habits, but we don't live like *this*.' He looked around, helplessly. 'I don't know where to start.' He picked up some papers and tidied them into a pile, but then had nowhere to put them, as the table was smeared with the same grey goo that lay in front of the grate.

Johns took pity on him. 'I admit, Dominus,' he said, 'that I had come to speak to you about your lamentable attendance at my lectures lately, as well as those of my colleagues. I felt guilty enough about letting myself in and when I saw the state of the room I concluded that you probably have enough troubles as it is.'

Marlowe looked around, still disbelieving. 'Who could have done this?' he asked. 'We hadn't even packed poor Henry's things away to give to his parents when they get here, if they come. What will they think when they see his clothes covered in ashes and beer like this?' He picked over a pile of stockings and shirts. 'I can't even tell which are his. To make things worse, some of these things are Ralph's.'

'Ralph's?' Johns asked, with a raised eyebrow.

'Yes. Dr Steane brought some of his things round the other day. He didn't know who else would have them, with Ralph an orphan. Sir Roger Manwood, who was his guardian, won't want them, I don't expect. And now, we'll have to sort them out from this mess.' No one knew if Kit Marlowe was prone to depression or sorrow; his enigmatic face hid most of his feelings, unless he wanted them on show. But Johns could see that he was now at a loss. He stood up and started to pick up the clothes on the floor and pile them in one place.

'Michael, you are covered in ash,' Marlowe said. 'Your sleeves, look, and your hands are all grey with it.'

Johns looked down. 'It's hardly surprising, Kit, is it?' he said, rather crossly. 'Are you accusing me of making this mess?'

Marlowe dropped his shoulders and sighed. 'I don't know what to think,' he said, 'but, no, of

189

course I don't think you did this. I think someone has been here, looking for something,
something connected with the murders of Ralph
and Henry.' He looked at the professor. 'Somebody who can pick a lock, it would seem.'

Johns crossed the room, kicking aside tumbled
bedding and put his hand on the scholar's arm.
'Murders?' he said. 'The inquests said...'

'I know what the inquests said,' Marlowe said.
'The inquests are wrong. I know what the bastard who did this was looking for, too.'

'You do?' Johns said, not moving away. 'What
was that, do you think? And has he found it?'

Marlowe smiled. 'Ah, Professor Johns. No
one can catch me that easily. I will keep my
counsel on those questions if I may.'

'As you wish,' the Fellow said and went back
to gathering up the ash-soaked clothes. 'This
will cost a pretty penny to launder,' he said,
changing the subject ostentatiously. 'This bedding was only changed last quarter, I'm thinking.'

Marlowe looked around at the devastation and
nodded. 'I'll have to try and sweet talk the laun-
dresses,' he said. 'It's not as though I haven't
had to curry favour with them before.'

Johns scooped up a parcel he had made by
wrapping the clothes in a sheet. 'I'll speak to Dr
Norgate,' he said. 'I'm sure there must be some
fund or another to meet this contingency.'

Marlowe allowed himself a quiet laugh. 'Ah,
yes,' he said. 'The Maud Ashenden Bequest for
the Laundering of Scholars' Clothing Besmirch-

190

ed with Ash in the Commission of a Burglary.'

'The very one,' Johns said, smiling. 'Now, if you will gather up the rest, we'll go down to the laundry and start the sweet talking, before we have to see how much money will have to change hands.'

Marlowe did as he was told and together the two struggled down the narrow stair and across The Court to the laundry at the back of the kitchens.

From a dark corner on the lower landing, a dark figure watched them go. The wet ash had dried to powder on his hands and in his pocket a small book made a bulge, which he would soon be swapping, he hoped, for a purse of equal volume. Sadly, as he would soon discover, his employer would not be amused to be offered a small Latin psaltery, annotated by a boy chorister in the Cathedral at Canterbury. Thus, they would both learn a lesson. The burglar would learn, as he was removed from the town for indigence, whipped at the cart's tail, that it was unwise to annoy a powerful man. The powerful man would learn that it was unwise to send a burglar who couldn't read Latin to steal a book.

Joseph Fludd was miles away. His carpentry business had suffered in the last few days in favour of his constabulary duties and he had a job he had to finish in a hurry, being a new chair for the rooms of Professor Wilkes, of Jesus College. Fludd's purse had reason to be grateful to Wilkes's unparalleled gluttony, as he got through chairs at a rate of around three a year, each needing to be more reinforced than the last. Fludd loved his work, the sound of the lathe spinning sweetly on its spindle, the smell of the newly turned oak as the shavings flew like ribbons from the blade. Professor Wilkes needed oak these days; the softer woods buckled almost at once under his weight. Fludd hummed under his breath as the chair leg took shape under his hand. He raised the blade and stopped pedalling and the lathe slowed and stopped.

'Joseph?' Allys Fludd knew better than to speak to her husband whilst he was working the lathe. She came from a family of carpenters and knew only too well from the tales of some of her six-fingered uncles how dangerous that could be.

He turned. She stood in the doorway of his workshop, holding a tankard of ale and a plate of bread and cheese on a tray. 'Is it dinner time already?'

'No,' she said. 'I think this is by way of being breakfast, Joe.' She pushed aside some shavings and put the tray down on a half-finished chair. 'You've got to eat. You'll make yourself ill.'

'I do eat,' he protested. 'I ate...' He wasn't quite sure when.

'It's this constable nonsense,' she said. 'You've done it often enough, and that's God's truth. When they ask you next, just say no.'

He took a swig of ale, looking at her over the rim of the tankard.

'And don't look at me like that either, Joseph

192

Fludd. You can't woo me with those eyes any more.'

He lowered the tankard and his eyelids, his lashes lying on his cheeks like a girl's.

She boxed his ears, but lightly and with love. 'Well, perhaps you can, then,' she said. 'But it's because you can, Joe, that I worry about you. You can't keep on at this rate.'

He sat down on his working stool, putting the plate in front of him and tucking into the cheese, soft and tangy. He gestured to it, mouth full, nodding.

'I know I make good cheese, Joe,' she said. 'And good ale. And bread. And all sorts of other food. I make good children, too.' She tossed her head back to the house where their daughter was playing in the shavings on the kitchen floor and patted her belly where, hopefully, a healthy son lay. 'But for all you know, I may as well not bother. Talk to me, Joe. Tell me what's the matter.'

He washed the cheese down with the ale and wiped his mouth. 'I don't know where to begin, Allys,' he said. 'It's constable's worries. It's not for you.'

Allys set her feet firmly apart and folded her arms. 'I can be the judge of that, Joseph,' she said.

Joseph Fludd had chosen a strong woman for a wife on purpose, against his mother's better judgement. It had paid off, more or less, over the years. But every good thing came with a price and this was it. He sighed. 'Sit down, Allys,' he

193

said. 'Don't loom over me like that. You addle my brain.'

She sat on a bench and waited for him to begin.

'In all my years as Constable,' he said, 'I've never encountered what I have encountered in the last month. Three murders...'

She laughed, rocking back and slapping her knees. 'Three murders in a month. Joe Fludd, you need to have a think before you say things like that. You had three murders on one day of the Sturbridge Fair not two years ago.'

'Ah, yes.' He had no choice but to agree. 'But they weren't *murders*. Not like these. They were stupid drunks with knives killing each other. The three murders I have got on my mind are ... what's the word, when it is done secretly, cunningly?'

Allys shrugged. Either of those words would make it clear, to her mind.

'Clandestine. That's the word the scholars would use. Clandestine. Someone killed these people and did it in such a way that no one would know they had done it. Might not even say it was a murder, even.'

'But the inquests...'

'Suicide, found drowned, natural causes.' Fludd ticked them off on his fingers. He didn't need to burden Allys with the names, though they were all human beings once, with hopes and dreams and families of their own. Ralph Whitingside. Eleanor Peacock. Henry Bromerick.

194

Allys leaned forward, hand cupped theatrically to her ear. 'I don't think I heard properly, Joe,' she said. 'I didn't hear you say "murder" in that list.'

'No,' Fludd sighed. 'I know you didn't. And that's the problem. The suicide and natural causes were scholars from the university, different colleges. The found drowned was a woman from Royston, a nun.'

'A nun?' Allys was genuinely surprised by that. 'Not so many of those around,' she said. In fact, the last time she'd seen one, she was still a small child, knee deep in wood shavings in her father's workshop. 'Quite long odds on finding one drowned, I would think.'

'Don't mock me, Allys,' he said. 'Perhaps a nun is the wrong word, but she was certainly very religious. Had only been back in the county ... the country, I should say ... for a few days. Knew no one but her family...'

'But?' she said quietly. She loved her husband and didn't mean to scoff, but he sometimes took himself too seriously.

'But she had a rosary embedded in her neck.' He fingered his own throat in reminiscence. 'The scholars were both poisoned, or so they say.'

'They?'

'A scholar called Marlowe and Dr John Dee.'

Allys's eyes widened. Even here in Trumpington, that man's name was a byword for all that was unholy. She wouldn't show it, but suddenly Allys Fludd was afraid. 'The Queen's Magi-

195

cian,' she said softly. 'You mix in high circles these days, Joe.'

'Hmm?' Fludd's eyes were troubled and he crumbled a piece of bread between restless fingers.

His wife watched him for a while and then got up, went over to him and kissed him on the forehead. 'Joe,' she said, smoothing his hair back from his face. 'I can see you are worried and that worries me. Look into your murders, and when you do you will find they are a suicide, a found drowned and a natural causes. Stay away from magicians. Stay away from scholars. But mainly...'

He looked up. 'Yes?'

'Eat. Your. Dinner.'

He kissed her back and patted her backside, comforting, wide and warm. 'Yes, my love,' he said. 'I promise.' He watched her go, back into the yard with the cackling hens and the summer sun. But his eyes were thoughtful as he ate his bread and cheese.

It was chaos at Madingley that morning, largely because the dragon that was Ursula Hynde was roaring through the house. She was a large woman, reminding John Dee of those stately merchantmen that blew in from the Channel, three-masted and full-rigged. Dee and his old friend Roger Manwood had spent the last few days studiously avoiding her, closeted deep in their host Francis Hynde's study. But there was no comfort there today because on the bride-to-be's orders, every door in Madingley was thrown back; every casement opened wide.

The pair tried to have a conversation in the hall, then in the parlour, but her shrieked commands to the little knot of servants who followed her everywhere drowned out their attempts. A clerk did his best to scratch her instructions down as she hurled them out, another trying to keep pace so the man could dip his quill into the inkwell he carried for him.

'Those curtains will have to go,' she screeched in the Long Gallery.

Francis Hynde, who had taken what he thought to be refuge on a padded windowseat behind one such hanging, stuck his head out. 'Ursie, dearest sister,' he said plaintively, 'these hangings were chosen by my sainted mother and I love them dearly. They have hung here for thirty years and more.'

'So have the traitors' heads on London Bridge and it's all the more reason for them to go,' she snapped. She and her train swept on, nearly stamping on the Lord of Madingley's toes. The clerk scribbled. Hynde gestured to the man and he crossed out his scribbling. Ursula Hynde stopped, peered at the paper and pointed imperiously. The clerk rescribbled, shrugged apologetically at Hynde, ducked his head and the circus moved off once more.

Hynde looked after his sister-in-law with hatred in his heart and venom in his eyes. But discretion being the better part of valour, he withdrew his head, like a snail into its shell and went back to his book and a rather nice bottle of claret.

The guests were to arrive any day and it was irritating beyond measure that Roger Manwood had turned up like a bad penny, expecting hospitality on a royal scale. And even more galling that he'd offered that weird old cove from Mortlake a bed for a few nights. Hynde considered charging them, then lost that thought as the claret warmed his soul and clouded his brain simultaneously.

Dee and Manwood scuttled ahead of Ursula to Manwood's room, but mayhem met them there. A confused dove, destined for part of the wedding service and then for a pie, flew in through the open window and was fluttering in terror around the ceiling as an equally terrified maid tried to shoo it away.

As he did an about-turn in the doorway, Dee's swirling cloak did little to soothe either the girl or the bird and Dee and Manwood hot-footed it down the back stairs, to the consternation of Hynde's steward, who had an overdeveloped sense of where the nobs belonged. He backed into his room at the rear of the house and took refuge in yet more of Sir Francis's best brandy, despite the day being still very new.

Hurrying through the Physick Garden in their attempt to escape, Dee and Manwood eventually found the shade of a huge old oak and sank gratefully into the smooth-worn bark of the roots.

'God's wounds, that woman is unbelievable,'

grunted Manwood, peering anxiously round the bole of the tree. Despite putting some distance between themselves and the house, her hooting tones could still be heard.

'You've even got to feel sorry for Francis,' Dee said, rummaging in his pouch. 'And that's not something you'll hear often from me. I know he's a friend of yours, Roger, but...'

Manwood held up a hand. 'Dear boy, I'm with you all the way. He's not the Francis Hynde I used to know. Mind like a bodkin, witty, inform-ed. Look at him now,' he said, and he mimed swigging from a bottle in mid-air.

'Her, do you think?' Dee asked. 'Ursula?' It didn't take much of a seer to offer *that* inter-pretation.

As if he had called her from the vasty deep, Ursula Hynde's voice was suddenly very near. They cowered behind their tree.

'Do you call that a ha-ha?' she bellowed. 'It's a wonder my dear brother-in-law isn't a laugh-ing stock the length and breadth of the county. But there again, perhaps he is. Dig it wider. Deeper.' There was a pause. 'And five feet fur-ther from the house.' In the silence that fol-lowed, the men could hear, above the petrified beating of their own hearts, the whistling of the breath in her nostrils. 'Well?' she yelled. 'Get a spade, man. Don't just stand there!' It was all Dee and Manwood, married men of some standing and used to jumping to it, could do to stay hidden.

'Is Francis making all these changes?' Dee

asked.

'I hardly think so,' Manwood said. 'But, as you implied just now, she is the sister-in-law from Hell and the poor chap does seem to have taken to the bottle. But this chap she's marrying – Steane, is it? Blind, is he? Deaf? Desperate?'

Dee shrugged. 'This is no more my neck of the woods than it is yours, Roger. I only came because of Marlowe.'

'Yes.' Manwood became serious. 'You and I both. That's what I want to talk to you about. What *are* you doing, man?'

Dee had been occupied for the last few minutes stuffing dried herbs into a clay bowl with a stem attached. He now thoroughly alarmed the Justice of the Peace by striking a flint to a tinder and setting fire to the herbs.

'Do you drink smoke?' Dee asked him.

'Do I what?'

Dee inhaled fiercely at the narrow end of the stem and proceeded to blow smoke rings to the bright-green leaves overhead.

'Good God!' Manwood looked horrified.

There was a distant cry of, 'Look lively, you, man, there. That tree appears to be on fire. It will ruin the outlook if it burns down. See to it.'

'Now see what you've done,' Manwood whispered, and Dee lowered his pipe. Running footsteps over the grass alerted them to the approach of a gardener who appeared around the tree, carrying a skin of water. The two men shushed him frantically and he retraced his steps, eyes wide. They gave him a minute to get

200

away and strained their ears for more shrieks, but all seemed quiet for the moment.

Dee raised the burning herbs to his mouth again, and puffed, looking at Manwood over that hook of a nose. 'This is all the rage in London. Canterbury isn't exactly a distant star, Roger. I can't believe the craze hasn't caught on there.'

'Craze indeed.' Manwood was still staring at the contraption in Dee's hand. 'What's it for?'

'It calms the intellect,' Dee said. 'Sharpens the wits and focuses the mind. This is the tobacco plant – from Virginia in the New World. John Hawkins brought it back, ooh, twenty years ago now. I have Penn's and Lobel's herbal at home, but their drawings leave a lot to be desired, I'm afraid.' He puffed slowly, savouring the smoke. 'Francis Drake thinks it might be a curative.'

'What for?' Manwood asked.

'Oh, toothache. Worms, lockjaw, migraine. Umm ... the plague, of course, cancer, labour pains. And bad breath.'

'All those?' Manwood was staggered.

'None of them, dear boy.' Dee shook his head. 'That's just what Francis Drake thinks. And off the deck of a ship, the man's an idiot. Care to try?'

Tentatively, Manwood took the pipe and put it to his mouth. 'What do I do now,' he asked, a trifle indistinctly.

'Breathe in, man,' Dee said. 'Deep as you can.'

Manwood did so and immediately wished he
201

hadn't, coughing, spluttering and sneezing all at the same time.

'Stop that sneezing!' came a distant screech. 'I will not have my wedding day marred by illness of any kind. Find the source of the pestilence and have it removed.' There were no running feet this time and the men relaxed against the warm bark of the oak.

'God's breath,' Manwood finally managed to wheeze.

Dee chuckled. 'I'm not sure whether it's God's or the Devil's,' he said. 'It's an acquired taste, perhaps.'

'Acquired is the right word,' gasped Manwood, passing the pipe back. 'And I have no intention of acquiring it.' He wiped his mouth and eyes, trying to focus again in the hot July morning sun.

'Your loss,' Dee said with a shrug. 'Now, to cases, Marlowe. You knew this Whitingside well, of course.'

'He was my ward,' Manwood said. 'But I'd be lying if I said he was like a son to me.'

Dee knew that. Roger Manwood was one of those people who made the bringing up of wards a business proposition. That was why they had a court for such things in London.

'But he lived in my house for ... ooh, let's see...' He let his head rest back against the tree trunk. 'It must have been four years. He was one of several wards at the time. I've given it all up now of course. At my age I'm getting tired of young people. They're too damned earnest and holier-than-you for my liking.' He glanced sideways at his old friend; almost *everyone* was holier than John Dee. 'I've just got the one now, Joyce. A couple of London merchants have expressed an interest, but I'm holding out for Lord Scrope; he's in the market for wifey number three, you know, turning heads at Court, that sort of thing. Such a vain bastard.'

'Whitingside,' Dee reminded him. How this man was able to focus on the job in hand on the Bench was beyond him. Scourge of the night prowlers indeed!

'I know what you're after, John,' Manwood said, sitting upright again. 'You want a nice little motive on a pewter platter, all parcelled up with ribbon. Well, I'm afraid the sordid world of murder doesn't work like that. Oh, you've got the easy job. Anybody can tell *how* a man was killed ... well, almost anybody. No, the problem is why. The Ralph Whitingside I knew was typical minor gentry. Same class as you and me. He was a bit wild, you know. He and young Marlowe sowed a few wild oats, I shouldn't wonder.'

'But Marlowe's younger, surely?' Dee checked.

'By two years, yes. Whitingside saved him from drowning once.'

'So Marlowe feels he owes his soul something.' Dee was gazing into the middle distance, beyond the warm stone that was Madingley with its green cupolas and the stable wing beyond, trying to establish events in his mind.

Manwood always became uneasy when John Dee started talking about souls. If the Queen died tomorrow, the Privy Council might have the magus burnt. The scourge of the night prowlers liked to keep a back door open in this relationship, just in case. He didn't press the point further. 'There was talk of a girl,' the Justice suddenly remembered. 'Some bad feeling between Whitingside and Marlowe. What *was* her name?'

'Marlowe and a girl?' Dee frowned.

Manwood raised an eyebrow but said nothing.

'And of course you knew the other one – Broderick – didn't you?'

'I did. Nice enough lad, I suppose, but there was always something ... bovine about him. He didn't sparkle like the other King's School lads.'

'Marlowe most of all.' Dee puffed his pipe.

'Ah,' Manwood chuckled. 'There's no one like Kit Marlowe. Mark my words, John, that man has greatness in him.'

'Or a short end,' Dee said.

'You spoke to this local Constable, didn't you?' Manwood asked. 'About Bromerick, I mean?'

'I did,' Dee confirmed.

'Any good?' Manwood asked.

'For a provincial Constable, very,' Dee said. 'But he's got his hands full with some woman found in the river.'

'Any connection?' Manwood wanted to know.

Dee puffed deep on the pipe, much to his friend's disgust. 'I can't see how. Constable

204

Fludd has found her relatives – they came from Royston, I believe. There's no evidence she knew Whitingside or Bromerick or any of them. It is, as the Papists used to have it in connection with the Eucharist, a mystery.'

Manwood leaned forward. 'I told Marlowe he was on his own,' he said.

'So did I,' agreed Dee.

'And yet, here we are, on a summer's day, nonny-nonny, trolly-lolly, fretting about him.'

'Oh, I'm not fretting about Marlowe,' Dee said, blowing smoke again. 'But I'm a man who likes answers to riddles, Roger. I can't let things go.'

'Riddles, eh?' Suddenly Francis Hynde was there, still clutching his bottle, joining them where they lolled in the sun in his best hiding place. 'I love a good riddle.' He smiled beatifically at them. 'I have a good one. Wait a minute ... it's about ... no, it's gone.' He tipped the bottle up, a proof of hope over experience as it had been empty for some time. He frowned at the men, seeming to register them for the first time. 'You shouldn't be here, you know,' he announced. 'It's very dangerous. This tree's on fire.' And with that, he passed out neatly across their legs and began to snore.

Dee glanced down at his host, then pointed to the edge of the Physick Garden where dear Ursie was still marshalling her troops. 'And talking of riddles,' he said, 'what are the odds of foxgloves growing at Madingley, when they shouldn't be here at all?'

ELEVEN

No one went out that night. At least, not the Parker scholars. A couple of sizars from 'F' staircase had sneaked out behind the night soil men and Marlowe had watched them go, holding their noses at the same time as keeping their eyes open for the prowling Proctors. He had tutted and shaken his head. Each generation had to learn their own lesson; it was no use telling them. Not only would Lomas and Darryl be waiting for their return, the smell of them would make the hunting easy.

'And you say he asked for me by name?' he said, turning from the window where his reflection flickered for an instant, four times in the thick, uneven panes.

'He did.' Parker was munching an apple. 'When we asked him why he wanted to know, he said he'd heard the name somewhere, from someone in London and he couldn't remember who.'

'Who do you know in London, Kit?' Colwell asked, plucking idly at his lute.

Marlowe shrugged. 'Nobody,' he said. 'What did you pair of innocents abroad tell him about me?'

206

'Nothing,' Parker said, perhaps a shade too quickly.

'Liar,' Marlowe muttered.

'Well...' Colwell was working out his defence, long learned in the School of Logic. 'He seemed such an honest fellow. Ex Granta man. One of us.'

'One of us is dead, Tom,' Marlowe said softly. Any further conversation seemed pointless after that. Colwell twanged the lute strings once, twice more, then put the thing down. They all heard a dog barking in the distance, out along the High Ward in the July darkness and the rattle of a cart creaking its way home.

Marlowe fished idly in the bag that Dr Steane had brought them, handling Ralph Whitingside's handkerchiefs and gloves. He hadn't really noticed the mirror before. None of the Parker scholars had one and the teaching of the churches now was that such things smacked of vanity and vanity was fast becoming a sin above all others, even though Marlowe was constantly telling the boys that the only real sin was ignorance. Marlowe found himself smiling, not at his own crooked reflection in the mirror but that Ralphie would have checked his own very carefully before slipping over the wall for a night on the town, combing the elegant moustache, curling the well-placed ringlet. What a waste it all was. Marlowe tossed the thing casually among the papers on his desk.

Suddenly, he stiffened, catching his breath despite himself.

'Kit?' Colwell caught the movement.

Marlowe grabbed the mirror again, angling it against the parchment. Then, he brushed it all aside – his scribbled poetry, his jottings on the Queen of Carthage, even some university lecture notes that he was supposed to be working on. And he hauled out Whitingside's journal. He nodded to himself, smiling grimly.

'Kit!' Colwell shouted. 'What the Devil...?'

'Tell me about the Dark Entry,' Marlowe said.

'What?' Parker had stopped munching and waited, not noticing the trickle of juice working its way down his chin.

'Come on, Kit,' Colwell said. 'You know as well as we do. This is not the time for schoolboy reminiscences.'

'Oh, but it is, dear boy. Matt? The Dark Entry?'

Parker sat upright on his bed. He put down his apple core and wiped his chin. He was as game for riddles as the next man. 'It's the name we all had, all us King's scholars, for the entry to the school from the cathedral cloisters, through Prior Sellingegate.'

Marlowe nodded. 'What do you remember of it, Tom?' he asked.

Colwell hadn't moved.

'Come on, man!' Marlowe was shouting now. 'You walked through those arches every day of your life for five years. Think!'

'There were five arches,' Colwell said, quietly, sending his mind back in time, 'from Prior Sellingegate. It was very dark in winter. In the

208

freezing mornings. I used to run.'

'Why?' Marlowe asked.

Colwell looked at him, then at Parker, then away, looking at no one, confronting his own past. 'I didn't like it,' he said. 'When you're eight, silly things frighten you.'

'Henry knew that,' Marlowe said. 'He'd tease you, wouldn't he? Play jokes. Jump out at you in the darkest recess?'

Colwell nodded and shuddered, as though someone had walked over his grave. 'I'd forgotten all about it,' he said, 'until now.'

'What's all this about, Kit?' Parker wanted to know.

'Come here,' Marlowe said and the boys clustered round him. He held up the mirror against the page. 'Who was working on this bit?' he asked.

Colwell looked shamefaced. 'I should have been,' he muttered. 'But ... Henry was. This was the bit he gave to Johns who said he'd pass it on to a colleague.'

'Well, Professor Johns should be ashamed of himself.' Marlowe tapped his arm affectionately. 'Matthew Parker, how is your Greek?'

'It's backwards!' Parker roared as if he'd discovered the origins of the universe and the elixir of life in one rapturous moment. 'Ralphie wrote this bit backwards. *That's* why we couldn't make sense of it!'

'Backwards–' Marlowe tilted the mirror – 'and slightly at an angle, with the letters jumbled for extra effect.'

'A cypher.' Colwell's eyes shone as brightly as Parker's. He straightened, adopting Gabriel Harvey's stance and tone. 'Well, come along, Parker. Out with it. For a grandson of the Archbishop of Canterbury, this should be a piece of piss.'

All three howled with laughter.

Parker said. 'Wait a minute ... *apenanti skoteinos eisodos*.' Then he frowned. 'Opposite of the dark entry. What does that mean?'

'Think!' said Colwell, tapping himself on the forehead with his knuckles. 'What's opposite the Dark Entry? Umm ... the Cloisters. Er ... tomb of Prior Chillenden.'

'No, Prior Markham.'

'Ah.' Colwell's mind was racing ahead. 'But which side are we talking about? What if he means the school side? That'd be the Almoner's Chapel.'

'No, you clod.' Parker hit him with his apple core. 'Strangers' Hall is immediately opposite...'

Marlowe held up a hand. 'Shut up, both of you!'

They looked at him.

'What if "anti" doesn't mean literally opposite? Tom, your memories of Dark Entry haunt you still, am I right?'

Colwell nodded.

'Matt, what about you?'

'I was brought up in those buildings,' he said, whatever childhood fears he'd once had banished now. 'From the time I was still in hanging sleeves, I used to totter that way. I remember

210

splashing in the puddles.'

'I remember something else.' Marlowe was suddenly far away. 'It was a night in July...' he looked out of the window where the moon was gleaming silver on the rooftops of Corpus Christi. 'Ralph was with me.'

'You were there at night?' Parker asked. 'You never boarded, Kit, did you?'

'No. Dr Rose had kept us behind one night. Ralphie was always getting us both into trouble. He'd smashed a window in Strangers' Hall and when Rose caught us, denied all knowledge. Since I was with him as well, Rose decided to flog us both.'

'That sounds like him,' Parker muttered.

'We were going home.' Marlowe recalled it as if it were yesterday. 'Rather more quietly than usual, perhaps. We saw two figures in the Dark Entry. A man and a woman. We thought they were fighting. Ralph ran off and fetched one of the servants from the school to help the woman. He left me there alone and I was sure the man was going to kill her. She was screaming and I didn't know what to do. Well, I was only ten. But when the servant came back with Ralph, he laughed at us and sent us round the long way out of school. Ralph and I talked about it a lot for ages, wondering if the man had been arrested, whether the woman was all right.' Marlowe laughed, at the children he and Whitingside once were.

There was a silence.

'But what were they fighting about?' Parker

asked.

Marlowe looked at him in astonishment. 'Er...'

'Oh, I see!' Parker realized his stupidity and Colwell pelted him with cushions.

'You can tell he's the grandson of the Archbishop of Canterbury, can't you?' Colwell laughed.

When they had control of themselves again, Colwell wiping his eyes on the hem of his gown, Parker was still confused. 'So ... what does Ralph mean, then? *Apenanti skoteinos eisodos.* They *weren't* doing it? And who are they? And why Canterbury? God, Kit, we're no further forward, are we?'

Marlowe looked at him, the worried scholar under the thatch of hair. 'I don't know, Matty,' he said. 'But Ralph's trying to tell us something.'

A silence filled the Corpus night. Marlowe flipped the journal backwards and forwards, worrying the problem in his mind. Then he clicked his fingers at Colwell. 'Ralph's letters,' he said. 'Remind me what we've got, Tom.'

Colwell riffled through them. 'Er ... tailor's bill. One from his cousin. Various estate matters for the bailiff. Woodland ... drainage ... something about enclosure of land.'

'What are you thinking, Kit?' Parker asked.

'Who's the tailor?'

Colwell checked. 'Tate of Mercery Lane,' he said.

'Does a good ruff,' Parker remembered.

'And the cousin?'

212

'Jeremy Whitingside.'

'Where does he live?'

'Hawe – isn't that Manwood's village?'

Marlowe nodded.

'Of course!' Colwell blurted out. 'Kit, you've got it! Ralph owed the tailor, didn't he? Unpaid for doublet and hose or something.'

'That's right.' Parker took up the theme with enthusiasm. 'And cousin Jeremy – if he's Ralph's only relative, he stands to inherit on Ralph's death. It's a conspiracy. Tate and Jeremy worked together. Ralph wasn't paying his tailor's bill, but that wouldn't matter once Jeremy got his hands on Ralph's lands. Brilliant!'

'And no doubt,' sighed Marlowe, 'Ralph's bailiff was in on it, hoping for a better master and he could supply the foxglove tincture.'

The others looked at him.

'Lads, lads,' he said patiently. 'Have you learned nothing from Johns over the last three years? Cousin Jeremy has sizeable estates at Hawe. After Manwood and the church he's the leading landowner. He wouldn't cross the road for Ralph's few acres, let alone kill him, especially as they're miles away from his own. And Master Tate may be a chiseller, but I don't have him down for a cold-blooded killer. Neither of them had easy access to Ralph here in Cambridge, so short of hiring a sworder...'

Silence again. Professional killers were beyond the experience of any of them.

'And what about Henry?' Marlowe asked.

'Throw him into the equation and all ideas float out of the window.'

'So, what are you saying?' Colwell asked.

'The cypher.' Marlowe turned to the journal again. 'What else does it tell us?'

'Dark Entry,' Parker muttered. 'Tombs. Five arches. Ow, Kit, that hurts.' Marlowe had grabbed his arm and his fingers were digging in to the muscle above the elbow.

'Five,' he hissed. 'Five.' He looked at the lads, their faces glowing in the candlelight. And he held up an index finger. 'Ralph Whitingside,' he said. A second finger joined the first. 'Henry Bromerick.' His ring finger jerked upright. 'Thomas Colwell,' he said.

Colwell blinked.

Marlowe raised his little finger. 'Matthew Parker.'

The boy licked his lips as Marlowe's thumb came to the upright.

'Christopher Marlowe.'

'Five,' Colwell mouthed.

'Four Parker scholars and an odd one,' Marlowe said with a nod. 'Whatever this is about, gentlemen, it's to do with Canterbury. And none of us is safe. Tom, are you carrying a dagger?'

'I can be,' Colwell said.

'Matt?'

'Kit,' the boy said, 'you know I never...'

Marlowe leaned forward. 'These are not normal times, lads. We must all watch our backs.'

They all jumped as the sounds of a scuffle

214

outside in The Court told them that the night-ride of a couple of Corpus sizars had come to a sticky end.

The Parker scholars were all agreed – if they had to be inside on a sparkling midsummer's morning, there were many worse places to be than the soaring beauty of King's College Chapel. Marlowe was very familiar with its vaulted ceiling and oak-lined calm, Colwell and Parker less so, but even so, he couldn't help but sit, head back, eyes half closed, letting his mind soar amongst the carvings so high above that they were always hidden in a dim fog of twilight and the smoke of dying candles.

Dr Falconer, halfway between Marlowe's spinning imagination and the soaring height, ensconced in his organ loft, was letting his mind and fingers run free, with trills and arpeggios and variations on a theme by Thomas Tallis, an overrated composer to his mind, but nonetheless worth plagiarizing if there was any chance of getting away with it. His music wound itself into Marlowe's imaginings and added depth and breadth to the pictures unrolling in his head.

There was an abrupt discord which brought the choir to attention, and then the dot and carry one gait of Dr Thirling was heard making its way up the nave. A rustle of papers and a soft oath confirmed it was the choirmaster; despite climbing the shallow steps to the choir many times a day, the third one, slightly higher than the others by a merest whisker, almost always got him, to the perennial amusement of the choristers. After a short pause, the Fellow appeared in the gateway in the Rood screen and approached his lectern, his conducting staff in one hand, his music, all anyhow, in the other. His gaze raked the faces turned expectantly towards him.

'Gentlemen.' He smiled briefly and sketched a bow. 'I am so sorry to keep you waiting, but–' and he thwacked himself on the thigh – 'this leg of mine needs exercise and I lost track of time on the Backs on this beautiful day. It doesn't matter, does it, how often one revels in the beauty...' a skirling chord from above brought him back to the task in hand. 'Yes, well, enough of that, perhaps.' He cleared his throat and began again. 'Thank you for your time this morning. I would particularly like to welcome Master Marlowe, and Master ... umm.'

'Colwell,' Tom called.

'Colwell and Master ... umm,' he continued.

'Parker,' Matt said, quieter, waiting for the punch line.

'Oh, Parker. As in Parker scholar? The Archbishop of...'

'Yes. Canterbury. Grandfather.' Matt was seriously considering changing his name. Something with no connection with anyone famous. He had quite liked the name Walter Ralegh; that would be a good one. No one had ever heard of him.

'I see,' said Thirling, turning to the decani side. 'Gentlemen, would you like a short practice with just the men's voices, or shall we just take it at a run?'

The rather decimated King's gentlemen muttered between themselves, the general consensus being that on the run was fine by them and were they getting paid cash for this and was it time and a half? Thirling chose not to hear – finances were for other people, not artistes like himself.

The choirmaster tapped his staff briskly on the floor. 'Gentlemen of Corpus Christi, are you familiar with *If Ye Love Me*?'

The three looked at each other and then nodded to Thirling. It had been a favourite with their choirmaster at Canterbury, a complex piece which when sung well reduced congregations to tears with its sweetness. When sung badly, tears sprang to the eye as well, but in response to the dissonances, which could break windows at quite a distance.

'Thank you, gentlemen. On my count and...' Thirling raised his staff to Falconer, who gave them their note, long, high and lingering. The cantoris trebles came in like larks, to be taken up in thirds by the decani and then the men. The words and the melody wound on to their conclusion, ending with a harmony so sweet that it sounded like one note, sung by the angels over the Rood screen, their wings pointing to God.

The note died away to silence and Thirling stood there, swaying slightly, thumb and fore-finger pinched together, staff raised, eyes closed. The choir held their breath.

'Beautiful,' he said. 'Absolutely perfect.' The makeshift choir smiled at each other and relaxed. 'And *again*,' Thirling cried. 'On my count and...'

Richard Thirling was quite right, the Backs were very beautiful on that lovely summer morning. Benjamin Steane strolled along, hands clasped lightly behind his back and felt he had not a care in the world. He had just had a note delivered that morning by a galloper from Canterbury to confirm his bishopric, and, though it was only Bath and Wells, rather than the Winchester for which he had hoped, it was still a bishopric and more than anyone else at King's College had. It was not in his nature to skip, but had it been, he would have been skipping now. And add to that, he told himself, the fact that he was to be married in just three days. If his bride was not a beauty, then at his age, did that matter? She had lands, she had money, she was willing; ample attributes, he thought, ample. A smile played on his lips which his enemies would have immediately labelled smug – and they would have been right. A faint song was borne on the breeze from the Chapel, just odd notes, rising and falling. His smile broadened, thinking of the size of the choir at Wells, the sweeping steps to the Chapter House, the Abbey at Bath, sweeping to the river ... the bishop's palace, full of Ursula's beautiful furniture. He stopped, rose up on his toes and took a deep breath. Benjamin Steane was a happy man.

Ursula Hynde stepped from her carriage at the end of Queen's Green. Only Ursula could consider a few days at the sprawling Madingley being cooped up, but that was how she had described it to her long-suffering brother-in-law. She had not taken, as she had put it to her maid servant the night before, to Francis' friends Sir Roger Manwood and that nasty Dr Dee. They were, in order of mentioning, fat and loathsome and scrawny and loathsome. It was something in the way they looked at her; they seemed to be undressing her with their eyes. Ursula Hynde was many things, but she was not a good judge of men's expressions. Looping up her skirts out of the grass still damp from the morning dew, she strolled along the water's edge towards the town. She had been so busy arranging the wedding – there was so much to do, Francis had let the place go to wrack and ruin, old curtains hanging in tatters, staff out of control, trees on fire ... it was not work for a sensitive woman like herself, on the verge of marriage after so many years alone. She sighed, then brightened up. In the distance, she could hear a faint thread of song, coming from King's College Chapel, grey and high and solid in the morning sun. How lovely it sounded, flickering in and out of hearing across the water. She allowed herself a smile; despite the work and the worries, Ursula Hynde, soon to be Steane, was a happy woman.

'Ursula?'

Her head snapped up. Who was this, that he

felt he could be so informal? Then she smiled. 'Benjamin! How lovely to see you.' She turned and beckoned her maidservant nearer. It was so easy to lose one's reputation. She looked flirtatiously at the river flowing between them, she on the Town side, he the Gown. 'How can I get across?'

The maidservant thought for one horrible moment that her mistress was going to throw herself on the mercy of the Cam, with its darkling waters and deadly currents but no; Steane was pointing to his right, to where a bridge spanned the river into the college grounds and the sheep munched the sweet grass.

'Cross the bridge,' he called. 'I will open the gate.'

The two women walked briskly along the bank, keeping pace with Steane, who was walking quite slowly as he tried to cultivate a suitably bishoply gait. When they got there, he was wrestling with the gate latch. It was quite obvious from their side how it worked and Ursula Hynde had to bite back a peremptory remark, couched along the lines of what sort of idiot was he?

'Just a minute, dearest one,' Steane said, as the gate finally yielded and he flung it open so the women could pass through. He looked at the maidservant. 'Must ... umm...?'

Ursula looked the woman up and down, as if to appraise her for sale. 'Dorcas?' she asked him. It wasn't the woman's name, but Ursula Hynde had better things to do than keep learning

new ones and her maids had a strangely short
tenancy in the job. 'I'm afraid she must, Benjamin,' she said. 'I have my reputation to consider. You hear such things about these
colleges.'

It was as well that Mistress Hynde was not a
mistress of men's faces, because the expressions
which flitted across Benjamin Steane's told a
very clear story, which Dorcas – whose real
name was Anne – could easily read. In defer-
ence to them both, she took a step back and turned to admire the view, but stayed within earshot.

'Your maidservant has a sensitive soul,'
Steane murmured, taking the arm of his bride-
to-be and retracing his former path along the
riverbank.

Ursula looked down and simpered. Steane
tried to find it attractive in this woman, over-
weight, overbearing and easily overwrought. He
hardly knew her, had been introduced to her at
Madingley the year before and had earmarked
her as future bishop's wife material. It was the
way of the world. He had heard a fund of stories
on the top table at King's and other colleges,
about senior men who had been seduced into
taking a young wife, after years of celibacy, only
to have her make a cuckold of him with any
number of lusty young servants. He risked another glance at Ursula from under his lashes.
Even if she tried, the servant would have to be
particularly lusty to keep his end of the bargain
with Ursula.

But he wasn't unkind, at bottom. Even his

enemies would only label him as rather unusually single-minded. He thought that perhaps that was what had drawn him to Ursula. She too knew what she wanted and set out to get it; she would be an ornament to him as his wife. And if the Queen didn't want to acknowledge her, as he had heard was often the case with bishop's wives, well, Ursula was difficult to ignore.

'The river is so lovely,' Ursula remarked, thinking that the silence had gone on long enough.

'It most certainly is,' he replied, with a dip of the head. 'But not, perhaps, so lovely as in Bath.'

Ursula Hynde was ever so slightly deaf in one ear. She was therefore shocked to hear a man of the cloth allude to bathing and blushed accordingly. 'Why, sir,' she said, 'I bathe when called for, to be sure.'

Steane was nonplussed for a moment, then caught up with the side-turning the conversation had taken. 'No, dear sweet one,' he said, racking up his volume a notch. 'Bath. Aquae Sulis. The town of Bath. Where I shall be bishop, along with Wells, of course.' He smiled benignly at her.

'Oh.' She let the disappointment show. 'Not Winchester?'

'No, goodness me, no,' he said, squeezing her arm. 'Very unhealthy. Damp. And such low-life living around the Buttercross there. No, no, Bath is much better for you, dearest.'

She looked up at him. He really wasn't too bad

222

looking and not too old either, compared with some. She smiled. 'How kind you are, Benjamin,' she said, and patted his hand as it just managed to emerge from under her left breast. 'I think we're going to be very happy.'

'I'm glad you think that,' he said. 'I think we will be very suited. I hope that I can live up to the standard set by your first husband.' He felt her tense. 'I'm sorry, my dear,' he said. 'Have I upset you?'

Trailing behind them, Anne grimaced. Oh, no, the stupid fool had mentioned husband number one. Now they were in for hours of weeping, if she was any judge. She rummaged in her bag and brought out a kerchief which she handed silently to her mistress, who blew her nose into it in a not altogether bridely way. Startled mallards flew up from the reeds.

'May we sit down somewhere, Benjamin?' the woman asked. 'I feel a little faint.'

He looked around and saw a felled tree at the edge of the path and led her to it, thoughtfully spreading the hem of his gown for her to sit on. He perched alongside her, tensing his legs to keep the trunk level as it took her weight. 'Rest here,' he said. 'What is it, dear heart? You must tell me; after all, in three days, we will be man and wife.' He felt a small chill go down his back.

She blew her nose again and cleared her throat. 'My first husband was a prince among men,' she began. 'Older than me, of course, much older, but very gentle and courteous. He

223

didn't ... trouble me.' She blushed and looked down.

Steane patted her hand, in some relief. He hadn't planned to trouble her too much either. 'There, there,' he murmured, in his best pastoral voice.

'We had a beautiful home, while we waited for him to come into his inheritance at Madingley. He looked after his father's affairs in Cambridge and London. He used to bring me presents when he had been away, jewels and books. He brought me a parrot once.' She gave a resounding sniff and smiled through her tears at Steane. Her reminiscences had made her look younger and he almost loved her then.

'And then...?'

'He died.' She could hardly choke out the words. 'He had been out all day hunting. When he came in, he said he was feeling tired and would go to bed. I sat by the fire with my maid-servants and we sewed and chatted. Laughed.' She seemed to be reciting a long-learned piece, which had no relation to her, and yet it was the story of the beginning of many lonely years. 'Then, his manservant came running in. He said ... he said his master was taken very ill. I ran to him. He was writhing on the bed. He reached out for me but, as I stepped forward, he took a huge breath in.' She stopped and even the maid-servant, who had heard this many times before, had tears in her eyes. 'It was his last. He died.' Then, reputation or not, Ursula Hynde leant against the shoulder of the Bishop of Bath and

224

Wells-to-be and wept, for all those lonely nights, now hopefully almost at an end.

And Benjamin Steane put his arm round his wife-to-be and wiped a stealthy tear away with his free hand. He had no idea whether he could be a good husband. But this fat, annoying, bossy woman had somehow just made him want to do his best to be just that.

TWELVE

Constable Fludd heard them before he saw them. Shouts and whoops and clarion calls told dozing Cambridge that a troupe had come to town. They threw up dust as they rattled through Trumpington, their great carts groaning behind the heavy plod of the oxen. Dogs ran by them, barking and yelping and small boys and girls ran with them, laughing and calling to the spotty youths in their dresses and the jesters in their greasepaint.

There had been rumours for days that a theatre troupe was on its way. It was supposed to come for the Sturbridge Fair, but a horseman had arrived to tell the Mayor that a number of the chorus had gone down with something nasty they'd picked up in Chelmsford and, not to worry, it wasn't the plague. It wasn't even contagious. It just put actors off their stride and could the Mayor be patient for a few days more.

The truth was that the Mayor could have been patient for ever. The man was not only torn between Town and Gown, he was harangued on a daily basis by the Puritan persuasion, who wanted him to shut the taverns and take the pews out of the churches. A troupe of travelling players was the last straw. On the other hand, plays brought crowds and crowds brought money. The Mayor's message to his Constable was that the company could come and the company could perform, providing their paperwork was in order.

'I shall need to see your papers,' Fludd told the player king as he swung down from the leading wagon. Behind him the seamstresses called and whistled. Some of them didn't seem to know one end of a needle from another. The drums beat incessantly with a rhythmic, hypnotic pulse and each deafening clarion blast was matched by shouts and general hysteria.

'Lord Strange's Men?' Fludd checked, having seen the seal on the parchment.

'And they don't come any stranger!' The man nudged him in the ribs. 'Ned Sledd, sir, at your service,' he said, and he bowed low, doffing his plumed cap so that it swept the ground. Fludd looked at the man's finery, the velvet and brocade, the silk and satin. He was breaking all the Sumptuary Laws rolled into one; the man was better dressed than the Chancellor of the University.

'Where are we to perform?' Sledd wanted to know.

'Parker's Piece,' the Constable told him. 'You can park your wagons nearby.'

'Excellent.' Sledd patted his arm and took his papers back. 'You won't mind if my people canvas the town?'

'Er...?'

'Walk the streets, man. Advertise. It's all about bums on seats, you know. Or feet on the ground for the poor buggers. Still–' he breathed in the warm midday air – 'it'll be an honour for them, eh? To stand for an hour or two to watch The Fair Maid of Kent? I don't suppose you get much real theatre this far north, do you?'

Fludd was stung. He'd lived in Cambridge all his life and here was a strolling player talking down to him. 'Well,' he said, 'we have the May Day festivities – and the colleges perform their own stuff.'

'Oh, really!' Sledd laughed, shaking his head. Then, he was serious and closed to his man. 'Tell me,' he said. 'You're the Mayor's man, I assume. His factotum?'

'I am Constable of the Watch.' Fludd was on his dignity. He hadn't warmed to Sledd at all.

'Of course you are,' Sledd patronized. 'How many taverns do you have? Fifteen? Twenty?'

'Enough,' Fludd told him.

'Good, good. What about trugging houses?'

'Sir?' The player king had lost him.

'Stews, man.'

Still nothing.

227

'Brothels!' Sledd whispered in the Constable's ear.

'None,' Fludd told him flatly.

'None?' Sledd mouthed, but no voice came out.

'This is a respectable town, sir. You're lucky we're letting you in.'

'No, no,' Sledd said, laughing. He'd heard this before, more or less at every town they visited. 'It's you who are lucky. Have you any idea of the skills my troupe possess? Dancing, singing, agility of body, memory, skill of weapon, pregnancy of wit. They are like springs of pure water–' he was getting carried away with his own rhetoric and flung his arm wide – 'which grows sweeter the more they are drawn from.' He let out a breath, dropped his arm and turned to Fludd. 'And we are bringing all this to you Cantabrigensians for the most trifling sum.' He moved closer to Fludd. 'What's the Mayor's cut? Ten per cent of the gate?'

'I believe so, sir,' the Constable told him.

'And yours?' Sledd thought it best to check in advance.

'I don't take bribes, sir,' Fludd said, looking him in the eye.

The eye widened in disbelief and Sledd spread his arms wide.

'Come on, Ned,' a squawky lad called to him from the first wagon. 'My arse is killing me on this thing.'

'Keep your wig on, Thomas. I am in the presence of that rare beast, an honest Englishman.'

He put his plumed hat back on with a suitably theatrical flourish. 'You'll have to excuse him,' he said, nodding towards the boy. 'He's playing the lead tomorrow. It's gone to his head rather.'

'You mean ... *he's* playing the Fair Maid of Kent?'

Sledd frowned. 'Of course,' he said. 'You don't think we'd be so perverse as to put *females* on the stage, do you? What do you take us for, man? There are laws in this great country of ours.'

Sledd moved away to mount the wagon, then turned back to Fludd. 'Are you *sure* there aren't any trugging houses?'

The camp fires of Lord Strange's Men flickered in the cooling night air on the level open space that was Parker's Piece, on the edge of the town. In the circle of carts and wagons, their carpenters had been hammering and sawing all day, adjusting the travelling stage they'd brought with them for the Fair Maid of Kent. Striped awnings flapped slightly in the breeze and rattled the painted flats that had been lashed to the wooden O.

All day the children and men of Cambridge had found reason to go there, snooping, prying, staring at the actors as they went through their paces, making passes with their swords and dancing to drum and fife. The women went nowhere near, not during daylight, for fear of what their neighbours would think. They just quizzed their menfolk on their return. What was the play the company was putting on? Was Lord Strange there himself? How handsome were the leading men? And would there be fireworks?

Kit Marlowe left it until nightfall to make his own visit. For most of the day he'd been closeted in King's Chapel, more for Ralph Whitingside's than Benjamin Steane's benefit, although it would do the dear, dead man little good now. It was good to stretch his legs, striding past the flaming torches that marked the edge of the ground. Laughing girls passed him, nudging each other at the handsome roisterer in his doublet and colleyweston cloak. But they were otherwise engaged already with the lads of Lord Strange, even if one of them was wearing a dress.

He suddenly felt a bit of a fool. In his satchel he carried a manuscript on parchment – A True History of Dido, Queen of Carthage. He'd been scratching away at this for nearly a year, when he should have been learning his Horace and his Aristotle. Yet he was drawn to the theatre like a moth to a flame. And now the theatre had come to him, with all its magick and its fire, right here on Parker's Piece.

He looked across to the stage, silent and deserted now under the moon, waiting for the trumpet blast that would open the theatre and release the crowds. Instinctively, he crossed to it and stood looking up at the flats, with their palace stairs and turrets and the silver birches of his own home county.

A movement caught his eye and he turned fast,

making sure his back was to the woodwork. He saw the swirl of a short cloak and the flash of an earring in the half darkness. But this was no player-king, no lord of the boards. For a brief moment, he looked at a pale reflection of himself – another roisterer in doublet and cloak and carrying a satchel just like his.

'I hope you've made your peace with God,' he said in a steady, level voice.

An answer rang back. 'Kit? Kit Marlowe – is that you?'

'You know perfectly well, it is, Robert Greene,' Marlowe answered. 'But you can call me Machiavel. Or avenging angel, as you prefer.'

'Kit!' Greene emerged into the full glare of a brazier's light. 'It's been ... what?' He held out a hand.

'Nothing like long enough,' Marlowe said, ignoring the offer of friendship. 'But I must admit, I admire your nerve.'

'Er ... do you?'

Marlowe looked at the frozen smile on the man's face. 'You can't have forgotten our last conversation,' he said. 'The one where I told you I'd cut your pocky off if I saw you again.'

'Ah, now, Kit,' Greene trilled, a little more falsetto than he'd hoped. 'That was so ... two years ago. All's forgiven, surely? Old friends like us...' He dropped his hand at last.

'You haven't got any friends, Robyn,' Marlowe said. 'What you do have is the brass neck to steal my poetry, pass it off as your own and

231

then pretend that nothing has happened.'

'No, no,' Greene protested. 'There's been some mistake. A misunderstanding.'

'What's in the bag?' Marlowe asked.

'The ... er...' Greene seemed to have forgotten he was holding it. 'Oh, nothing, just some college notes. I'm reading for my Master's degree now, at St John's.'

'Kicked you out of Italy, did they?' the Corpus man checked.

'Kit...'

Marlowe suddenly lunged, snatching the satchel from Greene's grasp and hauling it open.

'You've got no right, you murdering bastard!' Greene yelled and in an instant there was a dagger in his hand and he was running at Marlowe. The Corpus man feinted with his cloak and wrapped it over Greene's head before kicking him in the backside so hard that he sprawled on the ground. Marlowe tugged the papers from Greene's satchel and read the first page by the firelight. 'Friar Bacon and Friar Bungay,' he said. 'More arrant tosh, Robyn?'

Greene was scrambling upwards, looking frantically at the same time for his dagger. Nobody turned their back on Kit Marlowe when his blood was up. Marlowe was quietly turning over the pages, reading the odd line here and there. 'At least,' he said, 'it seems to be *your* tosh. There'd be no point in pinching anything as bad as this.'

He stepped back. Simultaneously, he and Greene saw the dagger at Marlowe's feet.

232

Marlowe kicked it up and the Johnian caught it, unsure what would happen next.

'Tell me,' Marlowe said. 'Did you bring this bit of nonsense to sell to Lord Strange's Men? See if you could make a name for yourself? Oh, Robyn, really!' and he shook his head, tutting.

'Well,' Greene said, petulantly. 'What are you doing here? What's in *your* satchel?'

'This?' Marlowe held it up as Greene's pages began fluttering away on the breeze. 'Oh, just some college notes,' he said with a smile. 'I'm reading for my Master's degree now, at Corpus Christi. I'm finding the law particularly fascinating. Shame there isn't one about pinching other people's poetry.' His smile vanished and he stepped closer to Greene, who licked his lips and held his dagger-point higher. 'What did you mean, Robyn, a moment ago, when you were silly enough to lunge at me. I don't object to the use of the word "bastard" in the right context, although I suspect my father would. No, the word that threw me was the adjective, "murdering". Just who am I supposed to have murdered?'

But Greene was gone, leaving his opus scattered on the wind and only the piercing eyes of Kit Marlowe for memory.

At the stage, a single pair of hands clapped. Marlowe turned.

'Very good,' a voice said. 'I've rarely seen a man face a dagger like that before.'

'Who are you?' Marlowe asked.

The player king strolled into the light. The
233

frippery of the day had gone and he stood in his shirt and breeches, a tired look on his face. 'I am Ned Sledd.' He bowed extravagantly. 'Of Lord Strange's Men.'

Marlowe bowed likewise. 'Christopher Marlowe,' he said, 'of no man's men.'

Sledd laughed. 'Good for you,' he said and looked the man in the face. Then he took his arm. 'Come, Master Marlowe, let's sink an ale or two. And you can show me what you really have in your satchel.'

'What the Devil is that?' Dr Goad was lost in the academic niceties of the philosopher Ramus and the sudden braying of the trumpets across the rooftops nearly made him drop his book.

'A play's toward, Provost,' Benjamin Steane told him, without looking up. The scholar's work he was marking was particularly awful, reminding him yet again of the sore decline at Cambridge University. He'd be glad to be in his mitre at Bath and Wells, where he'd never have to see another scholar's miserable scribbling ever again. 'Lord Strange's Men, I understand.'

'Strange?' Goad was alarmed. 'Ferdinando Stanley, old Derby's son?'

'The same.' Steane wasn't really listening.

'But he's a Papist, Benjamin. A recusant. What's the Mayor doing, letting people like that into the town?'

Steane looked up. 'I rather think Lord Strange's money is the same colour as everyone else's to the Mayor,' he said. 'And anyway,

234

Strange isn't actually with them. He's a poet himself, I believe, but he's a patron at heart. Bit of a soft touch, I've heard, given to lending money to explorers and similar mountebanks. Are you going?'

'Where?' Goad was on his feet, peering out of the window across the Cambridge rooftops.

'The play.' Steane was patience itself, but he quietly wondered how much more decline there could be before someone came to take Dr Goad away.

The Provost turned to him as though he'd been speared. 'Good God, no,' he gasped. 'What worries me−' he turned again to the window − 'is that rather a large number of our scholars seem to be on their way.'

Parker's Piece had not seen such a throng for years. The flags were fluttering in the breeze and the apple and pastry sellers were doing a roaring trade. Half Cambridge seemed to be there, paying their admission to the large men at the makeshift gate and jostling for position.

'How much?'

'This had better be worth it.'

'Do they all die in the end?'

'Will there be any fireworks?'

The hubbub of the groundlings rose in ever growing hysteria to the tiring room behind the flats where the Fair Maid of Kent was struggling into his stomacher. 'Buggered if I know how women wear these things,' he complained as a dresser laced him in. 'Good crowd, Ned?'

'Tolerable, Thomas, tolerable.' Ned Sledd was

235

playing the Fair Maid's father, complete with false grey beard and an outsize picadill.

'Any nobs in?'

Sledd craned his neck to the far side of the stage where a row of seats had been placed for the gentry. 'One or two,' he said. 'But you know they don't make an entrance until the last minute. Have you got that bit sorted in Act Two, Scene Three yet?'

'Think so.' Thomas was still having problems with his fol-de-rols.

'Tell me,' Sledd insisted.

Thomas frowned and blurted it out. 'Fie, my lord, whereof do you call me daughter?'

'Wherefore should I not?' Sledd fed him the line.

'Go to, go to,' Thomas scolded, without feeling. 'We are but ladies of the night.'

'What? Harlot, would you say?'

'Er...' Thomas was struggling already. 'Umm...'

'Come on, Thomas,' Sledd snapped. 'You knew this yesterday.'

'Yes, I know...'

'Two minutes of the clock, everybody,' somebody called.

'Um ... never breathe it, sir.' Thomas was on track again. 'Lest God in his Heaven, who is the father of all...'

'Father of *us* all,' Sledd insisted.

'All ... us...' Thomas ranted. 'What bloody difference does it make?'

'At a groat a line, *every* difference,' Sledd told

236

him. 'I've lashed out a small fortune on this tour, young Thomas and I don't want it buggered up.' He suddenly leaped for the lad's groin, fumbling under the placket of his skirt.

Thomas jumped and squealed.

'Just checking,' Sledd said. 'Falsetto, remember. Falsetto.'

The fanfare began, the brass flaring in the afternoon sun as the last groundlings scuttled in under the barrier.

'No!' Sledd hissed from backstage. 'Don't close the gates on them. Jack!' he called a minion to him. 'Get down to those idiots taking the money. *Everybody* in. We can squeeze a few more yet.'

And Jack dashed off. The fanfare seemed to be going on for ever and that was because the gentry were still taking their places on the stage. Sir Edward Winterton had left his regalia of office as the Queen's Coroner at home, but in every other respect, he looked resplendent. He'd even brought Lady Winterton with him – the one day of the year he'd deign to be seen in her company. She fussed around him, arranging the great sword he'd carried at Pinkie and curtsied to the Mayor and his wife, who smiled benignly. Coroner and Mayor – and Ned Sledd – knew that, technically, everybody had broken the law. The Fair Maid of Kent should have been performed in camera before the Mayor and his corporation, to check that the fare was suitable. As it was ... well, a sunny Saturday in a Cambridge summer. What could possibly go wrong?

Three or four rows back, the Parker scholars stood elbow to elbow with other Corpus men. As was usual in the rare meetings of Town and Gown, the college fraternities tended to cluster together, the arms of Trinity, Jesus, King's, Christ's, Corpus and the others on their sleeves. There was the usual bit of jostling from the lads of the town and the mob from the outlying villages seemed to have come prepared. Marlowe noticed, as did Joseph Fludd on the far side of the field with his under-constables, that the Dry and Fenny Drayton men carried quarter staffs and, judging by the bulges under jerkins, not a few of the lads from the Bedford Levels were sporting cudgels that day. Fludd checked his men again – five of them. Men in the crowd? Difficult to count, but he estimated at least two hundred. And he didn't even want to think about the women. The only woman he cared about was Allys, whom he'd told to stay at home with their daughter, their chickens and their unborn son. If things got nasty here on Parker's Piece, at least she'd be out of it.

But Allys Fludd wasn't out of it. She'd packed up a lunch of fresh-baked bread and good Stilton cheese and tied a flagon of milk to her bundle before setting off on the road from Trumpington, little Kate trotting beside her, babbling away with excitement. She'd never seen a play before and she had no idea her daddy had told her mummy not to come. It would be such an adventure.

The crowd clapped rapturously as the Pro-

238

logue stepped forward and bowed to them.

'Pray, gentles all,' he bellowed as the noise subsided.

'He don't mean you, mate!' a groundling yelled to the men around him.

Sir Edward Winterton tapped his foot in disgust. 'Shh, Edward!' his wife hissed, although the man had yet to open his mouth.

'Good crowd!' the Fair Maid of Kent beamed to Ned Sledd at his elbow.

The veteran player was less sure of that. 'We'll see,' he muttered. On Fludd's word, the little knot of constables broke up and took their positions at the edge of the crowd, walking softly and keeping their tipstaffs out of sight.

'Pardon us,' the Prologue went on. 'Our sorry postures and our feeble antics...'

'You got that right, son!' somebody else called.

'We come before you to present the story of Esmerelda the Fair Maid of Kent. And you shall see her played, and by her father twice betrayed.'

There was booing and hissing from the crowd. Nothing went down with country clods like a good villain. He duly stepped forward, Ned Sledd in all his Elizabethan patrician finery and a little servant scurried after him.

'How now, sirrah,' Sledd delivered, scanning the crowd below him. 'Where is Esmerelda, the apple of my eye?'

An apple accordingly whizzed through the air from somewhere near the front and the crowd shrieked its approval as it bounced and caught the servant a nasty one on the kneecap.

'Didst call, father and founder of our race?' Thomas tripped on with a full-blown falsetto, to the catcalls and whistles of the groundlings.

Edward Winterton had had enough. He was about to get up and remind the rabble that they were letting down their fair town – it certainly didn't look as if the Mayor was going to do it; the man seemed nailed to his chair – when a strangled cry broke from the crowd on Fludd's side.

'Harlot!'

Sledd spun to his prompter, hidden in the wings. 'That's not yet, surely?' he hissed. 'Not 'til Act Two.'

'Er...' the prompter was riffling through the papers balanced on his knees, desperate to make sense of what was happening.

'Whoredom!' the voice shouted again, taken up by others. In the centre, a group of black-robed clerics and scholars was forcing its way towards the stage.

'Uh-oh,' Marlowe muttered and half-turned to be ready for what was to follow.

'They're St John's men,' Parker said as the hubbub grew. One of them was up on stage, while others at the front were tussling with the groundlings who were draped on its edge.

'If you will tear and blaspheme Heaven and Earth,' the Scholar shouted. 'If you will learn to become a bawd...'

Roars of approval rose from the crowd.

'...if you will learn to devirginate maids...'

'I already know how to do that, sonny!' a Bedford Levels man shouted back to the delight of the men around him.

'If you will commit lewd and ungodly filthiness...'

'Well, there have to be some perks,' somebody else shouted.

The Scholar grabbed the Fair Maid of Kent and proceeded to haul up the lad's skirts. 'Sodomites!' he roared. 'All of them!'

Thomas pushed him away and tried to regain some composure. 'Do you mind?' he said in his own voice. 'There's nothing funny about Lord Strange's Men,' he insisted.

But the Scholar wasn't listening. 'Are we going to allow this filth in our town?' he screamed. 'Within the precincts of our University? On this very piece of land bequeathed to us by Archbishop Parker of blessed memory?'

'Oh, yes, wonderful,' Matt Parker muttered in the increasingly mutinous crowd. 'Let's bring granddad into this again, by all means.'

A fight had broken out below the stage where a Dry Drayton man was kicking a John's scholar for all he was worth. The muscular Christians of the college leapt to his defence and Fludd's under-constables darted through the swaying mob to prevent a murder.

'Ned?' the Fair Maid of Kent looked at his master for approval.

'All right,' Sledd sighed, pulling off his grey beard. 'The whole bloody thing's ruined now

241

anyway.'

And Thomas lowered his head and butted the John's man in the stomach, grappling with him until they both fell off the stage. Edward Winterton's sword was in his hand and at last the Mayor was galvanized into movement. He clapped his hands and attempted a calming speech, but nobody was listening. All over the crowd, fights were breaking out here and there. Dry Drayton men against the scholars; Bedford Levels boys against the scholars. Everybody against the Puritans.

'It's a little late for that now, Mayor,' Winterton yelled in his ear, trying to be heard over the din.

'Edward!' the Coroner's wife was bewildered. Doling out domestic violence was her meat and drink, but this was getting out of hand.

'Not now, dearest,' Winterton snapped. 'Mayor, get the ladies out of here, will you?' And the Mayor was only too happy to oblige.

On the edge of the field, Nicholas Drew, the ferryman, was trading punches with a couple of Jesus men. He really wanted to get across to the Corpus lads to give them a smacking for pinching *his* church. His wife stood behind him, fists clenched, ducking and diving for her husband. Then it was cudgels out and the clack of quarterstaff on quarterstaff, among the screams and cries.

'How are we doing?' The Fair Maid of Kent popped his head above the stage parapet. His nose was bleeding, but his stomacher and farthingale were holding up quite well.

'I don't know if you've noticed, Thomas.' Ned Sledd was kneeling on one knee above him, his temple dripping blood from a carelessly-lobbed stone. 'But Lord Strange's Men appear to be outnumbered about twenty to one.' He had a commanding view of the battlefield that was Parker's Piece from where he crouched and his troupe were in danger of being engulfed by sheer numbers.

'Rally with the boys on the right,' Sledd ordered, as much a general as a player-king if the need arose. 'I'll take the lot on the left. Push them all back from the stage area. I don't want to face his Lordship if they get their hands on our flats.'

Thomas complied, hauling up his skirts and shouldering struggling scholars out of the way.

'Not easy, is it, sonny?' a village woman snarled at him. 'Fighting in a skirt.' And she smacked a shovel down on the head of the Fair Maid of Kent. It was the last thing he saw for quite a while.

'We can't hold them on the left, Joe!' an exhausted under-constable stumbled alongside Fludd. 'We need the militia.'

Fludd looked at him. The man must have taken too many knocks to the head. 'Well, I'll just write a letter to the Lord Lieutenant, shall I?' he asked. 'Send a messenger to London for him? Wait for him to issue a commission of array? That'll be perfect. They'll be here in a month or so. Oh, and by the way,' he said, pointing to the melee, where men were knocking lumps out of each other, 'most of the Cambridge militia are already here!'

The constables knew only too well that fists, boots and cudgels would soon be replaced by knives and then things would get really nasty. Fludd sent his man back into the fray and clouted a man over the head with his staff. In the centre, Harry Rushe, his broken arm strapped into his jerkin, was kicking a Puritan in the groin. Meg Hawley, alongside him, was doing her best to drag her man away. Part of her felt sorry for him – he was at a serious disadvantage, after all, with only one arm. But part of her hated him for the lout he was, gouging the eyes of another scholar with his good hand.

One woman who wasn't helping her man was Allys Fludd. In fact, she'd only seen him once, before the trouble began and had done her best to shrink down in the crowd, hoping that little Kate wouldn't see her daddy and call out to him. But the excitement of earlier in the day had given way to terror and knots of people, some bleeding and hurt, were staggering away from the chaos on Parker's Piece. Allys was with them. She'd lost her bundle back in the terrifying, swaying mob and had held Kate to her, the little girl screaming and crying. If this was what a play was like, she never wanted to see one again.

'Hello, darlin'.' A Bedford Levels man stood in Allys's path. 'Now, where are you goin' in such a hurry?' He grabbed the woman's arm and pulled her to him. Allys bit the man's lip as it brushed her mouth and he pulled back, bleeding and swearing. In a second, he'd shaken his head and slapped her hard across the face, sending her reeling.

'Don't hurt my mummy!' Kate screamed at him, pounding his leg with fists and feet. He scooped her up and held her on high, dangling her at arm's length, laughing.

It was then that Fludd saw his daughter, being twirled like a puppet above the mob. He didn't remember the next few seconds or how he crossed that field, but the next thing Allys Fludd knew was that the oaf was lying senseless alongside her and her husband was straddling her, holding their daughter to him and soothing her crying. He snatched Allys to her feet and held them both tight.

A body collided with the little group and Fludd turned, staff at the ready to crack more heads.

'Good afternoon, Constable,' the scholar said.

'Master Marlowe,' Fludd panted. 'Enjoying the play?'

Marlowe smiled. 'I don't think much of the metre.'

Fludd was suddenly serious. 'Marlowe, my wife and child. Get them to safety, for God's sake.'

Marlowe looked at the Fludd women, one tiny, one heavy with child, both tear stained. 'It will be my pleasure,' he said and he shepherded them away.

'Joe!' Allys screamed, but Marlowe held her

fast, with little Kate clinging to her skirts. They all saw the man disappear into the crowd again, pulling fighters apart and laying about him with his tipstaff.

'Constabulary business,' Marlowe said, smiling. 'Calm yourself, Mistress Fludd. Your husband is very good at pursuing his enquiries.'

Gradually, the sounds of battle on Parker's Piece died away and Marlowe and the Fludd family joined the throng drifting along Silver Street. Occasionally, as they hurried west, there were shouts and roars as some new outrage was committed around the wooden O that had started the whole thing. Then, they were hurrying down St Edward's Passage and around the corner to the front gate of Corpus. It was locked. Marlowe drew his dagger for the first time that day and hammered on the gnarled old oak with its pommel. There was a grating sound and the grille slid back.

'College is locked, Marlowe,' Proctor Lomas grunted. 'You're on your own.'

'I've a woman and child here, Lomas,' Marlowe hissed. 'If you won't let me in, at least think of them. It's murder out here, man.'

Lomas grinned. 'Oh, you've got lots of ways to get in and out of Corpus, *Dominus* Marlowe. Why don't you use one of them now?'

There was a metallic clink as Marlowe's blade flashed upwards, catching the Proctor's nose along with the grille. 'Avert your gaze, Mistress Fludd,' he said. 'There are some things a constable's wife shouldn't see.'

Allys Fludd was made of sterner stuff. And after this afternoon, she'd seen enough for a lifetime, constable's wife or not. Marlowe had gripped Lomas' nose with one hand and held the glinting blade under his nostrils.

'Now, Proctor Lomas,' he said softly. 'You will very slowly raise your right hand and unlock this gate. If you don't, you won't be picking your nose for a while because you won't have a nose to pick.' And the blade edged infinitesimally higher.

Behind the gate, Lomas was on tiptoe already and he couldn't pull away for fear of the speed of Marlowe's knife. Gingerly, very gingerly, he turned the heavy key to his right and the door creaked open. Marlowe kicked it so that it slammed back on the Proctor and he ushered the Fludd women inside before locking it again behind them.

Briefly, he bent over the man. 'I promised you that there'd be a reckoning,' he said.

Professor Johns strode past the Proctor's Lodge at that moment and glanced at the scene that met him, Lomas lying groaning on the flagstones, holding his head.

'Lying down on the job again, Lomas?' he chirped. 'Tut tut.'

In another part of the field, a wheezing Sir Edward Winteron found a bleeding Joseph Fludd.

'Sir Edward,' the Constable shouted in his ear as all Hell raged around them, 'you shouldn't be

247

here. Go home, sir.'

'When you do, Constable,' the coroner shouted back. 'Tell me, is there still a cannon in Great St Mary's?'

'Yes, sir, a saker. It's in one of the outbuildings.'

'How many men to get it here?' Winterton wanted to know.

Checking the parish gun was part of the Constable's duties. The thing was eight feet long and weighed 1500 pounds. 'Four,' Fludd said, optimistically. 'Three at a pinch.'

'Three it is, then. Take two of your men and get it here. There'll be powder and shot with it.'

'Er ... I should point out, Sir Edward–' Fludd knew his local legislation – 'that that gun was placed there on the orders of King Harry. In case the French should invade.'

'Yes, laddie,' Winterton humoured him. 'I'm impressed by your grasp of history.' He looked at the man closely under the mask of blood. 'You weren't even born then, surely? I remember it as though it were yesterday.'

'That's my point, sir,' Fludd shouted. 'Nobody's fired the gun in forty years. As for the powder...'

'Bring it!' roared Winterton. 'It may be that just the sight of the damn thing will bring those rioting idiots to their senses. It won't be long before they start on the shops and God help us then.'

Fludd hauled two of his lads out of the fight and they ran across the field in the direction of the church of Great St Mary.

'Yes, that's it!' Harry Rushe and his fenland men saw them go. 'Run away, you tipstaff bastards!' And he swung back to the punching again.

Winterton had been right about the event, but wrong about the time. Even as Fludd and his men dragged the heavy saker across the market square and into Petty Cury, people were smashing windows and ripping down the market awnings, stuffing whatever they could into jerkin-fronts and aprons. Here and there, running battles broke out as shopkeepers fought with looters to the crash of glass and the clash of steel. Stallholders struggled to keep their frames upright and all the shutters came down in a rattle of bolts.

Fludd himself carried the powder and shot, a six pound iron ball that bounced painfully in the canvas bag at his hip as the constables negotiated the tight corner by Pembroke Hall at a jog. Even the wounded and the just plain scared who were hurrying or straggling homeward in the evening sun stopped short at the sight of the saker. No one had seen a cannon on Cambridge streets for years; some of the younger ones didn't quite know what it was. Fludd grabbed a couple of the more intrigued and dragooned them to putting their shoulders to the wheel.

Parker's Piece looked like a battlefield, with hats, clothes and rubbish lying everywhere.

Winterton had been defending himself with his sword while keeping an eye out for the gun. Now he launched himself in a tired run and helped Fludd and his lads to haul it into position. Those nearest broke off the fighting to stare at the thing, with its bronze barrel and studded wheels. But if Winterton had hoped its appearance would shock the mob into civil obedience, he was wrong.

He tossed his sword to a Constable and began tearing at Fludd's powder supply.

'Do you know how to fire this thing, Sir Edward?' Fludd asked him, now thoroughly alarmed at the proposition.

Winterton pulled himself up to his full height. 'Sir,' he said calmly, 'I fought at Pinkie. You never forget.' And he stuffed handfuls of the black powder into the muzzle. There were still cobwebs on the carriage and the nuts were rusted. Fludd didn't have a good feeling about this.

'Ball, ball!' Winterton shouted and Fludd rolled the shot down the hole.

'Ram!' Winterton ordered. 'Ram?' he asked, arms outstretched, looking wildly at the Constable. 'Where's the ram?'

'There wasn't one,' Fludd realized, all too late. He dashed across the field, disarmed a fenman of his quarterstaff and kicked the man in the groin. He threw the pole to the coroner who, improvising wildly, rammed the ball in place before Fludd packed in more powder.

It took several attempts to get the tinderbox to

flash, but once it did, Winterton applied the sparkling fuse to the touch hole and covered his ears.

'You're going to kill innocent people!' Fludd came to his senses seeing where the cannon was pointing, straight into the melee around Lord Strange's stage.

'They're expendable!' Winterton told him.

All four men stood with their hands over their ears, looking expectantly at the saker. The fuse appeared to be going out.

'Oh, bugger!' Winterton dropped his arms and went over to it. Before Fludd could stop him, the gun bucked, roaring with a dull crash and jerking backwards, carrying Winterton with it. The old man went down with a searing pain in his shoulder and back, but nobody was watching. As if in a dream, Lord Strange's stage blew up, flats collapsing in all directions and debris raining down on those nearest to it. Flames leapt skyward in the cannonball's path, burning gunpowder peppering the tinder-dry timbers and even setting fire to the grass.

The fighting mob broke with a cacophony of screams and shouts, sheer panic driving them from the field. In minutes, the only people left standing on Parker's Piece were five constables of the watch, bloodied but unbowed. There was an eerie silence for a moment, then the moans of the wounded rose here and there. Fludd patted the saker's barrel and realized the thing had split along most of its length. It could have killed them all.

251

He knelt beside Edward Winterton, who was lying on the ground, still clutching his arm. 'How did we do, Constable?' shouted the coroner, in the over-loud tones of the deaf. He shook his head, as a puppy will who has snapped at a fly.

'I think we did very well, Sir Edward,' Fludd told him, wiping the blood from his face. He looked on as the rioters, numbed and exhausted, began to drift away from the edge of the field. He faced the man to give his words the extra emphasis Winterton needed while his ears still rang. 'Very well.'

'I'd swear that was a cannon,' Roger Manwood said, strolling in the knot garden at Madingley.

'It was,' John Dee told him. 'A saker by the sound.'

'Some sort of celebration, Francis?' Manwood half turned to his host walking with them.

'What day is it?' Hynde often needed to be reminded of that.

'Saturday,' Manwood said. 'Sixteenth of July.'

'Hmm,' Hynde said, bending his memory to recall the saints' days celebrated in his youth. 'That would probably be ... not St Athenogenes, surely. St Faustus ... no, I can't think of anything that would warrant a cannon.' He sniffed the air. 'And a bonfire as well, unless I miss my guess.'

Dee, who professed to know nothing of such matters, could nonetheless think of another half dozen saints who had once shared this day, but kept quiet, for the good of his reputation.

The men stayed silent for a minute, waiting for another explosion, but none came.

Hynde shrugged. 'Can't be much. Come on, gentlemen, let's to billiards.'

It seemed like a good idea.

As the sun went down over Cambridge, Lord Strange's property was still blazing into the night, sending sparks into the evening sky. The streets were strangely deserted. The churches were cluttered with bleeding people, comforting others. Stallholders in the square were trying to assess the damage. The Mayor and his corporation were making the brave decision to leave it until the morning before making an appearance. The colleges had battened down their hatches and bolted their gates. Any scholars still abroad were strictly on their own and the Proctors had orders to admit no one.

'A woman and child, Michael?' Dr Norgate sat in his study at Corpus surrounded by the books he loved. 'This is very irregular.'

'These are irregular times, Master,' Professor Johns reminded the old man. 'Marlowe brought them.'

'I'm glad you raised the topic of Marlowe.' Gabriel Harvey spoke from the shadows for the first time. He'd been watching the fire-glow over the rooftops and couldn't think of a better time to consign a man he hated to Hell. 'I have evidence of his involvement in the death of the King's scholar, Whitingside.'

The other two stared at him.

'What evidence?' Johns asked.

'The word of a gentleman,' Harvey told him flatly. He closed on Norgate. 'I hate to have to bring this to your attention, Master, but I fear it all has to do with the crime of Sodom.'

Johns, the quiet, the sensible, the unflappable, stepped forward. He knew that if Marlowe had been there, Gabriel Harvey would be dead by now. He stood toe to toe with Harvey, eyes burning, fists clenched.

'This is a purely college matter,' Norgate said. 'And now is not the time to investigate, sir.'

Johns relaxed a little.

'But there will come a time,' Norgate said.

THIRTEEN

Ursula Hynde lay in her bed with the curtains drawn and the bedclothes up to her chin. Her linen cap was pulled down on to her forehead and tied tightly in place, to protect both her thinning curls and her modesty. It was her wedding day and she had been working tirelessly for weeks to make it perfect. Her dress was laid out in the next room, beaded and embroidered to such a depth that she could hardly move under its weight. Her bridesmaids had been gathered, chosen from the best families as befitted a Hynde, even if only by marriage. She even had three boys, kitted out in identical suits of clothes bought at huge expense, to help carry her train. They were lodged in a house in Cambridge; the proprieties were all-important to Ursula Hynde and she didn't think it was right that three adolescent boys should be in rooms next to three adolescent girls, although her knowledge of what might ensue was hazy, having been brought up very strictly before being married to an older man. But still, it wasn't right. So now, all she needed was a perfect summer's day. She called to her maid, who slept in a truckle bed in the corner.

'Dorcas?'

There was a sigh and a muttered word, which may have been 'Anne!' Then: 'Yes, mistress?'

'Draw back the curtains. What is the weather today?'

The maidservant whipped back the hangings of the bed. 'I have had the window curtains back for hours, mistress. The day is fine.'

'Why are you up and about so early?' Mistress Steane-to-be struggled upright in her feather bed and straightened her cap.

'I am packing up my bed, mistress. I must move my things up to the attic.'

'Why must you move your bed?' Ursula Hynde was confused. 'What will happen if I need you in the night?'

The maid blushed. Surely, after all the rushing about, the stupid woman had not forgotten she was to be married today? She looked at her feet, stuck for an answer and yet her mistress seemed

255

to be waiting for one. 'Tonight ... well, you will be married, mistress.'

'Yes.' The woman looked down her not-inconsiderable nose at the maid. 'I know that. What I wanted to know was ... ah, I see.' She drew herself up and spent a moment tidying her bedclothes to hide her confusion. Memories of her previous nuptials spread over her face in a crimson tide. Then her head snapped up. 'Get on with it then, girl. We don't have all day.'

The maid let out the breath she had been holding for what felt like years. 'I have done now, mistress. I thought you might like to break your fast in bed this morning.' She tried a small smile. 'As a treat. On your big day.'

Ursula Hynde allowed herself to smile back. The girl was right. It *was* a big day. She inclined her head. 'That would be nice, Dorcas. Thank you. That was a kind thought.' Then, to make sure the girl didn't think that her mistress was going soft: 'Run along, then. And make sure on the way that the bride's maids and men are up and ready. Tell them to eat a good breakfast; they won't be getting anything else once they have their wedding clothes on, I can assure them of that.'

Anne turned on her heel and trotted out of the room. In her opinion, the clothes they would all be wearing wouldn't show if anything dripped down them, so encrusted were they already with everything the dressmaker could inveigle to stick there. Her tastes were simpler and when it was her turn to marry – and she had her eye on

256

a very handy looking lad who worked in the stables – she wouldn't be got up like a dog's dinner. Just her best clothes, some friends in their best clothes, the man she loved and a few flower petals would do her fine. And she knew she would be happier than all the bishops and their wives in all their palaces. She smiled to herself and skipped off to hammer on bedroom doors and annoy the cook with requests for breakfast in bed.

Benjamin Steane had, as his beloved was starting to surface, been up for hours. His final Evensong at King's had left him feeling rather rootless and so, from habit, he had attended Matins and had watched the dawn light fill the windows of the Chapel as the service unwound itself in its time-honoured fashion. Standing in the chancel instead of in the choir had seemed odd at first, but he had derived comfort from the words echoing through the carvings and corners of the building which had been his home, almost literally, for years. As he left through the west door, he was stopped by more people than he knew he knew. By the time he had reached the foot of his staircase, he had been reminded, if he could ever have forgotten, that this was a Big Day.

Francis Hynde was happily eating breakfast at the head of the enormous refectory table in the Hall at Madingley. He gazed benignly down the length of the enormous board and was happy to see that Ursula was not present. She made him feel uncomfortable for many reasons, first and foremost because she had an expression permanently on her face which said clearly, if my husband had not died, *I* would be mistress here and then we'd see what's what! Well, soon she would be a mistress of a house far, far away and then he would probably never see her again. Francis Hynde heaved a happy sigh and took a huge bite of bread, smiling as he chewed.

'Francis looks happy,' Manwood remarked to Dee, further down the table.

'He has every reason to,' Dee said. 'With the wedding today, he can see the day when he is Ursula-free. He doesn't need a showstone for that. Perhaps he will cut back on the drink when he waves the happy couple off to their palace.'

'Palace?' Manwood looked dubious. 'Surely...'

'Don't forget, Stead, or whatever the man's name is, is to be a bishop. I doubt Ursula would have married him otherwise.'

'Any idea where of?' Manwood asked anxiously. 'Not Canterbury, surely? We're not talking about an *Arch*bishopric by default? I've heard of such things. And Whitgift's an idiot.' The idea of the dragon who had been making his life a misery for the last week as a neighbour made his blood run cold.

'Bath? Somewhere with a B anyway.' Dee had done a divination the night before and, throw it how he may, the apple peel had always made the shape of a B. Or an R. As he always told people,

258

it was as well to keep an open mind in these matters.

'Not Bromley?' Manwood had dropped his spoon.

'Is there a Bishop of Bromley?' Dee asked. There had been changes over the years, he knew that, but surely...

Manwood picked up his spoon again and shrugged, smiling. 'No, no of course not. I just...'

Dee patted his shoulder comfortingly. Manwood had had a particularly unpleasant time with Ursula Hynde, who had thought that he was a touch too tall and possibly an ell too wide to fit in with the wedding party. She wanted him to sit at the back. 'Don't fret, Roger. They'll be gone soon and it will all be back to normal. We can see Master Marlowe tonight and see if he has any more news for us. He won't let this matter rest until he has brought the murderer to book, you know that.'

Manwood smiled into his oatmeal. 'You're right there. He was always tenacious, even as a boy. I well remember...'

Dee saw the light of reminiscence kindle in the man's eye and changed the subject by causing the bread in the centre of the table to burst into flames.

'God's teeth, Dee,' Manwood said, as a man-servant doused the loaf with a pitcher of water. 'Do you have to do these things?'

Dee flicked his fingers and gave the resulting rose to one of the bride's maids sitting on his right. 'A rose for a rose, my dear,' he said to the startled girl. 'Got to keep limber, Roger,' he whispered to Manwood. 'If I don't behave like a conjuror, they may see through me.'

Manwood looked confused. 'What does that mean? You *are* a conjuror. Pure and simple, I know that.'

Dee looked down modestly. As long as even his friends thought him a simple conjuror, he was safe from the flames.

Across in the church of St Mary Magdelene, Doctors Falconer and Thirling were spying out the lie of the land.

'It's no good, Richard,' Falconer said, lounging at the end of one of the choir benches. 'It just isn't possible for the choir to process in. Look how small that chancel is; they'll have to elbow everyone aside just to get to their seats. Let's have them already in place when the congregation start to arrive.'

Thirling started to rock back and forth, testing his leg, a sure sign he was feeling fretted. 'No, no,' he muttered under his breath. 'The boys, the boys won't behave. I know boys ... they will secrete mice and frogs about their persons. They'll push and shove. They'll...'

Falconer got up and walked over to his friend and colleague. He really didn't feel quite up to snuff himself this morning and the last thing he needed was for the choirmaster to work himself into a frenzy. The sheer act of leaving college after the riot had unnerved them both and they had made sure their carriage doors had been secured fast. 'Sit down,' he said, pushing on the man's shoulder as he did so. 'It's true that boys will be boys, but really, Richard, I doubt that they can do much in the scope of the service here. And, with this rood screen in place, who's going to see them, anyway?'

'I will,' mumbled Thirling.

'And so will I,' Falconer said, gesturing to the tiny organ, its loft at ground level. 'We'll tell them in advance that any misbehaviour, *any* at all, will result in instant dismissal from the choir. None of them want to be sent home with their tail between their legs. Hmm?'

Thirling shrugged, with just one shoulder.

Falconer leaned in. 'Pardon? I didn't quite hear you.'

'Yes,' Thirling said, giving himself a shake. 'Yes, you're right. I'm sorry. But ... where shall I stand? I can't stand here.' He took up his usual position at the top of the chancel steps. 'The priest won't be able to get to the altar without squeezing past and you know how my leg...' He didn't have to finish. When he was carried away with his music, the slightest touch could have him toppled into the font.

'Simple!' cried Falconer. 'Stand facing this way.' He turned and faced down the church from the altar rail. 'Then, you can just step out for the music and then tuck yourself back afterwards, out of the way. You'll have somewhere to sit, as well,' he added, as a final temptation.

'It isn't really done, though, is it?' Thirling

261

said, dubiously.

Falconer spread his arms wide. 'Richard,' he said, 'the people here will never have seen such pomp, will never have heard such music. If the choirmaster is standing facing the wrong way, what of it? They'll never know. And also, you will be able to tell me when the bride is approaching, so I can begin my voluntary.' Personally, Falconer thought he would probably feel the ground shake as she approached, but it didn't hurt to have another pair of eyes helping out.

Thirling took up his putative position and practised stepping in and out. It seemed to work and he turned to thank his friend, who he saw to his horror, was doubled over on the bench, with his head between his knees. 'Ambrose!' he cried. 'Whatever is it?'

Falconer flapped him away with one hand. 'A spot of my old trouble,' he muttered, his voice muffled by cloth. 'I'll be quite all right in a minute. Why don't you go outside and see if the choir is in sight yet?'

'But, Ambrose...'

'Please. I'll be perfectly well in a minute. I just need some quiet.'

Thirling limped off down the church and Falconer gave a groan. What a day to have this happen. With luck he would get through the service. With a lot of luck he would get through the day. He wasn't sure whether crossing of fingers was allowed in church, but he did it anyway.

* * *

As the cart carrying the choir lurched towards
Madingley, Marlowe amused himself by trying
to identify the treble who would be sick first.
His internal competition became null and void
when two of the boys leaned over the side and
parted with their breakfasts simultaneously.
Marlowe comforted himself with the knowledge
that at least this time he had not had money on
it.

The cart was pulled by two elderly horses,
who seemed unable to get into step with each
other. Marlowe, despite being a Man of Kent
had not spent much time at sea and fervently
hoped he never would have to – the motion of
the cart was beginning to make him feel queasy
and that was without looking at the boys' green
faces. It was not a moment too soon that the
church of St Mary came into view. Richard
Thirling was standing at the lychgate, his hand
raised theatrically to shield his eyes from the
sun, already bright on this perfect wedding day.

'Master Marlowe,' he said, stepping forward
as the carter pulled his horses in. 'Umm...' he
nodded to Colwell and Parker. Parker was sporting a glorious black eye. He had more things on
his mind than remembering names today. He
didn't even care whether the bruise would show;
in other circumstance he would have moved
Parker from decani to cantoris, to hide the blem-
ish, but sufficient unto the day was the evil
thereof, and what was a black eye between
friends? The two boys who had been sick and

the ones who almost had stood wanly in a row, leaning against the rough stones of the low wall skirting the churchyard. 'Good journey?' A couple of dozen eyes swivelled in his direction, but that was all the answer he would have. 'Good.' He rubbed his hands together. 'Very good. This church, as you see, is rather smaller than we are used to, so I think we should go inside and let you get your bearings.'

'Are there benches?' the tiniest chorister asked.

Thirling bent down in an avuncular fashion and patted the child on the head. 'Yes, yes, there are benches.'

'Are they hard?' The cart had not been over-endowed with cushions and everyone had taken rather a bouncing.

Thirling was in a cleft stick – he knew that the seats were hard, and it was not in his nature to dissemble. But he also knew his schoolboys. 'Softish,' he said. 'As these things go.'

Muttering and grumbling the remnants of King's College choir shambled in to the church. From the lychgate, they could be heard greeting the organist and complaining about the hardness of the seats. Then, they went quiet. Thirling took a deep breath and stepped forward to go in. Before he could reach the door he stopped, hackles rising, as three voices rose in song. He instantly recognized *Libera me Domine*, set by Byrd. It was beautiful. It was in tune. It was taken from the Office for the Dead.

* * *

264

Ursula Hynde sat on her bed, looking out of the window. Smoke billowed fitfully from the direction of Cambridge. People were wandering about, looking aimless and in the case of her brother-in-law, rather the worse for drink. One of the bride's maids appeared to be eyeing up the shrubbery with the connivance of one of the bride's men. But Ursula Hynde didn't even see the flies in her ointment. She was getting married today and was suddenly scared out of her wits. She had spent so little time with her husband-to-be and none alone with him. She wasn't even sure she could pick him out of a crowd. She hardly knew him, let alone love him. Her other marriage had been long ago and far away and when she remembered her brief married days, she seemed to be standing off to one side, watching it happen to two strangers.

She leapt to her feet as the knock came at the door. She spun round, to see her bride's maids standing there, garlands of flowers in their hands. She stood rooted to the spot as they wound them around her neck and pinned one in her hair. She walked as one condemned down the landing and the magnificent staircase, as the girls prattled and sang. She was outside, crossing the park, she was nearing the church. She hung back, but the maids were relentless. Slowly but surely, Ursula Hynde approached her doom.

Benjamin Steane arrived at the church with only a few minutes to spare. The play and the riot which not so much followed it but took its place had made Cambridge a very difficult place to leave. He had no groom's man to accompany him; he was moving into a new life and could take no one from the old with him. Friends and colleagues were at the church of course, having come by carriage, cart, foot and horse. They were all seated when he arrived, and he had just a moment to tweak his unaccustomed finery into place. Adopting his new stately walk, he stepped down into the church porch and paused. A young girl of the estate plucked his sleeve and he turned to her for a moment while she pinned a sprig of honeysuckle to the shoulder of his gown. He blessed her solemnly and swept on to take his place at the front of the church at the foot of the chancel steps to await his bride.

Without making it too obvious, he looked around to see who was there. Goad, of course, seated to one side. Johns, such a nice man; when he had settled into the palace, Steane half thought he might offer him a post. Norgate, various scholars and people he had met but could hardly remember. Ah, Roger Manwood, he knew him. And a strange, grey clad man by his side with singed whiskers on one side of his face who was probably an alchemist of some sort. Winterton, sporting a sling and the look of a man who had no right to have survived the previous two days.

He raised his head to look at the altar. There was the priest of St Mary's looking imbecilically welcoming. Richard Thirling, facing down the nave, rubbing his eyes. A small choir, tucked round the edges of the Rood screen. A small frisson passed through him. Where was the organist? In fact, where was the organ?

But he needn't have worried. Thirling looked to his right and gave a small nod and music filled the church. There was a shifting of the air behind him and Benjamin Steane turned to find his bride beside him, covered in flowers and as white as a ghost, leaning on, or being leaned on by, Francis Hynde.

'Dearly beloved,' began the priest, and the marriage service had begun.

The rest of the day went by at breakneck speed for Ursula Steane. Taken back to her room by her bride's maids to change her clothes for something rather less crackly and more comfortable, although still glorious in crimson velvet, she sat down in the window seat whilst they brushed their hair and primped and preened for the dancing ahead. She had never felt her age as much as while she sat there, cooling her forehead against the glass, watching with unseeing eyes her guests walking the grounds of Madingley. She saw her husband, walking in the knot garden talking with Roger Manwood and John Dee. A little of her old self rose enough to the surface to remind her that she would *not* be welcoming either of them to the Bishop's Palace when she became its chatelaine.

She raised her hand to tap on the glass and felt a roughness on the pane. She looked closer to

267

see what it could be and saw that it was a
message scratched into the glass, long ago with
a diamond ring. It was a message from her
young self, or so it seemed; 'Ursul Black Sep
1555' it said, in shaky letters. 'I pmise to be a
good wife'. She remembered the tears she had
shed as she painstakingly scratched the message, so many years ago. But she took the message to heart, gave herself a shake and turned to
her ladies.

'Where's my dress?' she barked. 'Come along,
I have guests to greet.'

Anne, the maidservant, bent her head and
whispered to whoever was listening. 'She's
back! I knew it wouldn't last long.' Then, louder: 'It's here, mistress. Will you step into the
frame and we'll have you downstairs in the
shake of a lamb's tail.'

After some lacing and squeezing and up-
holstering, Ursula Steane was ready and, like a
galleon in full sail, she went out to meet her
husband.

He was still in the knot garden, standing in the
centre by the sundial, but was now talking to
some much more congenial people. His wife
didn't know who they were, but she was pretty
certain that they were more congenial, as they
were not Roger Manwood or John Dee. Her
skirts brushed the lavender bushes that lined the
paths of crushed shell in the garden and the sun
beat down. Steane either heard or smelt her
arrival and turned to her.

'Dearest,' he said, extending an arm and

drawing her into the group. 'May I introduce Dr Goad, Provost of King's College, who I believe you may already know.'

She inclined her head to the little wizened man. He was older than Methuselah. They hadn't met, not in all the man's nine hundred years, but she appreciated her husband's nice manners in assuming that they had. 'Dr Goad,' she said. 'So nice to meet you at last. Benjamin has often spoken of you.'

Steane raised an eyebrow. He had been right to choose this woman – she would make an excellent wife for a man in his soon-to-be-exalted position. He moved slightly to his left and said, 'Professor Michael Johns, Fellow of Corpus Christi. A most excellent scholar and friend.'

Johns was slightly surprised to hear this accolade. Although he had known Steane for a number of years, they had never been what he would consider friends. He had occasionally passed a particularly able student on to him, when he found that the pupil had exceeded his master, but that was all. Nonetheless, he smiled at Ursula and sketched a bow. 'Delighted to meet you at last, Mistress Steane,' he said with a smile.

She bowed her head. She hoped this wouldn't go on for too long. She'd never had much of a head for names and the sun was very hot on her back. Crimson velvet had been a bad choice for so warm a day.

'And finally,' Steane said, with the air of a conjuror producing a rabbit, 'and if I may be so

269

uncivil as to introduce them as a set, so to speak, Doctors Falconer and Thirling, who made such beautiful music possible at our wedding this morning.'

The two musicians bowed as one and extended their arms to where the choir stood in a motley group beside a table loaded with sweetmeats and flagons of drink. One of the King's men was engaged in a tussle with one of the boys, trying to remove a beaker of ale from the child. Falconer coughed to attract their attention and most of them gathered their wits in time to bow prettily to the bride.

'The choir,' Thirling explained.

Ursula Steane realized that there had been music at the ceremony. She had no ear for it, and anyway at that point was almost catatonic with fear. But, she was a lady, and knew how to behave. 'Beautiful singing,' she said. 'I congratulate you. I am sure my husband will make sure that there is a coin for everyone, before you return to Cambridge.'

Steane's eyebrows both went up at this; he had after all married her for *her* money, not so that she could disseminate his wherever she liked. He smiled, though, and nodded. An awkward silence fell on the group. Across every face the desperation of the socially inept flickered. Johns came to the rescue.

'Mistress Steane,' he said, then realized that he may have made a gaffe. 'Or should that be Lady Ursula?'

'Not yet, Professor Johns,' she said. 'Not until

270

my husband is enthroned as Bishop, which is not for a few weeks.'

'Ah,' Johns said. That would be a useful titbit to drop into the High Table gossip. 'So, where will you be staying until then? Here?'

She smiled. 'No, I think I have taken enough of my brother-in-law's hospitality as it is. Although, had things been different, I would have been mistress here.'

Johns looked interested. All grist to the rumour mill. 'Indeed?'

'My first husband ... but, no,' she said firmly. 'My first husband is a very old tale, Professor Johns, and often told. No, we will be staying in one of my ... of my *husband's* houses until the palace is ready.'

So, that was it. A rich widow. Johns arranged his smile to elicit more confidences. 'But, you know this house well?'

'Very well. I have spent many years here, all told, I should imagine. Let me show you the Physick Garden. It is quite unusual to find one in a private house, but Francis' mother was very interested in such things, God rest her soul, and planted rather a fine one over there, behind that wall.'

'I should be delighted,' Johns said, falling into step with her. 'My own mother was also rather fond of folk remedies. I well remember going to bed in winter with a mouse in a bag round my neck. It was a specific against the quinsy.'

Ursula clutched her throat. 'Did it work?' she asked.

Johns bowed, arms outstretched behind him. 'I stand here, Mistress Steane, without a quinsy to be seen. But if the mouse kept it away, I could not say.'

She laughed and went on ahead, through the wicket gate in the wall. She liked this man. Perhaps dear Benjamin could find a place for him, after his preferment.

The others standing in the knot garden watched them go.

'Johns is a very sound man,' Norgate said. 'Liked by everyone. A good scholar, too, although a little weak on Greek.'

'Weak on Greek,' spluttered the imbibing chorister on the other side of the planted square. 'He just made a pome, did you hear that? A pome.'

Thirling peeled off from the group. 'I apologize, gentlemen,' he said. 'I'm afraid young Kenneally is getting rather excitable. I will get the choir back to Cambridge now, with your leave, Dr Steane.' Although still-smouldering Cambridge was not the place he would rather be just at that moment.

'Oh, no, surely not,' Steane said. 'There are places for all of you at the table for the wedding breakfast. Please, do stay. Ursula will be so sad if you go.'

Thirling dithered. He liked a good blow-out as much as the next man and if the sweetmeat table was any guide, the dinner later would be a spectacular one. But, a chorister was drunk and had to be taken home. On the other hand...

'Dr Thirling?' A smooth voice carried over the lavender. 'If you will permit me, I have a plan.'

'Ah, Morley,' Norgate said. 'You seem to get everywhere.' He had hoped to avoid this meeting. Gabriel Harvey's words still rang in his ears – 'the crime of Sodom'. For an old man, Goad could still think pretty fast on his feet. 'The singing was exquisite, if I may say so, but I hardly think it appropriate...'

'I was about to say,' Marlowe said, 'that the boys could be sent home in the cart that brought us and the men could stay to eat. They have, after all, given up a day for the wedding and they have been accommodated at the table...'

'I can't send the boys home alone!' Thirling said, aghast. 'Anything might happen. There is still a lot of unrest in the town. There's talk the rioters have hanged the Mayor.'

'I'll go with them,' Marlowe offered.

'You?' Norgate was puzzled and aghast in equal measure. This didn't sound like the roisterer he knew and secretly admired for his cheek. But it did sound like the murderer and pederast of whom Harvey spoke.

'Yes. I have had rather a sad time lately, if we take one thing with another. I think I may be a ghost at the feast and we don't want that. It would be my pleasure to make sure the boys got home safely.'

Thirling and Falconer looked at one another. Neither of them wanted to make the journey home on a jolting cart, riding into God-knew-

273

what and yet they, like Norgate, could not quite square their view of Marlowe with the offer he had made. But, a decent dinner is a decent dinner.

'Thank you, Master Marlowe,' Falconer said quickly, before the scholar could change his mind. 'That is very decent of you and I'm sure the boys will be safe in your charge.' He raised his voice. 'Boys! Gather round.' He set about counting heads and making sure he had a full complement before sending them off on the road.

Marlowe marshalled the children into a short column of two and marched them round the corner of the building to the stables beyond where the carts were waiting. 'Up you jump, boys,' he said, and walked round to where the carter dozed on his bench.

He was just hopping up into his place when he heard his name being hissed from behind a bush. He looked around vaguely.

'Yes? Who is it?'

'Kit. It's me. Roger Manwood.'

The Corpus scholar leaned sideways and could just see the man sticking out through the foliage. 'Why are you hiding in that hedge, Sir Roger?' he asked.

'Why are you leaving Madingley? We need to talk.'

Marlowe sighed. 'Of course we do. That's why I'm leaving.'

The bush trembled and John Dee's head appeared through the top branches. 'I tried to tell him, Master Marlowe. He wouldn't believe me.'

'Well,' Marlowe said, nudging the carter into what passed for action. 'Explain to him, will you? If I'm not away soon and with as little conversing with bushes as possible, this whole subterfuge will be pointless. I'll meet you back here later, when all these people have gone. Cockshut time.' He turned to the carter, who was sitting, whip raised, ready for the off. 'Are we going or not?' he asked. 'Only at least two of these boys are as pissed as owls and the sooner we get them off your cart and into the sick room, the better. Unless you like swabbing out your cart.'

The carter needed no second bidding and with a lurch, they were off, rattling along country lanes.

Kit Marlowe sat silently as the carter urged his horses along the dusty road. He only spoke twice and both times it was to demand that the boys were quiet back there and that they should stop vomiting. The carter was impressed that they obeyed both instructions without question, and he had to agree with them that there was something about Marlowe that brooked no argument. The streets were eerily quiet for a Monday and the hoofs and wheels were loud as the cart clattered into the School of King's, Marlowe yelling for a porter to fetch someone from the dormitory, a bedder, a sizar, anyone who could take the queasy children and put them to bed. That done, he considered his re-sponsibilities covered and strolled around the corner to Hobson's stables in Trinity Lane.

'Ho!' he called. 'Anyone there? I need to hire a horse for the night.'

A groom, no bigger than one of the trebles, emerged on bowed legs from behind a partition and pointed wordlessly to the horse nearest the door, a spavined-looking creature with a dull coat and a mean eye.

'No,' Marlowe said, patiently. 'I need a horse with some go in him, not this...' he waved a hand, lost, for once, for words.

The groom hoiked and spat into the gutter. 'This is Hobson's,' he said, as if that was explanation enough. 'You get the one nearest the door and no argument. You want to pick and choose, go somewhere else,' he continued, and he hefted his pitchfork over his shoulder and turned to go.

'While this one is next to the door,' Marlowe said, reasonably, 'you'll never hire out another mount. Not that it will be here long, I think. It'll drop dead soon and how will that look, a dead horse in your doorway?'

'Look ... *sir*–' the groom managed to get a world of derision into that single word – 'with what's been going on these past days, you're lucky we have a horse in the place. It's this one or nothing.'

Marlowe peered past him and saw, at the back of the stables, in the shadows, a likely looking mount, black as night and with a look of the Devil about him. All in all, a suitable horse for the night's black doings. 'What about that one?'

he pointed into the gloom.

'You wouldn't want that one, sir,' the groom said, spitting again. 'He's a demon to ride and anyway, he belongs to a visitor to the town, a Francis Hall, staying at the Swan.'

Marlowe looked around. 'Is he here?'

'Not at present,' the groom said. After Marlowe's question, he had heard, faintly the chink of coin and it was coming from the region of Marlowe's hand. 'He hasn't ridden him in a day or two. I expect he would be grateful if you gave him a bit of a run.'

'My thoughts exactly,' Marlowe agreed, opening his purse and foraging for the coins which had been his pay for the wedding. The groom's hand came up with lightning speed and, quick as a wink, the coins had disappeared into the man's jerkin-front.

'Will you take him now, sir?' he asked, suddenly deferential.

'What's the time?' Marlowe asked the man.

As the groom opened his mouth to speak, a clock chimed overhead, four times, sweet and crisp. 'Half past three of the clock,' the man said.

Marlowe looked puzzled.

'They keep that clock fast,' the man said. 'It stops people being late. Everyone knows that.'

'If everyone knows...'

'Ar?'

'Never mind. So, it is only half past three. Can I leave this horse here for an hour or so? It's a trifle early for my needs just yet.'

277

'Ar. That's up to you. You've paid for the day. But don' forget, we close the doors at seven.'

'Is that seven by this clock, or seven by the other hundred clocks in the town?'

'Seven by this clock.'

'So, at half past six, you close the doors.'

'Ar.'

'So, I must get back to you by half past six.'

'No need, really,' the man said. 'I shall be here. I live here. I just was saying we close the doors at seven.' There was a pause. 'By this clock. And I ain't taking no chances after cock-shut. There's people in this town that's aggriev-ed. They want to hang the Mayor, you know.'

Marlowe smiled a wintry smile and patted the man condescendingly on the shoulder. 'I'll make sure I get back before then,' he said, and made his way to the Swan.

FOURTEEN

The Swan was always quiet in the middle of the afternoon and especially so in the aftermath of a riot. Almost by definition, the regulars had been affected most severely by the violence, either because their stalls had been destroyed by random looting, or because they were habitual drunkards who had been too slow to move out of harm's way.

Meg Hawley was leaning on the counter which ran along one side of the room, polishing a pewter mug which was marred by an enormous dent in one side. At a brief glance, Marlowe suspected that the dent would fit, almost perfectly, the side of someone's head.

'Hello, Meg,' Marlowe said. The girl didn't raise her head, but polished even more furiously. 'Quite well, I hope,' he added. 'Not affected by–' he waved his arm behind him as if to encompass the whole town – 'recent events.'

She looked up at him, meeting his gaze full on. 'I'm well, Master Marlowe, thank you for asking,' she said. 'Harry is in the lock-up. My father has a bad sprain to his back, but that's his fault, silly old fool.'

'Harry's in the lock-up?' Marlowe was surprised to say the least. 'But, surely, he has a broken arm.'

'It would take more than a broken arm to stop Harry,' Meg said, ruefully. 'But that isn't really my problem any more.'

Marlowe raised an eyebrow. 'No?'

'No. I'm tired of the fighting, Master Marlowe. I don't want my...' her hand stole, almost involuntarily, to her waist. She gave herself a shake and looked again into his eyes. She saw honesty there, and trustworthiness that perhaps few others could see. 'I don't want my child to be brought up by Harry Rushe, and that's the truth,' she said. 'He won't grow up to be like his father if Harry Rushe puts his name to him.'

Marlowe stepped back a pace and looked

279

again at the girl. He was far from being an expert, but he thought that he could see a thickening there that had not been there before. His next remark would take careful planning; he needed to talk to this girl some more, to ask her things which would be sensitive and personal. He couldn't afford to annoy her, and yet – the question had to be asked.

'How can you be so sure this child is not Harry's? I assume you are saying it is Ralph's?'

The girl put down the mug. If she polished it much more, she would wear it away. In a low voice, she said, 'If you were me, Master Marlowe, with a child in your belly and no husband, would you rather that that child would grow up to be like Harry Rushe, or like Ralph Whitingside?' She put her knuckles on her hips and stepped back a pace as she waited for his answer.

Marlowe's problem was that he was not in love with Ralph Whitingside. They had been friends for so long he knew him inside out, the bad as well as the good. And, on balance, Ralph just came down on the side of the angels, but just barely, by only a whisker. But for a moment, he looked through the eyes of her love and gave the right answer. 'Ralph's,' he said and risked placing his hand on her stomacher. He looked up at her and smiled. 'He even looks like Ralph.' She laughed. 'Yes,' he said, removing his hand, 'he has his father's nose.'

'Thank you, Master Marlowe,' the girl said, resuming her polishing. 'I knew *you* would

280

understand.' She lowered her voice. 'I've told
Ralph,' she whispered. 'He's very pleased.'

'That's ... wonderful,' Marlowe breathed. This
might well put the cat among the pigeons. He
had heard, when he was at home, listening to his
mother gossiping over her sewing with the
maids, that sometimes being with child made
women mad. He would just have to trust that she
could make sense of his questions and answer
them right. 'Can we sit down?' he asked her.
Another thing he had picked up was that women
sometimes swooned when in Meg's condition.

She looked from side to side, back and forth.
'I think we can, Master Marlowe,' she said. 'We
are having a quiet patch just at the moment.' She
led the way over to a seat in the corner.

'May I ask you some questions?' Marlowe
said. 'About the days before Ralph died.'

'Of course,' she said. 'But I only saw him
once, as I told you.'

'You started to tell me. I didn't hear the whole
story, though, did I?'

'You stopped me,' she said, testily. 'I was
quite willing to tell you. There was nothing in it
to be ashamed of.'

'I'm sure there wasn't,' he said, quickly. 'But
... will you tell me now?'

She gazed into the middle distance, as if the
scene were printed on the air. 'We went outside,'
she said. Then, she glared at Marlowe. 'We
didn't always go outside, you must understand
that, Master Marlowe. It wasn't just about that
with me and Ralph.'

He smiled encouragement. She had forgotten that he knew Ralph even better than she did, and it was always just about that with Ralph.

'Well, we found a quiet spot and I lifted up my skirts. I ... well, I wanted it to be like that, that night. I hadn't seen him for a while and I admit I was in need of him...' She looked down and blushed. Marlowe could almost hear the 'but' hanging in the air.

'But ... when I unlaced him, he ... was not in need of me.' She lifted her chin defiantly. 'I was angry, Master Marlowe. I thought he had already been with someone else. I dropped my skirts and came back inside. And ... I...' She buried her head in her hands and cried, almost howling the words. 'I never saw him again. I never said I was sorry.'

Marlowe put his arms around the girl and she burrowed in to his chest. He stroked her hair and murmured, as he did to his sisters when they were sad. Soon, she struggled up for air. He looked down at her and tucked a curl back up under her cap. 'Better now?' he smiled.

'I never saw him again, Master Marlowe,' she whispered, her eyes big and dark with tears.

Again, Marlowe was on a cusp. If he told her that Ralph Whitingside had been less than lusty that night because he was already dying, and not because he had come to her fresh from another bed, she would feel even worse than she did already. He couldn't swear to that, but Dee had suggested that this would be a symptom of poisoning by foxglove. He took refuge in his own words. 'Love is childish which consists in words.'

She sat up. 'I beg your pardon, Master Marlowe?' she said. She narrowed her eyes. 'Ralph told me you were a poet. Are you quoting from your poems at me?'

'A play,' he muttered. 'Currently in the hands of Lord Strange's Men.'

She flicked him with her wash-cloth. 'Don't talk of players to me,' she said. 'We have been cleaning and scrubbing for nearly two days because of what those wastrels brought here – rioting and looting.' She jumped to her feet, every inch the busy cellar maid. 'Let me get on with my work.' She rubbed the last of the tears from her eyes and bustled away.

Marlowe smiled to see her go. He didn't need Dee's showstone to see that any child of Meg Hawley's would grow up big and strong, whoever his father was, and that she would survive. He turned towards the door.

'Master Marlowe?' she called.

'Yes?' He didn't turn to her, but paused in the doorway.

'I didn't speak to Ralph before he died,' she said. 'But I speak to him now.'

His shoulders slumped. Poor deluded girl. But he decided to let kindness prevail. 'That's good, Meg. That must comfort you.' And he stepped out into the afternoon light.

'Oh, it does, Master Marlowe,' she said, polishing her mug. 'It does.'

* * *

It was still early to be going back to Madingley – it was no good wearing dark clothes and riding a black horse if arriving in broad daylight – so Marlowe took a walk along the Backs. It had always soothed him and had the added attraction that he wasn't overlooking, and being overlooked by, his own college. The sunlight was golden, almost thick with motes of dust and ash still settling out of the air after the uproar of the days before. College servants were working in most of the grounds as they swept down to the river; the crowds had not been concentrated here, but stragglers had managed to get across the river and had either hidden there overnight, lighting small fires and making shelters, or had abandoned looted goods, to be collected later. Some of the meadows had been gouged by running pattens, others had been more unlucky, and windows were being covered up temporarily by planks of wood.

King's had been quite badly hit, although the Chapel was untouched. Marlowe assumed it had been used, as other churches had, as a meeting place for the injured and disoriented. This would probably explain the piles of clothing he could just see in the entryway leading to the side door from the gate in the fence. Then, suddenly, his heart gave a lurch, as the pile of clothing moved and he realized that what he had been watching was a college servant taking a rest in the shade. The man looked at him, straight into his eyes and leaned forward with his finger to his nose. Across the grass and echoing through the arches, Marlowe heard his stage whisper: 'Don't tell on me, Master.'

Marlowe waved to him and walked away, back round to Trinity Lane and Hobson's Stable. He had a lot going on in his head, and wanted to put it all in order before his meeting after dark with Manwood and Dee. A ride in the countryside would perhaps put it all in perspective.

Soon, he was clattering down the road out of town, glancing through the windows of the Swan as he passed. Although he had no feelings other than friendship for Meg, it would have been nice to see her before he left town, but she was nowhere to be seen.

In the ale-soaked shadows of the Swan, Francis Hall turned to Meg. 'I do believe I've just seen my horse ridden down the street,' he remarked, calmly.

'Sir?' Meg was startled. He didn't sound half upset enough. 'Are you sure?'

'Certain,' the man said. 'Young man, dark eyes, small beard, long hair, about so tall.' He sketched a size about equal to his own in the air.

'That could be any one of the scholars in this town,' she said with a laugh. But both she and Francis Hall knew that it could only be Kit Marlowe.

Francis Hall's horse was a magnificent stallion and Marlowe, an occasional rider at the best of time, found that he had to concentrate every second of his time on its back to prevent it having its way and going wherever it wanted to.

Its coat was deepest black and its mouth was as soft as silk. Once he and Marlowe had agreed to differ, the ride was smooth and, high above the cow parsley and ladies' bedstraw, Marlowe was able to organize his thoughts, with the soft clop of the animal's hoofs in the thick summer dust as counterpoint.

The sun started to go down just out of the corner of his left eye as he ambled towards Madingley and, with perfect timing, it slipped below the horizon in a blaze of sky blue pink just as the chimneys and copper cupola of Madingley came into view. There was still rather a lot of light in the sky to approach the house, especially on this horse, which had been drawing looks from everyone he passed on the road, so Marlowe started looking around for somewhere to tether him for a while.

Suddenly, the horse's head went up and he gave a snicker. Marlowe hunkered down in the saddle and drew in his knees. Pulling the animal to a stop, he slid down from its back and looped its reins in the hedge as he went to investigate what had startled it. As he peered through the interlaced twigs of a quickthorn, he saw a low building in front of him, painted white, but crouching under such a heavy thatch that its walls were in permanent shadow. The small windows were lit with candles as the night drew on and a bench was attached to the wall, running the length of the front of the building to each side of the door, which stood open, invitingly. The raised voices which had made the horse shy

286

were raised in friendship and, on the slight summer breeze, came a smell of ale and a whiff of a fragrant herb burning. He laughed quietly to himself out of sheer relief and crept back to the horse.

'Come on,' he said to it, clicking his tongue. 'Here's somewhere I can leave you, and wait until dark as well.'

The animal nudged his head with its nose and the two travellers walked round to the back of the inn, where the stable lad was delighted to take over the care of such a lovely creature. 'I'll be back for him later,' Marlowe said. 'Here's a coin for you to be going on with. I'm not sure when I can get back.' Then the reality of his situation hit him; he was going off to meet a murderer. 'If I'm not back by tomorrow night, take him to Hobson's in Trinity Lane.'

'Ride him there, you mean?' the lad asked, struggling under the weight of the saddle.

'Or carry him, if you'd rather,' Marlowe said.

'Kit,' came a quiet voice came from behind him. 'That was unworthy of you. Apologize to the boy.'

Marlowe spun round, his hand on his dagger hilt, to see Manwood and Dee standing in the stable yard. 'Why are you two here?' he asked. Then, over his shoulder: 'Yes, sorry, ride, of course.' He stepped out of the stable and closed to the men. 'I was on my way to Madingley,' he said quietly.

'We weren't expecting you this early,' Dee said. 'We thought you would wait until dark.'

Marlowe looked at the sky which was getting darker by the minute. 'It is dark, or would be by the time I got to the house. So, as I said, why are you here?'

'Come into the inn with us,' Dee said. 'We have ordered some food and some more ale. We'll eat and talk.'

'Ordered food? Surely, there was the wedding breakfast all arranged...'

'Come inside, Kit,' Manwood said. 'We can talk there. But meanwhile, have you discovered anything?'

'I have discovered that Ralph was impotent just before he died.'

Dee nodded to himself.

'I'm not sure whether I need that information,' Manwood said, prissily. To him, Ralph Whitingside was still the lad he had sent off to Cambridge years before.

'I need it,' said Dee. 'It is the last brick in the wall of my diagnosis. Although by no means a certainty, I think we can now consider that the cause of death of the two scholars is poisoning by foxglove.'

They all ducked their heads to enter the inn and waited a moment to get used to the light from the candle sconces on the walls. Looking back through the doorway, it was clear that night had finally fallen. The landlord scurried forward.

'Gentlemen,' he said, with a touch of relief in his voice. 'There you are. I feared you had gone.' And left me with all this food and ale already drawn, was the rest of the message, unsaid.

Manwood was immediately expansive. 'No, no, my good fellow,' he said. 'We ordered the food and we will eat it. And now we have someone else to help us, so it will not go to waste.' He looked around. 'Where is it?'

'I have taken the liberty of laying out the food in the back room,' the landlord said, opening a door in the far wall. 'I thought you would be more ... private, there.'

The back room was small, but tidy, with a table set against the wall, groaning with sallets and capons, tongue and pie. A savoury custard quivered gently in a bowl to one side. The sight of the food made Marlowe realize how hungry he was; he hadn't eaten that day at all and his memory of meals over the preceding days had been sketchy. There had been some soup and bread before the play, he remembered, but that had ended up tipped over someone's head.

Dee noticed the gleam in the scholar's eye. 'Tuck in, Kit,' he said, kindly. 'Perhaps like me you think better on a full stomach.'

A smaller table had been drawn up at the end of the trestle, with wooden chargers on it, along with three wickedly-pointed knives. Obviously, the usual customers at this inn were not the kind to bring their own weapons, and for that all three men were grateful; it was good to be able to eat and drink without keeping an eye on the door.

'So, Sir Roger, Dr Dee,' Marlowe said, 'what has happened at Madingley that has made you come here for your wedding breakfast?' He knew it was not in Manwood's nature to spend money where money need not be spent. 'No Will Nicholson to put his hand in his purse?'

'Up at the Hall,' Manwood said testily. 'Some maid or other had need of his services.'

The men looked at each other and then seemed to come to a decision. 'Sir Roger will tell what there is to tell,' Dee said. 'He may have noticed things I missed.'

All three men knew that this was a polite fiction at best, but nonetheless, Manwood began. 'It all started shortly after you left,' he said, addressing his tale to Marlowe. 'I'm not sure whether you noticed, but Professor Johns and the new Mistress Steane went off from the party to look at the Physick Garden.'

'Is that where they were going?' Marlowe said. 'I saw them walk off.'

'No one thought anything of it,' Manwood continued. 'Johns is well known as a very gentlemanly ... er ... man. So, after you had gone, everything went very well for a while. Hynde had arranged for some girls to circulate with wine, and of course it went to some heads rather more than to others.' He smiled a reminiscent smile. 'Professor Goad, for example, had to be taken inside to lie down.'

'And Falconer and Thirling,' added Dee.

'To be fair to Dr Falconer,' Marlowe said, 'he was not well before we even began the wedding ceremony.'

'Yes, I did discover that,' Dee said, 'when I

290

examined him. Poor chap has been bedevilled by ... but that is by the way and something which perhaps is best kept between him and his physician. Thirling, though, was taken very poorly, and I was hard pressed to tell if it was the wine or the oysters, but it was certainly one of those, as that was all he had taken.'

'Oysters?' Marlowe asked, with a raised brow. 'Where did he get oysters from? There were none on the choir table.'

'Ah, well,' Manwood said, resuming his tale. 'It seems that Dr Thirling is, like the oyster, a native of Whitstable and so whenever he sees them, he can't resist. There was a whole dish of them on the table set for the servants, and he did rather make a pig of himself.'

'So, all very sad,' Marlowe said, 'people getting drunk, ill and similar, but there is still nothing that I can see that would have made you both leave the house.' It all sounded pretty much like a routine wedding to him. He had seen things in his years as a treble which would make the prissy Manwood's eyes pop.

'He's coming to that,' Dee said, getting up to refill his plate.

'I'm coming to that,' Manwood said. 'In the middle of all this, what with Goad singing something we were shocked to find he knew, and Falconer falling in the carp pond and Thirling ... well, we will draw a veil over that. In the middle of it all, no one saw for a moment when Johns suddenly appeared in the gateway leading from the Physick Garden, with his robes all anyhow, calling for help.'

'Steane went wild,' Dee said, putting in his groatsworth. 'Went for him, like a madman.'

'No, no, you've got that wrong,' Manwood said, pausing to pick bits of venison out of his teeth with the point of his knife. 'He didn't do that until Ursula appeared behind Johns, with *her* gown all anyhow and her hair in her eyes.'

Dee shrugged. 'Sorry,' he said. 'That's the only bit I saw.'

Marlowe's eyes were wide. 'Professor Johns attacked Mistress Steane?' he asked, agog.

'No,' Manwood said. 'No, that's not how it was.'

'Mistress Steane attacked Professor Johns?'

'No, not that either. It turns out that she swooned from the heat, and the excitement I suppose, and in trying to stop her falling, Johns had grabbed a handful of her dress and it tore. She grabbed some of his robe and it did the same. She didn't accuse him of anything, but it was quite a shock to see Steane in such a temper. I always thought he was the mildest of men.'

'I've certainly never seen that side of him,' Marlowe said, 'although I can't say I know him well. I have usually only seen him conducting services at King's and there isn't that much scope for temper at evensong.'

'It rather broke the party up,' Manwood said. 'Francis Hynde has gone off somewhere with a bottle or two, Steane and his good lady have taken themselves off to bed. In the event, Ursula apparently didn't give her bride's maids her garters as is the custom and I don't suppose for a moment anybody wanted Steane's codpiece. The guests have all gone home, those within a reasonable distance, anyway. Falconer, Thirling and Goad are still having a lie-down although I should think they will be stirring soon. John gave them a tincture.'

'Just a spot,' Dee said. 'They will indeed be waking shortly. Johns stayed with them, so that they had someone other than the driver with them on the way home. I'm not sure about Norgate? Do you know where he went, Roger?'

'He went earlier, I think,' Manwood said. 'I started to lose track, at the finish.'

Marlowe blew out his cheeks and looked from one to the other. 'I'm not sure I can match that,' he said. 'All of my news is older than this, of course, and as such doesn't have the dramatic attack.'

Dee blinked. 'Kit, have you fallen among players or something?'

Marlowe blushed and looked down. 'No, no. A little poetry, that's more my métier.'

Dee looked dubious, but motioned him to continue. When would people realize that it was pointless to dissemble with Dr John Dee, the Queen's Magus. He knew everything; especially through the clear glass of hindsight.

'I've taken it as read that Ralph and Henry were poisoned,' Marlowe said. 'Henry was working on Ralph's journal when he died ... although I'm not sure that that is pertinent, because we all knew that Tom was supposed to be doing it. We managed to piece together the conundrum that Henry was working on – it was Greek, in a mirror, and not very good Greek at that.'

'What did it say?' Manwood leaned forward, a dripping spoon of custard halfway to his mouth.

'Well, we can't be sure that the translation is completely right, mostly because it doesn't make sense, but it seemed to say "opposite the Dark Entry". We have thought of what is opposite the Dark Entry, but it is just a couple of tombs and that makes no sense.'

There was a pause, then Manwood gave a shout of laughter.

'Is that a joke?' Dee asked, looking at the Men of Kent.

Marlowe bit his lip and then, smiling an embarrassed smile, told Dee about his childhood gaffe.

Dee looked at Manwood and they nodded at each other.

'After you,' Dee said, magnanimously. He had tired of Manwood's reminiscences over the last week, but the man's memory had come up trumps this time.

'Perhaps the tombs don't make sense, but does this?' Manwood asked. 'Kit, you thought that the couple in the Dark Entry were fighting, but in fact they were fornicating. So, might Ralph have seen a couple who he *thought* were fornicating, but who he realized were actually fighting?' He sat back, and waited for the reaction.

'The woman in the river!' Marlowe said, suddenly.

'Fludd's case?' Dee checked.

'Yes. Even Edward Winterton thinks there is something suspicious about her death, but instructed a verdict of "found drowned" to protect the family.'

'Where would Ralph have seen it, though? It could have been anywhere,' Manwood said.

Marlowe clicked his fingers. 'I was on the Backs this afternoon and I saw what I thought was a pile of clothes, but it was a college servant. It was in the cloister along the side of the King's meadow, leading from the gate to the Chapel.'

'That doesn't narrow things down at all,' Dee complained. 'I know in my day that was a short cut for every Tom, Dick and Harry.'

'True,' Marlowe said. 'So in that case, Ralph possibly told the wrong person what he had seen. And that person is the one who killed him.'

The silence was palpable. The men could hear the pinging of the candle sconces as the hot wax ran over the metal. They could hear the birds shifting in their nests in the chimney. They could hear their own hearts beating.

'Oh God's teeth!' Marlowe suddenly shouted and Manwood almost died of shock. 'I'm sorry, Sir Roger,' Marlowe said, contrite. 'I didn't mean to startle you. Henry asked one of the Fellows to help him with the translation when he took it over from Tom.'

'Who?' Manwood and Dee shouted together.

Marlowe sat back in his chair and sighed. 'The same man I found in my ransacked room one night, waiting for me. The man who had been kind; too kind, perhaps.' The answer was in sight but it gave him no pleasure. 'Michael Johns,' he said.

FIFTEEN

Ambrose Falconer sat in the carriage and couldn't remember when he had felt more ill than this. His trouble was very long-standing and an unexpected fit of it had robbed him of the post of organist at Canterbury Cathedral, many years before. His general malaise had not been helped by the fall into the carp pond; as he had sunk below the murky surface, he thought he saw his whole life flash before him and could certainly feel the nibble of fishy lips on his cheek before two of Francis Hynde's gardeners had fished him back to the world, coughing and spluttering. They had manhandled him into one of the second best guest bedrooms and that strange, slightly singed little man in grey had come to see him. For some reason that he still couldn't fathom, Ambrose Falconer had told him every symptom of his trouble and the man had told him to drink the contents of a small package dissolved in wine and then, dried and dressed in one of Francis Hynde's second best guest robes, he had fallen into a sleep like death. But now he was awake and dressed again in his own clothes, which were still very slightly damp about the seams and the dreams that had come to him in his long sleep still lingered at the corners of his eyes. He groaned and sat patiently, waiting for what would happen to him next.

Richard Thirling sat in the carriage next to Ambrose Falconer and couldn't remember when he had felt more ill than this. He often had attacks of whatever it was that made his leg give way, which was sometimes accompanied by singing in the ears; he had always attributed that to years as a choirmaster. But this afternoon, at the wedding breakfast, he had suddenly been spectacularly sick all over the second cousin twice removed of the bride. He had been removed with not too much ceremony by two of Francis Hynde's grooms, who had taken him, up the back stairs, to a second best guest bedroom, where he had been stripped of his clothes and put to bed. Just as he was drifting off into a troubled sleep, he would jerk awake as his muscles spasmed and arched his back. Then he would shiver as though with ague and drift off, until the whole sorry business would start again. There was a bucket strategically placed at his bedside, but he usually missed his mark, with a muttered apology to the empty room. His memory was unclear after the first visitation of whatever this pestilence was; one minute he was

297

talking to the wedding party, the next he was in bed. Then, he thought he could remember, a strange grey man had materialized and had made him vomit some more. There was talk of oysters and wine, but he had to say no; he really wasn't feeling all that well.

Professor Goad sat in the carriage and couldn't remember when he had felt more ill than this. He had absolutely no memory of the whole sorry day and just closed his eyes and hoped to die.

Michael Johns stood talking to the groom who would be driving them home. He was trying to persuade the man to let him ride up on the outside bench, where the groaning and the belching and the general stench would be less noticeable, but the man was adamant. It just wasn't done in Sir Francis Hynde's employ that gentlemen rode with grooms up front. He would have to travel with the other ... gentlemen – the pause was small but telling – in the carriage. Sighing, Johns turned away from the man. Surely there must be an alternative to getting into that noisome box and holding his breath the whole way to Cambridge.

Marlowe, Manwood and Dee reluctantly left some food, just a little, on the trestle in the inn and prepared to leave. The landlord was so ecstatic and lost in his cloud of cuckoo-dreams of having at last broached the world of quality clientele that it was not for some time that he realized that no one had paid.

They left Marlowe's horse behind, as Manwood and Dee had their own way of getting back into the park. A path wound through a small shrubbery between the church and the inn, which came out at the back of the stable yard. Manwood and Dee did have the grace to admit that it was possibly easier to use in daylight than it was in the dark, but eventually they were walking on cobbles and no longer had to pause every few yards to disentangle themselves from the clutch of brambles. As they walked, swearing under their breath every now and again as a mistimed branch whizzed back from the grip of the man in front, they made plans. Marlowe and Manwood were dagger men, at bottom. Subtleties suggested by Dee were, in the final analysis, too slow and not foolproof. The murderer – Marlowe still had trouble naming him as Johns, even in the teeth of the evidence – had killed at least three times to their knowledge and could easily be planning to kill again. Dee favoured a more oblique approach. He had, after all, tinctures by the dozen, incantations galore, which could bring the soul of a man to its knees and make him tell the truth though it condemned him to eternal damnation.

Manwood hadn't liked the light in Dee's eye, the way he rubbed his hands together. It smacked of heresy, necromancy and the rest; a good dagger-point at the throat would achieve all that and more and no risk to anyone's eternal soul

299

except that of the murderer.

They were still discussing it, although an eavesdropper may have chosen to call it arguing, when they stumbled on to the cobbles of the stable yard. There were no carriages to be seen and even the grooms seemed to have gone to bed.

'Where was their carriage?' Marlowe asked, urgently.

'Here,' said Manwood, spreading his arms.

'I should have given them a bigger dose,' Dee said. 'But with Falconer, I had to be careful. It could have killed him in his condition. And of course, Thirling...'

The other two waited. Finally, Manwood could bear it no longer. 'Yes? Thirling? What about Thirling?'

'Thirling might have been poisoned,' Dee said slowly. 'I assumed it was the oysters or the wine.'

'Poison has to be given to the person somehow,' Marlowe said. 'With Ralph and Henry, we couldn't tell when or how they had been given it. But I know that Dr Thirling had not eaten for hours before we got to Madingley, so he must have been given a dose there.'

'But why didn't it kill him?' Manwood asked.

'Because,' Dee said, 'tincture of digitabulum takes varying times to kill – and because I gave him tartar emetic when I went to see him after he was taken ill. It got the poison out of his system when only a little had been absorbed.'

'So who gave it to him?' Marlowe wanted

300

to know.

Manwood was confused. 'Haven't we decided it was Johns?' he asked.

'Was Johns near Thirling when he ate or drank?' Dee asked. 'I can't remember, but I don't think he was. He had already gone off with the bride, I *think*. And he couldn't have just put the poison in some food because if he had we would have a house half full of the dead and dying.' Dee wished he had a showstone which would clarify the past in the way that it clarified the future.

Marlowe was almost hopping with frustration. He had missed a vital clue because he had had other clues to find. Why had neither of these stupid men...?

'Shhhhh!' whispered Manwood, peering through the shrubbery. 'There's someone creeping out of the side door of the house. Whoever it is is making for the stables.'

'Can you see who it is?' breathed Marlowe, who had his back to the building and was loath to attract attention to himself by turning round.

'No. He's going into the tack room. It's probably just a manservant on some assignation with a scullery maid. Shhhh ... No, he's coming out again...'

'Turn your head away,' Marlowe said. 'The moonlight reflecting in your eyes will give us all away.'

Dee looked at the scholar with new eyes. 'Master Marlowe,' he whispered. 'I believe you have done this sort of thing before.'

Marlowe lifted a shoulder in recognition and bent his head towards Manwood's shoulder, whispering, 'What's he doing now? Can you see who it is?'

'He's saddling a horse,' whispered Manwood. 'I still can't see who it is ... he's keeping to the shadows. Where is he going?'

'To get Thirling,' Dee whispered back. He risked a glance out of the corner of his eye. 'It could be Johns, I suppose. It's hard to tell in this light. He needs to finish off Thirling, to stop him telling what he knows.'

The sensible Justice of the Peace rose up inside Roger Manwood. 'Aren't we perhaps getting a little overexcited?' he asked quietly. 'There may be a perfectly simple explanation.' He wondered what would happen if people at home in Canterbury heard of him skulking around stable yards at dead of night and accusing reputable members of Cambridge colleges of murder.

Marlowe pulled the two men aside into the shadows. 'Sir Roger, there is no simple explanation. Creeping about and saddling horses by moonlight is not normal behaviour. Murder has been done three times. We couldn't stop them happening, but this fourth one we *can* prevent. My horse is ready for me down at the inn. If I run now, I can be on its back and waiting to follow before this man passes that way. It is hard for one man to saddle a horse, and if it is Michael Johns he isn't used to it.'

'If?' Dee said.

'Yes. If. That will leave me time.' The older men started to complain, to argue that they should just stop the man and see what he was up to.

'He'll say he was up to have a midnight ride, after the stresses of the day. We have to catch him red-handed or we won't catch him at all. Go into the house, but don't raise the alarm. Just tell Sir Francis. Then, get a carriage, or a horse if you're able.' Marlowe remembered the time slip journey with Dee, but put that out of his head. 'Get into Cambridge as fast as you can and raise the Watch, Constable Fludd for preference.' Then he was running on tip toe along the edge of the shadow of the stable wall. And he was gone.

The stable boy at the inn was in seventh heaven. He had never even been near a horse this beautiful before, let alone had one left in his care. And if that scholar, the one with the scary eyes, hadn't come back by tomorrow, he would be able to ride this lovely beast all the way to Cambridge. He started to plan his route, the slow way, the most meandering way he could devise...

'Boy!' Marlowe's voice cut through his reverie. 'Is my horse ready?'

With a sigh, the lad got up from where he sat in the stall and wordlessly handed Marlowe the reins. The dream had been nice though, whilst it lasted.

The animal had liked the boy. He had been

kind and had apples in his pocket, a little wizened at this time of year, but a nice change from oats. But Marlowe was exciting, leaping on to his back and then keeping him, like a coiled spring, back from the light that spilled in through the stable door. Soon, in the distance, the beat of a horse's feet thrummed through the night, first as a tremor in the horse's fetlocks, then as a sound that anyone could hear. The stallion whickered and tossed its mane, but Marlowe kept him reined back until the hoof beats began to recede, dopplering into the distance. Only then did he give the horse his head and how they flew, eating up the dusty road on the way to Cambridge, still outlined on the night sky by the few desultory fires still burning on the outskirts.

Every now and again, Marlowe reined his mount in and they sat, like one exotic creature, ears cocked to judge the distance and direction of the other rider. When they were too near, Marlowe walked the black, only breaking into a canter when the sound was faint enough. Once or twice, the lead horse stopped also, and Marlowe could imagine the rider twisted in the saddle, listening for the hoof beats which were following him. But he always set off again, Marlowe like an echo in the night.

A gap in the hedge gave him an idea and he urged the stallion through it and into the field beyond. They couldn't keep up the speed on the more uneven ground, but what they lost in speed, they made up for in not having to stop, because the horse was almost silent in the soft meadow grass.

Soon another sound could be heard over the beat of the galloping horse, the creaking leather, plodding feet and rumbling wheels of the carriage bearing the Fellows back to Cambridge. Marlowe could faintly hear their querulous cries to the groom to go more slowly and not to rock about so much and he knew they were really close. He couldn't hear the other horse any more. Either he was waiting for Marlowe, knowing he was being chased, or he had fallen into silent company with the carriage, waiting to carry out the rest of his murder when he got the opportunity.

Slowing the horse to a walk, Marlowe had a chance to listen to the beating of his heart; this could so easily be a trap. He had enemies of his own. There was more than one way to skin a cat, and ... had it been Tom? Matt? ... had reminded him that there were five arches in the Dark Entry and five scholars, now reduced to three. Was the woman in the river a red herring? Were Manwood and Dee really on his side, or had they been part of an elaborate plot all along? The stallion tossed his head as the reins drew tighter in his soft mouth as Marlowe clenched his fists. The sound of the tiny bells jingling on the bridle brought him down to earth, with his heart thumping. Of course this wasn't about him. This was about a murderer and stopping him from killing again.

The scholar strained his ears in the darkness

and could hear nothing except the diminishing sounds of the carriage, making its way back to Cambridge and safety, if safety lay anywhere in these days. The voice in his ear was quiet as voices went, but sounded to Marlowe's strained nerves like a pistol shot.

'Good evening, Master Machiavel,' Steane breathed in his ear. 'Taking the air?'

Marlowe swallowed, but his voice came out sounding cooler than he felt. 'Doctor Steane. May I take this opportunity to congratulate you on your nuptials. Too excited to sleep, I imagine.'

The man chuckled. He liked a good adversary. Eleanor hadn't counted, not at her death or ever. Ralph Whitingside had given him a few nasty moments, but the greedy sot would drink anything in the right shaped bottle and so that had been easy. Bromerick was such a crawler and when he had started talking about the journal, an inn was the natural place to do it and tipping the tincture into his ale had been the work of a minute. Then, it had all started to slip.

'Too excited indeed, Master Machiavel. My bride is ... modest in her needs and I find I have time on my hands.' He looked at Marlowe's horse appraisingly. 'You have a nice mount, I see. He didn't come from just inside the door, I'll wager.'

'Nor did yours,' Marlowe countered. 'He's a good horse, but he will be still done up in the morning. And don't forget, I have witnesses that you left the house tonight.'

For the first time, Steane's gaze flickered. 'I don't think you do,' he said finally. 'Who else was abroad at that time?'

'Sir Roger Manwood and Dr John Dee,' Marlowe said. 'They are rousing the house as we speak.'

'And for what?' Steane spat. 'To tell them that I am out for a ride and that you have chased me like a maniac with, no doubt, the intention of stealing my purse, or worse.'

'No. To tell them that you are a murderer, at least three times over. More if Doctor Thirling still succumbs to the poison.'

Steane's head snapped up. 'Might he?' he asked. Then, sensing his mistake: 'I certainly hope that Doctor Thirling recovers. It would be a great loss to King's if he should not.'

Marlowe pulled at the left hand rein and turned his horse's head, reaching as he did so for Steane's rein. 'I'll keep you company back to Madingley, then,' he said. 'You can tell me all about your plans for your bishopric. Bath and Wells, did I hear?'

Steane yanked his rein out of Marlowe's hand. 'We'll do no such thing, Master Marlowe,' he hissed. The tip of a dagger pricked Marlowe's thigh as the horses pressed together. 'I think the best thing we could do would be to dismount – very slowly – and then you will walk with me into the woods over there. Then–' he reached round behind him and unhooked a coil of rope from the back of his saddle – 'you will loop this over a branch and, if you would be so good, you will hang yourself with it. I had earmarked this rope for Thirling, but it will do as well for you. Another sad inquest for Sir Edward Winterton to get wrong, another suicide among the Parker scholars.' He jabbed the dagger a little harder and Marlowe felt hot blood run down the inside of his leg and soak into the saddle. 'But hardly surprising with the rumours flying about you in your college and indeed all over the University. The shame of it. Sodomy in Corpus. Hanging is too good for you, they'll say. But never mind, you will be dead and from what I also hear, you will have no soul to go to Purgatory or anywhere else, so not too much harm done. You're very quiet, Master Machiavel.'

'Doctor Steane,' Marlowe said smoothly, 'my death is neither here nor there, in the scheme of things. I would rather live, that I will allow, but if I have to die to prove you a murderer, then so be it.'

Suddenly, the dagger was at his ribs. 'And how will your suicide prove me a murderer?'

'I told you, I have witnesses to the whole thing, you leaving Madingley, me following. There is Dee, Manwood, the stable lad. There were probably a few drunks sitting outside the inn who would testify to our chase. Are you going to poison and drown the whole world, Doctor Steane?'

'Damn you, Marlowe,' Steane snarled, jumping from his horse on to Marlowe, his weight, not skill, carrying them both to the ground. The startled animals jolted away as the pair rolled in

308

the grass. Steane's knife flew into the darkness and his hands struggled in the excess material of his wedding clothes to find Marlowe's throat.

'You're very strong, Dr Steane,' Marlowe hissed. 'But you are rather older than me and I think in a straight fight, I will surely win.'

'But this isn't a straight fight, Master Marlowe, is it?' Steane gasped. He was straddling the scholar, his arm pressing down on his windpipe. He weighed almost half as much again as Marlowe and had taken him off his horse with Marlowe underneath him. And he knew from experience how to choke the life out of another human being. Marlowe wriggled and twisted like a fish on a line, scrabbling with his hands in the dirt to find anything he could use as a weapon. The field had not been ploughed that year and had been left to meadow, so not even a sod was hard enough to do any damage. But the soft soil could be his weapon even so. Gathering up as big a handful as he could, Marlowe raised his hand and rubbed the dirt, with the broken flints and shards of old corn stems, into Steane's eyes. It wouldn't blind him, but if it just made him raise his arm for a second, Marlowe's youth and agility would do the rest.

The Fellow howled as a broken snail-shell scraped the cornea of his left eye and he let go with an oath. As quick as a flash, Marlowe had wriggled free, unsheathing his dagger as he did so.

'Now, Dr Steane,' he said, moving closer, the weaving blade catching the light as he twisted it in his hand, ever closer to the man's throat. 'It will be a long walk still into town, so I think we should start now.' He reached down to haul the man to his feet.

'I don't think I want to go to town with you, Marlowe,' Steane grated, still rubbing his eye. 'I want you dead.' He grabbed the scholar's proffered hand and yanked down hard. Marlowe's dagger pricked the older man's sleeve and blood spurted, black under the moon. 'Oh, oh, see what the wicked Machiavel has done to me?' he shouted to the stars. Then he turned his face back to Marlowe and his eyes shone. 'I think that the coroner's jury at your inquest will be very sympathetic to see me, a Bishop-elect, sitting in the court, cradling my injuries. All I had done was to go for a ride to calm away the stresses of the day, when suddenly, I was set upon by a known roisterer, drunkard, pederast and liar.' Suddenly, there was a second dagger glinting in his hand; in another second the point was at Marlowe's throat. 'Drop the knife,' he growled.

'Not very bishoply behaviour, some might say,' Marlowe said tightly, trying not to move his throat too much. He let the dagger slip from his grasp.

'Hmm, perhaps not. We'll see when this night ends who has the sympathy, Marlowe,' Steane said. 'Now–' he whacked each horse on the rump and they wheeled towards the road, one heading for Madingley, the other for the town where its owner waited patiently – 'as I think I

310

have already explained, we will go to those woods over there, where you will be so good as to hang yourself.'

'I know when I'm beaten,' Marlowe said dully and, turning, started to make his way to the woods.

'And I know that means you're not,' Steane said. 'Even so, I will not tie you up. You have been a challenge, Master Marlowe, and so for that reason we will walk along like old friends, talking as we walk. I shall enjoy that because the life I have been living and, I fear, the life I have yet to live, is a lonely one.' He made an expansive movement that pricked Marlowe's throat painfully and made a small trickle of blood run into his soiled ruff. 'I will tell you the story of my life, shall I?'

'I would prefer you not to,' Marlowe said. 'As a playwright, I might feel the need to use it some day and then where would that leave us all?'

'I would enjoy watching that, Master Marlowe; what a pity you won't live to write it. Let me tell you a story then, as though it is some other man's life. Then tell me if you think it would make a good play. But keep walking. We are nowhere near the trees yet.'

Marlowe trudged on, his mind whirring. It must be possible to get away from the older, heavier man, but it would perhaps be wise to hear his story first. He would need the details to prove his case, when this was all over and done.

'Once upon a time – you must correct me, playwright, if I use the wrong words – once

311

upon a time there was a very young priest. He had known that he would be a priest almost from when he could talk. All second sons in his family became priests. It was just the way of things. If there were two daughters, the second would become a nun. So, one son to breed, one daughter to look after the parents when they were old, one son to be a priest and make his mother proud, one daughter never to be seen again. Any other children were extra, but in my family there were only two sons.'

'This story is very slow,' Marlowe said, carefully. 'The audience would have thrown some rotten fruit by now.'

'Patience, playwright, patience. Then, in this family, a terrible thing happened. The eldest son died, leaving just the priest to do all those things; to breed, to care and to make his mother proud. But before he had to decide whether to renounce the priesthood, a marvellous thing happened which solved everyone's dilemmas. The boy-king Edward came to the throne and priests could marry. It was a wonderful solution, especially since a beautiful girl lived just over the hill and the young priest had loved her and she had loved him since they were children.'

'So they married,' Marlowe added. 'And they all lived happily ever after. That play's too short. No jester? No lover dying from a broken heart? You would need another one to fill the time, or the audience would want their money back.'

'Ah, but wait. This is real life, so the story is not over. The priest and his lovely bride were married, but no sooner had they done so than the king died and his sister Mary came to the throne. The fires were stoked again, men were burned as heretics, priests must be celibate. There were many ways of managing this situation, many left the priesthood or just carried on as before, with wives become housekeepers and no one any the wiser. But this young priest and his bride were very devout. They saw the world in black and white whereas you and I, Master Machiavel, we know that it is all grey, don't we, like cats in the night?'

Marlowe couldn't nod, but gurgled assent in the back of his throat.

'The priest left his wife back at her parents' house and ran far away, to a town where no one knew his name or what he had done and he did well. Mary died and Elizabeth came to the throne and many priests married, but he had almost forgotten he had ever had a wife. She had probably remarried, he told himself. It would be best not to meddle with her life any more. He was clever and learned quickly and soon he rose in the church. Then, one day, when he was within an inch of what he had always wanted, a bishopric, with a rich wife in the offing, he was walking along the riverbank when a woman called his name.'

'His wife?' Marlowe asked. They were nearly in the trees and he needed to move this narrative along.

'Indeed, his wife. She had entered a nunnery in France as a lay sister, but was back now to care for her old father. She didn't want anything from me. Her life of contemplation had made her happy with her lot and she would not have said a thing. But ... I am not a trusting man, Master Machiavel, I didn't trust her then and so I killed her. I twisted her Popish rosary around her neck until she stopped breathing and I pushed her body into the river.'

'You say that very easily,' Marlowe said. 'And I notice that the young priest has become a character much closer to home.'

The knife point pricked again. 'Don't play with me!' the man snarled. 'Now–' he glanced up briefly to the towering elms – 'do you want to die in the middle of this wood, or on the edge?'

'On the edge.' Marlowe could just make out the black tower of St Stephen's and the turreted colleges beyond. 'But the edge facing the church. It's where my friend is buried, after all. I would like to be near him, at a time like this.'

'The church, Master Marlowe?' Steane sneered. 'Don't tell me that you have decided to embrace religion in your last moments.'

'God is forgiving, or so I'm told.'

The Fellow sighed. 'I believe he is,' he said. 'I hope he is ... As you wish, Master Marlowe. Walk on a little, then and I will tell the rest of the story. What I didn't realize was that Ralph Whitingside had seen what I had done. He knew that it was me, under the darkness of that archway and he came to tell me so. He would, he said, have to speak to Goad. I brazened it out and he

314

went off, to see that jade of his from the Swan, I expect. While he was gone, I went to his rooms and put poison in the brandy he keeps there.'

The edge of the wood was showing brighter against the dark. 'And Henry?'

'Ah, yes, Bromerick and that bloody journal. I was afraid that Whitingside would have written down something incriminating and Bromerick was idiot enough to show it to Michael Johns, who told me about it, hoping I could help. It was all so perfect. I arranged to meet Bromerick to discuss it. Foxglove in the ale. That was it.'

'That was it?' Marlowe spun round with no care for his safety. 'That was *it*? That was my friend, not just a problem for you to do away with.'

Steane pressed him up against a tree, the knife to his throat, pressing under the angle of his jaw. 'Do you think that the rope will hide the pricks of the knife? I hardly care if it does or not, Master Marlowe. I just want you *dead*!' The last word echoed round and round the trees like a banshee's wail.

'Thirling?' Marlowe ground out. The pain in his leg and his throat was washing over him and the loss of blood as it still ran down his leg into his boot was making everything seem faint and dreamlike. But he had to know.

'Thirling also saw me with Eleanor. Like Whitingside, he didn't know quite what he had seen, until that stupid village girl pinned that weed on my shoulder this morning.' Both men paused. Could it really have only been that

315

morning? 'It made him realize what had been going on, but not that I had killed her. He accused me of "dalliance". Me, a Bishop-elect. He had to die.'

Marlowe sagged suddenly at the knees and took Steane by surprise. It was enough and the younger man turned to run clear of the trees, hobbling across the uneven ground below the church wall. As he stumbled and tried to find his footing, he heard a scream behind him which turned his blood to ice. Rolling over, his arm up to defend himself, he saw Steane staggering away to his left, eyes wide with horror, arms up with palms outwards, to fend off some dreadful thing. Twisting back to see what Steane was seeing, all the scholar could make out was an indistinct white shape, moving along the churchyard wall, on a path which must meet with Steane.

Marlowe scrambled to his feet and ran round behind the man and off at an angle, to head him off at the end of the churchyard wall, but put his foot in a hole and fell heavily, a searing pain screaming up his leg to his groin. Gingerly, he eased his foot out of the hole and gently massaged his ankle. It wasn't broken, but wouldn't be taking him anywhere fast tonight. As he sat on the dampening grass, rubbing his leg, he realized that he had stepped in a collapsing grave, that a mouldering hand was just below the surface. Even the dead seemed to be on the murderer's side tonight.

Steane and the white shape had disappeared.

Marlowe knew the story now, but he still had to prove it. Steane's flight would make it hard for him to carry on with his life as he had planned it, but Marlowe didn't want him to still be drawing breath when the dawn came up. He had no time for trials and inquests; he knew how wrong they could be. He wanted to take a life for those of his friends; not an equal count, but as equal as he could make it.

Slowly and in enormous pain, he hobbled across the seemingly endless distance of the Potter's Field and rounded the corner of the wall. Using the gravestones to support him, he limped around the uneven path, gasping as his foot accommodated the pebbles on the ground. He was almost at the eastern end of the church when he heard a drawn out whistling noise above him and he looked up to see the bulk of the flint-spattered tower looming against the stars. A strange shape was approaching, pale and getting bigger against the dark wall. Then, suddenly, with a sickening crunch which shook every synapse in his body, it landed at his feet, with a warm spatter of something which he knew could only be blood. Some self-preservation deep in his soul kept his eyes heavenward for another minute of sanity. They met the eyes of Meg Hawley, wide with terror and far away at the top of the tower. Reluctantly, he looked down and saw, spread over far too wide an area, all that remained of Benjamin Steane.

317

SIXTEEN

The summer sun was beating down on the oak door of the Great Hall of King's College that Wednesday afternoon and the whole town seemed to hold its breath. There was just the faintest breeze to carry the murmur of voices drifting out through the single open window high up in the transom. There was the distant tap of a gavel, and then the doors were flung open and a mixed gaggle of people spilled out into the hot air.

'Well, Master Machiavel.' Sir Edward Winterton, still wearing his sling, turned to Marlowe. 'As First Finder, what did you think of my ... the jury's verdict?'

Marlowe squinted up at the sun, then turned to the coroner. 'Suicide sounded a very fair judgement to me, Sir Edward. His widow won't like it, of course, but she would have liked it less if he had lived to stand trial.'

'That's what I thought,' Winterton said. 'I try to be merciful.' He paused and looked at a distant rooftop, pursing his lips. 'I know what you're thinking, Master Marlowe...'

'No. I don't think you do, Sir Edward. I think that ... bearing in mind what I saw, and what you

318

chose to ask me not to repeat in court, I think your verdict ... I mean, the verdict of your jury, was very merciful indeed. And if the guilty have not been brought to justice by a human court, I should think that as a Bishop-elect he would be expecting to be judged by a higher one.'

'Guilty of *felo de se*, you mean, of course,' Winterton said, still keeping his eyes elsewhere.

There was a silence, then Marlowe said quietly, 'As you wish, Sir Edward. Amongst other things, but I think as we understand each other, we can leave it there.' He extended his right hand, then pulled back, remembering Winterton's injury. He laid his palm gently on the man's shoulder instead, a breach of protocol which Winterton acknowledged with a smile.

'Take care, Master Machiavel,' he said. 'God go with you, if you would like him to.'

Marlowe turned to find Dee hovering behind him.

'A reasonable verdict, taken all round, do you not agree, Master Marlowe?' Dee said. 'Old Gerard was right, then, in a way – foxglove is good for those who fall from high places.'

Marlowe looked closely into the man's eyes and saw the message beneath the words: that this was the best we could expect; that Winterton had done his best to atone for the wrong verdicts on Ralph Whitingside, Eleanor Peacock and Henry Bromerick; that he and Marlowe knew more than could ever be told, out loud and in the light of day. Accordingly, Marlowe's reply

319

was simple. 'Yes, Dr Dee. A reasonable verdict.' Then he looked closer, not into the eyes but at the face. 'But ... you don't look well. Have you had a shock? Are you ill?'

Dee put a hand on Marlowe's arm and the scholar could feel it shaking. 'Are you sure you are not a magus, Kit?' he said, with a hollow laugh. 'I have had a shock, yes. My manservant was waiting for me this morning when I got up. He had ridden through the night to tell me ... well, to make the story short, Master Marlowe, my house has burned down. To its very cellars.'

Marlowe was appalled. The house, although he had been often disoriented in its labyrinthine corridors, had been a marvellous world of exotic things, sights and smells that he knew he would now never experience again. 'How did it happen?'

Dee drew him to one side. 'Do you know a quiet inn?' he asked.

'We could go to the Swan,' Marlowe offered. 'I need to speak to Meg if I can. She will find us a quiet corner, if there is one to be had.'

Dee nodded and the two walked through the afternoon streets, through market stalls, miraculously restored, through geese and sheep being herded by their new owners to their fate. It seemed nobody had hanged the Mayor after all. Neither man spoke, each being busy with his own thoughts, until they were ensconced with an ale each in a quiet corner of the inn, with the back of their settle turned out into the room, for added privacy.

320

'How did it happen?' Marlowe repeated. 'Is everyone well? Helene ... your servants?'

'Everyone got out. They are staying at one of my other properties in London, just a small house, but all of my papers, my potions ... everything has gone. Many of the things I work with are rather easily ignited; the place went up like a torch, or so I'm told.' The magus slumped on his seat.

'I don't know what to say,' Marlowe said. 'But, you haven't told me; how did it happen?'

Dee closed to him. 'That's the thing,' he said. 'I have started the rumour, which will be all over England before the summer is done, that an angry mob overpowered my grooms and put torches to the house.' He looked up briefly. 'I have a reputation to keep up; people must be afraid of me, if only slightly, otherwise I am just a magician, doing tricks for a meal and a bed.'

Marlowe smiled. As a conjuror of a different sort, playing people and words off against one another to keep ahead of the game of life, he understood. But he still didn't know what had happened. He opened his mouth to ask again, but Dee raised a hand to forestall him.

'You must promise not to tell a soul.'

'I promise.' And Kit Marlowe kept his promises.

Dee stared at him for a long minute. 'Do you promise not to put me into one of your plays, even?'

'I don't write plays,' Marlowe said. 'I am a poet, at best. I saw what happened to Lord

Strange's Men. A theatrical life is not for me.'

Dee knew what his showstone had told him about Marlowe and shrugged. He had less faith in it now that it had not foretold the fire. He drew a deep breath. 'It was the cook,' he said, baldly. 'And her perpetual toast.'

'Toast can't burn a house down, surely?' Marlowe sat back. It seemed unlikely.

'No, it can't,' Dee agreed. 'But a candle can if the manservant who should have been watching the house to make sure that if the curtain was blown into the room because the window was left open and touched the flame and caught alight was put out straight away was having toast.' He gasped at the end of his mammoth sentence which had been punctuated by ticking each brick in the wall off on his fingers.

'Ah. I can see how it happened now.'

'The curtain in question then flapped in the wind against a particularly fine stuffed vulture which was hanging from the ceiling. The moss with which it was stuffed caught fire and before they knew it ... the beams were alight and in a matter of hours, the house was gone.'

There seemed nothing to say, so Marlowe sipped his ale and kept quiet.

Then Dee brightened up, however falsely. 'To get back to the inquest, though, Kit. There seemed to me to be ... a lot missing from your testimony.'

'A little. Possibly a little.'

Dee waited patiently.

'There was...' Marlowe weighed his words

and began again. 'When I broke away from Steane, at the edge of the wood, something frightened him, so that he ran towards the church.'

'Did you see what it was?'

Marlowe could picture it quite clearly in his mind; a nebulous white shape, which had risen from the ground over Ralph Whitingside's grave and had skimmed along the boundary wall, heading for the gate into the churchyard proper. It must have reached it a second at most after Steane had disappeared into the blackness beyond the yews. If it had a face, he had not seen it. 'It was...' he sketched a helpless shape in the air. 'It was white,' he said, finally. 'That's all I can say.'

Dee slapped his knee and made the ale jump in the jug. 'I knew it,' he almost shouted. Then he remembered the need for secrecy. 'I knew it,' he repeated, in a whisper this time. 'It was the soul of Ralph Whitingside. I *knew* that I should have completed that banishment rite, hedge priest or no hedge priest.'

Marlowe looked at the man. He seemed quite sane, most of the time, and yet it was hard to swallow his belief in souls and wandering spirits. He dropped his voice so low that it was just a breath in Dee's ear. 'I rather thought it was Meg,' he said.

Dee bridled. 'When you are an expert in raising the dead, Dominus Marlowe,' he said, sharply, 'then I will take your advice on these things. Why would Meg make Steane scream and run for his life?'

'Because he *thought* it was the soul of Ralph Whitingside,' Marlowe said. 'It hardly matters, does it, whether it was or not?'

'It matters to me,' the magus said, in a huff. 'And it matters to all those who use that church, unless they mind a shiftless ghost attending their services when it fancies.' He picked up his ale mug and drained it. 'But, I must be away. My manservant is sorting out the horses at the livery and I have a lot of work to do when I get home.'

'And when do you expect to get home, Dr Dee?' Marlowe said, drily.

'First thing tomorrow, Master Marlowe,' Dee said with a twinkle. 'It would be sooner, but I have decided to take the scenic route.' He stood up and looked down at the scholar. Dee could see, all laid one over the other, the boy he had been and the man he would, with the grace of something, possibly God, become. 'Travel safely, Kit,' Dee said.

'And you, too, John.'

They clasped hands briefly, then, with a smile and just a hint of saltpetre and a shower of sparks for the look of the thing, the magus was gone.

'You're very quiet back here, Master Marlowe.'

The voice came from above his head and behind him and he twisted his neck to check who it was.

'Meg!' he said. 'Can you come and sit with me?'

'I can,' she said, 'but only for a minute. I had the afternoon off for the inquest, but I am back at work now, officially.'

'Officially?'

'Well–' she patted her stomach – 'I won't be working, here or in the other way, for much longer. So it doesn't matter if Jack Wheeler tells me to go today; it will all be the same in the end.'

'What will you do?' Marlowe knew there should be some sort of justice for Meg and her baby, but didn't know how to make it happen. In fairy-tales, he would have married her himself and they would have lived happily ever after, but this was no fairy-tale.

'Sir Roger Manwood has offered me a place in his house,' she said, 'but I'm not sure. It's a long way from home and ... well, I'm not sure why he did it.' She bent closer. 'I'm not sure what he's after.'

'Justice, of a sort,' Marlowe said. 'Don't forget that you ... well.' He dropped his voice until she could hardly hear it. 'You did ... kill Benjamin Steane.'

She looked at him, her eyes wide. 'Don't say that, Master Marlowe. Anyone could be listening. I thought when you didn't mention it in the inquest...'

'It doesn't mean I don't know, though, Meg,' Marlowe said. 'I had to tell Sir Roger and Dr Dee; they had been helping me with the case from the beginning, they deserved to know.' He clapped her on the shoulder. 'Go to Sir Roger's

325

house. He lives in acres of woodland, with a lake, a stream, everything that little Ralph could want as he grows up. And ... don't forget the baby's father grew up there too. It will be like a homecoming.' He didn't tell Meg Sir Roger's feelings about children; there would be plenty of occasions, he felt sure, when she would discover that for herself.

She looked dubious still, but nodded, for the baby's sake. 'Anyway, I didn't kill him. He fell...'

'He fell because you hit him with a candlestick, Meg, and please, don't interrupt.' He held the hand she had raised and trapped it in her lap. 'You did what I was trying to do, and so I will never tell another soul. But, one thing I have to know. Tell me how you got ahead of him up the tower. You were behind him when you ran through the gate between the yews.'

'What?' Meg Hawley was confused. 'I was in the church praying for Ralph when I heard someone scrabbling at the door. I was frightened and wanted to hide from whatever it was outside. I was already halfway up the tower when he crashed in, babbling and crying, begging someone to leave him alone. That was you.' The statement was more than half question.

'No,' Marlowe said, feeling the hairs begin to rise on his neck. 'At that point, I was limping across the field. I had put my foot in ... in a hole. I could hardly walk.'

'Well, who was it, then?'

'I don't know,' he said, slowly.

'I backed up the stairs,' she told him, 'and halfway up, in the bell loft, I found an old candlestick. I picked it up in case he followed me and he did. But it was not following so much as that he was also hiding from someone, the person he had been shouting at in the church.'

Everything around them had seemed to go very quiet, as though the whole town held its breath.

'I got to the top of the tower,' she carried on. 'I looked over and saw you come through the gate.' She stopped, frowning. 'Who was it, then, in the church?'

Biting his lip, Marlowe shook his head and gestured for her to go on.

'I heard the trapdoor slap back and Dr Steane was suddenly there with me, on the leads. He was running, running at me, with his hands out. He was screaming at me to leave him alone, which seemed a bit strange, because he was chasing me. I hit him with the candlestick. I was so scared. He ... he...' she broke down and covered her eyes.

Marlowe held her to him. He knew what had happened next. The sound that Steane had made as he hit the path would be with him for the rest of his days. He remembered Meg rushing out of the church. He remembered holding her against his chest so that she couldn't see the broken thing on the ground. He remembered the roughness of her cloak against his cheek Her black cloak. Over a black dress.

* * *

'I thought I'd take this opportunity to say goodbye, Michael.' Marlowe held out his hand. The pair stood in The Court, near the buttresses that had so often hidden roistering scholars creeping back after dark.

'Goodbye?' Johns frowned. 'But Kit, your degree? Your Master's?'

Marlowe shrugged. 'After the last few days,' he said, 'I've rather lost the taste for scholarship. But I wanted to apologize.'

'Apologize? What for?' Johns asked.

'I thought it was you. When I found you in my rooms that time ... It all seemed to fit at first.'

Johns shook his head. 'I played my part,' he said. 'Giving Henry's translation to Steane...'

'You couldn't have known,' Marlowe said.

'Well, then.' Johns suddenly couldn't find the words. 'Look after yourself, Dominus Marlowe. If you should ever change your mind...'

And the pair shook hands, the roisterer scholar and the quiet man who loved him.

Tom Colwell and Matt Parker were waiting by the front gate, still in their grey fustian, still waiting for their degrees.

'Lads–' Marlowe spread his arms – 'I'm away.'

'Where to, Kit?' Colwell asked. Corpus and Cambridge would never be the same now.

'Who knows?' Marlowe shrugged. 'I have charges to answer from Edward Winterton and Gabriel Harvey. I doubt the law will let me get far. Tom,' he said, and hugged the man, 'you

328

know, it wouldn't surprise me to see you in old Norgate's chair one day. Keep up the good work. Matty.' He held the boy close to him as the tears welled in Parker's eyes. Marlowe held him at arm's length, frowning. 'Now then,' he scolded, 'remember where you are, man. Your grandfather was Archbishop of Canterbury, for God's sake.'

He turned across the flagstones. 'When they give you your degrees, lads,' he shouted, 'have a swig from the auroch's horn for me, will you?'

And he was gone, through the gates into the High Ward.

Christopher Marlowe, Secundus Convictus, Bachelor of Arts of Corpus Christi College and a scholar of the finest university in the world was travelling south through Trumpington. He left his books behind him for Colwell and Parker and had thrown, in time-honoured tradition, his grey gown into the Cam to float, like the bodies of the drowned, downstream. All he took with him were the clothes he stood up in, his roisterer's doublet and colleyweston cloak and the swept-hilt rapier that was once Ralph Whitingside's slung over his shoulder. The rattle and groan of carts and the lowing of oxen made him stop and stand to one side on the road.

Lord Strange's battered company plodded past him, wagons tied with rope and clothes patched and stitched. There was no fanfare now, no clarion call and absolutely no fireworks. It would be a long time before Ned Sledd allowed

329

any frivolous fires near his company. The seamstresses who had seemed to be anything but as they all rode into Cambridge were now quiet and actually *sewing*. The Fair Maid of Kent, on the lead wagon, peered at Marlowe through two black eyes and nodded to him.

'Master Marlowe.' The player-king stood on the last wagon in line, as his driver hauled on the oxen rein.

'Master Sledd.' Marlowe bowed.

'I'm afraid your play was lost,' the actor told him. 'In the fire. Dido, Queen of Carthage. A shame – it had promise. Never seen a metre quite like it before. A mighty line, sir, a mighty line.'

'These things happen,' Marlowe said with a smile. 'I have other plays. Other lines.'

It was the player-king's turn to smile. 'Come with us, then. You're wasted in this backwater.' He waved a dismissive arm at Cambridge, already a distant jumble of golden buildings in the evening sun. 'Come to London, Kit. The city of gold. The city of wonder. I'm looking for a new playwright.' He stopped and sighed. 'And I expect others will be too, once they know Kit Marlowe's in town.'

'All right, but I'm not a playwright,' Marlowe said and swung the sword on to the baggage behind Sledd before climbing up alongside it. 'And no promises,' he said. 'I never make promises I can't keep.'

'Good enough!' The player-king laughed and threw the man an apple.

They had bumped and rattled their way out on to the open fenland, waving to the few people who were still stage-struck enough to line their route. Marlowe had a special wave for Constable Fludd, not so much stage-struck as he stood in the door of his carpenter's shop as making certain the players were really leaving town. He stood under the thatch of his cottage with his wife and daughter at his side and Allys Fludd waddled away, as women with child do, to feed the chickens near cock-shut time.

Soon, Cambridge was just a shapeless mass in the dying sun. Marlowe only now realized how exhausted he was and he dozed, lying on the rolls of singed curtains in the back of the cart. He was woken sharply by something nibbling at his fingers, deftly extracting the apple core that still lay there.

He sat bolt upright to see a fine black stallion pull its head away at a jerk from its rider. The man was a gentleman, in black velvet finery and he was leading another horse.

'Dominus Marlowe?'

'Who wants to know?' His mother had always warned him about strange men on the road. Pity he hadn't listened.

'Your fellow Parker scholars would know me as Francis Hall.' He pulled his horse alongside the wagon's rear wheel and leaned across. 'But it's actually Francis Walsingham, Privy Councillor to Her Majesty, Elizabeth, by the Grace of God.'

Marlowe was still sitting upright. 'What

business do you have with me, sir?' he asked.

'Her Majesty's business,' Walsingham said.

Marlowe looked into the man's eyes. They burned as dark and enigmatic as his own. 'You're the spymaster,' he said softly.

Walsingham laughed. 'Ah, you playwrights,' he roared. 'Always the dramatic. I've been looking for you.'

'Why?' Marlowe asked.

'Let's just say,' Walsingham said, leaning forward in the saddle, 'I believe you are the kind of man who can effect Her Majesty's business well. Very well.' The spymaster sat upright again. 'The pay's not good, Marlowe,' he said. 'But I can guarantee you a life like no other.'

'I am not exactly a free agent, Sir Francis,' Marlowe said. 'I have various charges pending against me.'

'If you are referring to Edward Winterton and pulling a knife on him, it's gone. I have had a word with Edward. He understood.'

'He...?' Marlowe was amazed.

'He works for the Queen,' Walsingham explained. 'As do we all. As for Dr Gabriel Harvey...'

'Yes?' Marlowe leaned forward.

Walsingham smiled. 'Let's just say, he'd rather like to be Master of Corpus Christi one day. He's gone too.'

Marlowe chuckled. 'Once,' he said, 'all I wanted was to take my first degree. That achieved, my second. Then–' he waved to the theatrical pile on which he rode – 'I had dreams of writing plays and poetry – all fire and air, eh?'

Walsingham steadied the stallion. 'I see no reason, Master Marlowe, why Her Majesty's business could not be fitted in around your second degree and your writing for the theatre, if you wish. After all, God gave us twenty-four hours in any day.'

They rode on for a moment in silence. 'Well, Machiavel, Kit?' Walsingham leaned in again. 'What do you say?'